To Ashley
Thank you for
the support!

In Absence of Fear

CELESTE CHANEY

Celeste G. Chaney

ISBN: 0996824308
ISBN 13: 9780996824309

Library of Congress Control Number: 2015917192
LCCN Imprint Name: Corner Canyon Press

For Ted.

PART ONE

We are born into this world unarmed—
our mind is our only weapon.

—Ayn Rand, *Atlas Shrugged*

How does a government keep its citizens safe?

Crime prediction. Threat mitigation. There are leading indicators. Behavioral patterns that signal a plan to bomb, the desire to murder. A comment in a forum. A purchase at the hardware store. A detour on the way to work. Together, they tell a story. But they are not enough.

Once the threat is identified, action must be taken.

1

THE DATA FEED continued to crawl, an overlay against the late-morning sky rendered by windowless walls. Marus sat in his fluorescent-lit workstation, eyes fixed on the massive screens in front of him. Algorithms weighted millions of individual data points, parsing and analyzing to predict patterns and determine possible outcomes. The code did the work, but as senior algorithm architect for the predictive policing program, he guided it. Inhale, input. Exhale, output. He thought in variables and values. Saw sequences in his sleep. Ones and zeroes. Black and white.

When he was a boy, he wanted to be a fireman, as most boys do. Why was that? Why do most boys wish to be firemen? It was noble to put out fires, yes. But, it was nobler to prevent them.

Murderers, bombers, burglars, rapists, and kidnappers were halted before they struck. The program led police right to them. And yet, the Protectors had only scratched the surface. External indicators pointed to plotting criminals, but the system hadn't eliminated all danger. Unplanned crime still ripped families apart and threatened the order of the State.

The Internal Indicator Initiative, coined "I3" by the State, would change that. The Protectors had been able to distinguish various physiological responses that preceded violent behavior. Hormonal influx, brain activity, and an accelerated heart rate were among the most rudimentary. In time, the State's scientists would identify others. The system would make it easier by flagging patterns they'd initially missed. Statistical significance would ensure inclusion. The program would adjust. Bigger, faster, more secure. Machine learning at its finest.

It was Marus's job to lead the design, analysis, and implementation of I3. It had taken months—years—of testing and refining the code. A lot longer than he and his team would have liked, but he had to make sure the technology was exact. There was too much at stake. Not only the safety of his family, his friends, and citizens across the State, but also their freedom. Misattribution or a faulty diagnosis could put the wrong person behind bars. That ripped families apart, too. He hadn't been willing to take that chance.

Now, I3 was ready. *Finally.* Another month or so and it'd be going gold. He'd be able to take a deep breath. Take his wife and child and father and head south. A beach somewhere. Their first vacation in years. They'd spend a week, maybe two, swimming and sunbathing. Beachcombing. Cade would like that. Collecting shells and other treasures. They'd eat shrimp and sea bass and large plates of crab. He could almost taste the butter, the spongy white flesh breaking apart in his mouth. He and Shey would make love every single day. And then, after a good, long sleep he'd get back to work. Iterations and updates would be necessary. Several hundred Saturdays just like this, but it was in the name of a future free from fear.

The ninth floor was quiet, except for the faint purring of the machine. Its heat radiated from the floor and the walls. Warm-blooded. All around him, slender necks on the ceiling pivoted silently. Dozens of tiny cyclopes twisted to watch as he worked. He didn't mind.

Show the boss I'm here. On a Saturday.

He looked at the clock. Cade's soccer game was about to start, if it hadn't already. Sometimes they'd begin a half hour late. Sometimes five minutes early. It was hard to tell. Seven-year-olds, he found, were unpredictable. It was best to hurry. His fingers floated across the keyboard, melodious in their tapping.

One more thing. One more line. One more reason I'm the best they've got.

His phone came alive beside the mouse. Shey's face appeared on the screen as it quivered. The game must have already started. He finished the update and logged off. Jacket in one hand, phone in the other, he started for the elevator. The phone displayed his favorite picture of her. The light was just right, illuminating emerald eyes, tinting her brown hair red. He slid the bar green and put the speaker to his ear.

"Hey, I'm just walking out."

"Marus, Cade's not here," she said, her voice a frantic staccato. "I don't know where he is."

"What?"

Entirely unpredictable.

Once Cade had wandered out of the apartment and ridden the elevator up and down, up and down, until an elderly woman heading to the fifteenth floor took his hand and rode down to the lobby, where she deposited him at the front desk.

This isn't a playground, young man, she'd said

I was just making sure it worked, he'd told her.

Marus could hear clapping on Shey's end of the line. A whistle.

"Joey's mom gave him a ride this morning. I just got here, and he isn't here."

"Have you checked ChildSafe?" Marus asked.

"Yes. It says his last tag was here. But I've looked everywhere. The school is locked, and the game's already started. I don't know what to do."

"Sometimes it lags. Maybe he wasn't feeling well, and another parent took him home. ChildSafe probably hasn't registered it yet."

"Marus…" Shey hesitated for a moment, as if trying to make sense of something. "I found his ball in the parking lot. *He left his ball.*"

He could hear her breath, quick and desperate. She was moving around frantically, he could tell. Her boots made a swishing sound in the grass as she walked the length of the field. The clapping grew distant.

It wasn't like Cade to miss a game. But it had happened before. Strep throat and a fever of 102 degrees had benched him, but his ball was another matter. The ball changed everything. Since his idol, soccer star Luca Valdetti, had given it to him, the ball never left his side. To Cade, sheer proximity to it ensured stardom. He'd even tried to take it into restaurants.

"*Oh*," Marus said, turning. He hadn't made it past the break room. "Okay. Call the police." He hurried back to his desk. "Get it into the system. I'll be right there."

"Okay," she said.

"Shey—"

"Yeah?"

"Everything is going to be all right."

She breathed deeply into the phone, an unspoken prayer that he might be right.

"I love you," he said.

"I love you, too." She hung up.

He turned on the machine and logged back into the system. At the top of the feed, he saw Shey's call. Her elevated heart rate, a violent line drawn on the screen. His code at work.

He wasn't authorized to pull up specific user profiles, regardless of his relation to the person. Doing so was against protocol, and for good reason. The data wasn't meant for human eyes. ChildSafe was a separate application designed to equip parents with just enough visibility to be effective in their parenting role. It gave them access to a list of their children's geotags—the dates and times. It provided itemized cafeteria receipts so they could monitor what their kids ate and alerted them if their child had a fever. Unlike the Protector Program, the app didn't display communications or show other data from a user's iD. And, ChildSafe often lagged. Five minutes, maybe ten. Marus had never thought it significant before. But in situations like this, a few ill-informed minutes made all the difference.

Hacking the system to bypass permissions and view Cade's profile was a matter of identifying system exploits. He didn't have to guess where the weaknesses were. Having architected the code, he knew. Accessing the information wasn't a concern. It would take a matter of minutes, at most. And yet, he hesitated. Several seconds passed as he sat frozen in front of the screens.

There would be consequences. By dodging authorization, he'd be written up. He'd have to visit with a State counselor, explain the behavior. His permissions might be restricted temporarily until it was clear he wasn't a threat. No one was excluded from the Protectors' watch, not even a Protector. The algorithms never failed to do their job.

It took him four minutes to gain entry. He scrolled down to the *Tags*, revealing a chronological list of locations where scanners had tagged Cade's iD. The most recent, the athletic field at his school, St. Xavier Preparatory, was at the top of the list. Joey's mom had driven him there. Her car's GPS had appended the route they'd taken to his profile. Marus clicked on the map and traced it with his finger. A left, a right, and another left. Twelve minutes. No stops. The car parked in the lot. Cade was tagged as he ran by the bleachers. There was nothing else.

Point A: Home with Shey.

Point B: The soccer field at school.

As for *Point C*?

Without the data, Marus's guess was as good as any. *A friend's house? A convenience store? The restrooms?*

There were more than four million State-issued scanners within city limits, and thousands more that had been installed as part of residential security systems. And none of them had picked up Cade's iD in the past twenty minutes.

■ ■ ■

The drive from work to the soccer field took fifteen minutes. He looked at his watch. A total of thirty-five minutes had ticked away since Cade was last seen. Every last one of them counted. Every second from here out, counted.

Shey stood at the other end of the field, flanked by several bystanders and a few uniforms. A semicircle of concern. She wasn't looking at any of them. Her head bobbed and turned as she scanned the edge of the field, the bleachers, and the lot. Yellow and blue jerseys darted back and forth. A few parents clapped and shouted at their tiny players, but most were looking at Shey or glancing nervously at those clustered around her. A parent's worst nightmare, realized. Many of them were worried. Many more were relieved. *Not my child.*

Shey saw Marus walk onto the field and lurched forward into a half run, nearly colliding with a police officer.

They met at the curb, folding into each other upon impact. Her hair still smelled of the shower they'd taken before he left for the office. When she finally pulled away to meet his eyes, he saw something he'd never seen there before, a fear so great it pushed everything out. Even the light.

■ ■ ■

"I thought he was you," Joey's mom said, looking at Marus. "He had a cap on, and a brown windbreaker. I couldn't see his face."

"Where did they go?" The police officer was tapping at the glass in her palm. Pinned flat to her chest was the name *Muñoz*.

"They were walking away from the field. Over there." Joey's mom pointed to the far side of the parking lot. "The man had his hand on his back. Cade was holding the soccer ball."

The ball lay lifeless, stark white against the grass in front of them. Joey's mom eyed it as though it were a body.

"I thought he was Marus," she said again. Her face was red. Her eyes, glossy with guilt. "Like he was leading Cade away for a pep talk." She was shaking her head at no one in particular.

"And where were you?" Officer Muñoz glanced in Shey and Marus's direction.

A shrill whistle sounded from the plastic at the referee's lips. Shey jerked at the noise. "I had to finish up some work at home," she said. She, too, was staring at the soccer ball. A look of terror, taut across her face.

Officer Muñoz referred to her tablet. "And you got here twenty minutes ago?"

Shey turned away from the ball. She nodded. "I couldn't find him, so I checked ChildSafe. It said he was here. I found his soccer ball sitting in an empty parking space."

"And where were you?" Muñoz turned toward Marus.

"At the Protective Services Center," he said. "I'd just wrapped up some work when Shey called."

"You're a Protector?" The officer asked, though she held that exact information in her hand.

Marus nodded.

"All right. Why don't you two head over to your district station to fill out a report? Cade's iD hasn't been tagged since the school, but we've initiated a facial recognition search. If one of the cameras finds a match, we'll notify you. In the meantime, we'll issue an Amber Alert and pull back surveillance footage from the area. I'll come by your house later tonight—"

"Will it take that long?" Marus asked, one arm still firmly around Shey.

"It might." Officer Muñoz tucked the tablet under her arm. "It depends what we're dealing with. I'll call you if we learn anything before then."

"Okay. Thank you, Officer." He picked up the ball and guided Shey past the bright jerseys, away from the game and the fixed eyes of spectators, toward the parking lot.

He wanted to ask why she hadn't told him she couldn't take Cade to the game, or why she hadn't gotten there sooner. He wondered what work she'd had to do. Dissatisfied with her job, it'd been months since he'd seen her bring any work home. There were a lot of questions he wanted to ask, but, just then, she dropped to her knee, gagged, and spit up onto the asphalt.

"I'm sorry," she said, looking up at him.

He helped her stand again. "We're going to find him."

■ ■ ■

A fleshy man with thinning blond hair greeted Marus at the front desk of the satellite station with a disinterested mumble.

"G'day." He focused on the desktop screen concealed behind the high counter.

Marus nodded an unseen reply. "I need to report a missing person," he said.

Surprised, the man looked up at Marus and leaned in as though he had misheard. "A missing person?"

Marus nodded. "Officer Muñoz sent me."

"Uh...uh. Hold on a minute."

The man waddled hurriedly down the hallway until Marus could no longer see him.

Moments later, he returned, accompanied by a woman. The word *Sergeant* arced across the gold and silver plaque pinned just above her heart.

"Can I help you?" the sergeant asked.

"He can," Marus said, pointing to the blond man. "I already told him. I need to report a missing person...my son, he's been kidnapped."

An audible silence fell over the station. An officer lingered in the doorway. A woman looked up from the lobby, turning her ears. Even the hum of machines and radios seemed muted somehow. The sergeant glanced at the heavy, blond man.

"Get him a tablet, please," she said.

The blond man looked around, wide eyed, but didn't move.

"They're in the cabinet in the hall."

He stepped around her and shuffled back down the hallway.

"We don't get many of these here," she said in apology. Her brown eyes fell to the screen to see what the door scanner had registered. Seeing the seal there, she straightened. The thin black lines of her eyebrows knit together. "You work for *the State?*"

The blond man returned with a tablet and set it on the counter in front of Marus.

The sergeant picked it up, palming the thin glass as though it were an offering. She looked briefly at Shey, who was sitting in one of the rigid, blue lobby chairs with her head in her hands.

"Let me know if there's anything we can do," she said.

Your job, Marus thought. Though he took the tablet from her without a word and turned toward his wife.

The woman sitting several chairs over continued to watch. Her head swiveled in their direction. Hungry eyes glanced from Shey to Marus and back again when he looked up at her from the tablet. She started to smile and then thought better of it. Her lips retreated to the dull corners of her mouth as her thumbs ticked across her phone in excitement.

Marus angled his body away from her, turning to protect Shey from her view. Scanning his wrist with the iD reader affixed to the tablet, he pulled up his profile. He clicked *Reports* and selected the missing persons report Officer Muñoz had requested. Empty fields materialized on the screen. *Name. iD. Sex. Address. DOB. Height. Weight. Hair color. Eye color.* Information the Protectors already had. Information he had to provide as an exercise, a matter of formality. Busy work. Keep the victim's loved ones occupied. Ease their angst. He remembered discussing it in a procedures meeting. *Idleness leads to despondency. Despair creates an opportunity for people to doubt the system. Participation provides purpose. Purpose instills a sense of accountability.*

For everything, a cause and effect.

Last seen?

Marus had gone to work while Cade was still sleeping. The night before, he'd picked him up from soccer practice. In the car, Marus had listened to the news while Cade played a game. Had they talked? Had Cade said anything unusual? He couldn't remember. They'd had dinner as a family. Roasted chicken with mashed potatoes and carrots. Sometimes they'd play a game after the plates were put away, but this time Marus retired to the study early to return to his work.

What was the last thing he'd said to his son? Had he pulled Cade into his chest to say good night? Had he told him that he loved him? He was sure he would have, but couldn't actually remember.

Father: Last night, at home, before bed.

He pulled his collar open to the side and took a breath. Movement caught his attention, and he realized it was his own foot tapping. He held it still, pressing it firmly into the gray, industrial-grade carpet. The woman stared openly from her seat. He tried not to look at her as he typed.

"When did you last see him?"

Shey lifted her head from her hands. Her face was streaked, pink and pale, though the crying had stopped. "This morning," Shey said. "After you left. Joey's mom came at nine thirty."

"Why so early?"

She wouldn't face him. "I had to run some errands."

There was a moment of silence. The desire to say something more. Then it passed.

Marus returned to the tablet.

Mother: 9:30 a.m. today, at home.

"I should've taken him to the game," Shey said. "I should have been there from the start." She bent over in the tiny chair. Resting her elbows on her knees, she folded her hands and brought them to her forehead. It was a look of pleading. And apology.

He put both arms around her and pressed his lips into her hair. "Everything is going to be okay," he whispered. "I'm sure a camera or a scanner has picked something up by now. They're going to find him and bring him home."

He kissed the side of her head and let her go, returning to the screen in his hand. The Protectors had all of Cade's information, but accuracy was still important. Each field ought to be reviewed. *Discrepancy created delay. Delay meant death.*

Shey turned to face him. "Can't you do it?" she said. "Can't you look in the system and find him?"

He hadn't yet had the chance to tell her that he already did. That it was the first thing he'd done, and he'd come away with nothing.

Marus glanced over at the counter, meeting the blond man's gaze.

Once they were home, he'd lead her into the bathroom and crank on the shower. Through the steam, he'd tell her about his breach. What he'd seen. What he hadn't. And if Officer Muñoz didn't come up with something by the time she paid them a visit, he'd hack his way in and do it again.

"You've said it yourself: they don't know what they're doing. They don't know what to look for. But you do. It might mean his life, Marus. That could be the difference between life or…" Shey couldn't bring herself to say it.

The woman shifted in her chair and let out a little cough. Marus wondered how much she could hear. How much she'd already shared.

"He's our son. A child. It isn't like you're violating his privacy. I'm sure Devlin would understand."

Marus submitted the report and stood. "Come on. Let's go home."

■ ■ ■

By the time Officer Muñoz arrived, the sun had already begun to sink beneath the vast blue horizon. Marus left the officer standing in the kitchen and went to Cade's bedroom. Shey had been resting inside with the door closed for more than two hours. She didn't want to talk, and he hadn't known what to say.

He tried to remember the last time he'd heard of a child being kidnapped. What once was a common headline on the nightly news had become increasingly rare since the dawn of the New Era. Crime still clung like an infectious disease at the fringes of any city, but not here. The Isle was different. Scanner and camera placement was triple, maybe quadruple, what it was elsewhere. Same with the patrols. Even the bridges came up after curfew. And yet, Cade had been taken in plain sight, when the sun was at its highest.

Shey was cocooned in his green comforter, her eyes fixed on the darkening sky outside the window. A pale hand rested atop the soccer ball at her side.

"That police officer is here now."

She didn't move.

He lingered a moment in the doorframe. In the corner, a small reading chair was piled high with library books Shey and Cade had checked out. The world's most comprehensive library lived online, but Shey was insistent. She'd wanted Cade to see the weathered spines and smell the yellowing pages. The weight of a book was something to revere, she'd said.

The Luca Valdetti bobblehead stared back from the bedside table. Its plastic mouth was pursed into a dismissive grin that gave Marus an uneasy feeling.

As he made his way down the hall toward the kitchen, he could hear Shey get up.

"I should have known," he heard her say.

■ ■ ■

"Do you mind if we sit?" Officer Muñoz asked, gesturing toward the couch.

"The kitchen table," Shey said, emerging from the hallway.

The three of them sat. Marus pulled his chair closer to his wife. Muñoz set her tablet on the table's glass surface.

"We were able to track Cade's iD. He was tagged at Golden Bay Marina at 12:17 p.m. It was his last tag."

"Golden Bay Marina?" Shey leaned forward. "What do you mean his last tag?"

"By the time we got there, he was gone." Touching its screen, she brought the tablet to life and angled it toward them. "We were able to pull surveillance footage from both the school and the marina."

The camera at school was at the south end of the bleachers, but the view was clear. A man in a brown jacket with a blue baseball cap pulled low over his forehead walked onto the north side of the field. He cut a diagonal path toward the goal, exposing no more than a sliver of his bespectacled face to the surveillance camera. A moment later, Cade came over, dribbling the ball.

Marus felt the heat build beneath his collar. Shey's hand trembled in his own. He thought she was crying, but, when he looked, the only emotion wrung across her face was anger. *Rage.*

The man crouched down and picked up the ball. He said something to Cade and stood. With one hand at Cade's back and the other pinning the ball under his arm, he led their boy away.

"No one saw that? No one said anything?" Shey said.

I thought he was you, Joey's mom had said. And from a distance, the man looked like he could be Marus. He had the same build. The hair peeking out of the back of his cap was the same dark brown. Even his jacket looked a bit like the one Marus kept in the closet. And Cade didn't put up a fight. He appeared willing, even eager, to follow the man. But why? Hadn't they told him to never talk to strangers? Or did Marus have such faith in the system that he'd forgotten?

Shey read his mind. "I don't understand," she said. "He doesn't speak to strangers. We had that conversation."

Marus squeezed her hand. She was a good mom. He wanted to tell her so, but Muñoz interrupted.

"The same man was seen at the marina," she said, flipping the screen around to select another video. She turned it back toward them.

There was the sign, *Golden Bay Marina*. And there was the devil, strolling past it in his brown jacket toward the docks. But where was their son? The video ended. Muñoz set the tablet down.

"You said Cade was gone by the time you got there. But he isn't in the video," Marus said.

"Maybe he wasn't there at all," Shey added, nodding.

Muñoz folded her hands and rested them on the table. "He was tagged by a scanner near the dock."

"We didn't see the car they were in. Maybe there were others."

"Is it possible that the marina was one of several stops and *somehow* they evaded additional scanners?" Marus said.

"It would be unlikely given the sheer volume of scanners and cameras on the Isle," Muñoz replied.

"But it's possible," Shey said. "If someone knew where the scanners were and how to avoid them."

"Have you implemented checkpoints at the bridges?"

Leaning forward, Muñoz pressed her lips together. She looked like she wanted to say something but didn't know how. The words faltered before she could get them out.

"There's something else," she said finally, glancing back at the tablet. "I don't know how to say this." She met his eyes and then Shey's. "We've pulled Cade's Lifewatch feed for monitoring. A couple hours ago his heart rate—"

"No." Marus felt the air turn to lead in his chest. He pushed his chair back as if to rise. To leave. To pretend it wasn't real. But then he saw his wife.

"It stopped," Muñoz said.

Marus grabbed for Shey.

Encircled in his arms, she wailed. The tears fell, fat and hot, against his neck, pooling at his collar.

"*Oh God.* My baby. Our little boy."

Muñoz's mouth was open, but she didn't speak. The room seemed to spin around them. Shey's cries reverberated off of every surface. They became his own.

"I am so sorry for your loss," Muñoz said. She retrieved a small pack of tissues from her coat and slid them across the table. "The boats are out there now combing the bay. They retrieved an article of clothing."

Marus and Shey lifted their heads to look at the screen Muñoz was holding. Cade's navy blue soccer jersey was drenched, flung across a white table in the picture. The harsh light and ruler placed alongside the bottom edge made it foreign, and yet, it was unmistakable. It was Cade's.

"Can you confirm this belongs to your son?"

Marus wiped at his eyes. He nodded.

"Forensics found blood on the cloth. The DNA is a positive match. According to Lifewatch, the time of death was two fourteen p.m. We are still working to determine the cause, but as you know, it will be nearly impossible without a—a body."

She cleared her throat. "I know this is an incredibly difficult time." She set the tablet down. "Please let me know if there's anything I can do for you."

"You can find our son and bring him home," Shey said.

But she wasn't looking at Muñoz. She was looking at Marus.

2

TIME STOOD STILL. It was normal to feel as though life had stopped after the death of a child. *Normal.* Nothing would ever be normal again. How could it? His wife wouldn't talk to him. When she did speak, it was to herself. Barely audible, rarely coherent. Entire days were spent in bed, but never asleep. Sleep rarely came, and when it did it was punctuated by nightmares. Cold sweats. Even as it happened, he felt like he was watching from a distance. His own alternate reality. They'd miss breakfast, lunch, dinner, sometimes all three, without realizing it. His stomach refused to grumble. The slightest recollection, a sound or a scent, would cause him to tremble. Not tremble, *shake.* Uncontrollably. There was a numbness, a loss of circulation in his legs and arms. As though his heart had forgotten to keep beating. Some days he wished it would.

These things were supposed to be *normal.* He'd read that. Some of it he expected. He wasn't a stranger to grief. He'd been the child that lost a parent. He'd spent entire months out of school, locked in his bedroom. Nightmares and tremors plagued his childhood. As bad as it had been, this was worse.

To be the parent that loses a child. The grief and anger and despair dwarfed every other emotion he'd ever experienced. They said that time could heal even the deepest and ugliest of wounds. But could it erase the guilt, the unflinching feelings of failure?

The media wouldn't leave them alone. Everyone wanted to hear from the Protector who couldn't even keep his family safe. Marus had dodged dozens of reporters' emails and calls. Requests for interviews. Invitations to appear on TV shows. He'd seen the segments, other parents pleading on-air for their child's safe return. They'd cry into the camera and tell their lost little one *we love you* and *we'll find you.* If that script had been available to him, Marus would have gone on-air in a second. But his son wasn't coming home.

■ ■ ■

The grandfather clock sounded in the corner of the café, ushering in a new wave of customers from the autumn air. Marus watched from his seat by the window as they loosened the scarves coiled around their necks and sped toward a growing line at the counter.

Shey hadn't said much since ordering. She hadn't looked at him, either. Her eyes were red and puffy, though he'd swear she hadn't cried in days. Her breakfast sandwich lay untouched, cold and soggy, on the plate in front of her. The drink she ordered, a black coffee, had been refilled four times in the past hour. She didn't sip from the mug, but took long, desperate gulps as she looked out the window at the trees.

The park across from the Rose Café was the only true green space on the Isle. Sitting so close, the massive trunks and leafy tops blotted out towering concrete and steel. Sometimes, he could forget he was in the city at all. They'd sat in the same seats eight years earlier on their first date. *Loves the outdoors. Coffee fiend.* He'd read that somewhere on her profile. It was because of those trees, he'd invited her here. And it was because of her the Rose existed for him at all.

Now it was theirs. The place where they'd picked apart the past and considered the future. Where they'd talked about their families and their jobs and their dreams. A confessional of sorts. A place to ponder life and death. He remembered brisk mornings when they'd been the first customers through the door and quiet evenings when they'd shut the place down.

It was here, sitting in the same seats so many years ago, Shey admitted to loving him moments before he had the chance to do the same. They'd hoped and game-planned, choked back tears and told terrible jokes. One time, in a fit of laughter, Shey spewed coffee, dousing him and this very table. He couldn't recall what had been so funny but remembered succumbing himself as, in her hysterics, she'd struggled to sop it up. Countless conversations survived space and time and echoed now, alive and audible as they'd ever been. A gateway to the past. The memory of place.

He never would have imagined a scene like this. The stillness. A gnawing silence between them despite the clanking of cutlery that filled the Rose as Sunday brunch came into full swing. Plates of eggs, smoked salmon, potatoes and toast, came out from the swinging door in a procession to patrons waiting to devour them. Across the café, a gaggle of women broke out into a uniform titter as they smeared butter and crimson jam over slices of toast. A family of four shared pancakes two tables over. The little girl dumped syrup into her lap and started to cry.

He couldn't remember the last time he'd heard Cade cry. A boy with a stiff upper lip. A gleaming trail of snot or tears called attention to the occasional stifling of sobs. He was never very vocal about it. At least, not since birth.

Cade had come on a foggy April morning. Marus remembered with perfect clarity his son's first gasping screams, his swollen face and tiny feet, the dark brown hair plastered, thick and wet, atop the perfect globe of his head. Marus could still see the milky foam running down his chin as he luxuriated, eyes rolled back, in post-meal unconsciousness. Infancy had terrified Marus at first. He never knew quite how to hold him or whether he was being gentle enough. *You won't break him*, Shey used to say. He wasn't so sure.

Light through the café windows cast strange patterns on people's faces as they ate and drank, consumed wholly by the small screens in their hands or the conversations with those across from them. Marus watched, kicking his gaze from the women, to the family, the man talking too loudly into his cellphone, to an elderly couple silently sawing away at slabs of ham. The lives of the unaffected. The unaware. *The unconscious.* To them, it was just another Sunday. The world still spun on its axis. Life went on.

A couple tables over, a knife clattered to the floor, metallic against the tile. Startled, he turned toward the woman who dropped it, eyes sharp and accusatory. Shey didn't notice or didn't care. He'd never seen her so expressionless, so vacant. He wondered what his own face looked like. Did it betray the millions of thoughts he was thinking all at once? An amalgamation of notions and emotions woven into one horrific mask? Or had it singled out one, one feeling that dominated them all?

A few diners strayed from their plates to look at Shey, and then at him, and then back to their bacon and eggs. He knew what they were thinking: *liar*, or maybe, *cheater*. With Shey stone-faced as she was, that's likely what it looked like. But they were wrong. He wasn't those things, he was something worse. A father who hadn't been able to protect his child. A developer whose program hadn't done what it was supposed to do. A husband who couldn't comfort his wife. A failure.

A bit of light caught in Marus's eye. He dodged it and looked across the café, seeking its source. An angular man in a tattered overcoat sat hunched in the corner in front of the grandfather clock. He swiveled a spoon on its head, throwing light back at the window. His foot tapped rhythmically beneath the table to the mechanical clicking of the clock's gears. Tufts of straw-like hair stuck out from the hat he wore low above his brow. Lost in thought, the man observed the spoon with large and sunken eyes.

As if feeling Marus's stare, the man pushed the mug aside to dress his hands in a pair of black leather gloves taken from his coat pocket. He pulled them on with the precision of a surgeon, adjusting each fingertip just so. Appearing satisfied, he tidied his space, dropping his napkin into the mug and centering it at the edge of the table beside a half-eaten croissant.

He pulled the wool collar of the coat high upon his neck and stood. His shoes made a light tapping sound against the tile as he made his way to the door. He glanced at Marus and then to Shey before his slender frame moved through the door and across the street toward the park. When Marus looked, he saw Shey was watching the man, too.

"I wish you'd talk to me," he said, trying to catch her gaze.

She cupped the empty mug in her hands and continued to look out at the trees even after the man had ducked the foliage and vanished into the park.

The park wasn't really a park. Time had turned it into something else: a reminder or a warning. Maybe both. In the years that filled the space between that first date and this day, those towering trees, once noble in their stature, had taken on a manic, anguished quality. Had they always sprung haphazardly from the crusted earth along the perimeter, like tombstones enshrining the past? Or was it only now, now that the park symbolized so much else, that they appeared that way? Beyond the thicket, enclosed by a steel fence dotted with knots of colorful ribbon, remnants of a playground, several slides, a swing set, and a pavilion, were welded together in a tangled mess of sculpture.

Soon they'd go with their own ribbon, a dark green. Cade's favorite color.

"Maybe we should start thinking about a ceremony," he said.

Shey set her mug down. "You mean *a funeral?*"

He didn't know what he meant. Funerals were supposed to provide closure for the living, a way to move forward. Had that been the case after his own mother's death? He couldn't remember.

"Mothers shouldn't have to bury their children," she said looking back toward the trees. "Besides, we don't have a body to bury."

He swallowed dryly, angling his mug to examine its silty bottom. "You're right."

"Why do you suppose that is?" Shey asked.

"What?"

"Why do you think they haven't found his body?"

Marus had pondered the same question many times. He'd deferred to the search engines. The bay averaged a depth of 43 feet, but its deepest point, underneath North Bridge was 360 feet. There was the tide to consider, too. And sharks. Not many in the bay itself, but even one would be enough.

"Maybe he's still alive."

"Shey—" Marus reached for her hand. "You saw what Officer Muñoz showed us. His jersey. The blood."

"People bleed, it doesn't mean they've died."

"Lifewatch showed that his heart stopped."

"Muñoz didn't show us his Lifewatch data," she said.

"I saw it."

Shey looked at him, disbelieving.

"I did. I saw it with my own eyes."

"Just because the system says it, doesn't mean it's true."

"The data doesn't lie." Immediately, he regretted the words.

"*Data*—" Shey began.

"I didn't mean it like that."

"So Cade's just a statistic now?"

"I'm sorry, you know I didn't mean it the way it sounded."

She exhaled audibly. Her shoulders went rigid. The wall grew taller.

"It's my fault. If 13 had gone live when it was supposed to, none of this would have happened. If we'd pushed it a year ago, most of the bugs would be resolved by now. 13 would've detected imbalances. It would have warned us. That guy never would've had the chance to so much as step near a child. Devlin was right. I should have listened. I should have just—"

"*Devlin,*" Shey scoffed. "You think Devlin gives a shit about the people?"

"*Shey.*" Marus nodded toward his cellphone on the table. Anyone could be listening. Even Devlin. He picked it up and powered it down.

"How many people would've been wrongly prosecuted if 13 went live then? The program isn't exact. You've said that yourself. Even now, after all the hours you've spent, *thousands* of hours, and it isn't. There will always be errors."

"I can fix them."

"You can't fix everything, Marus. The work gives you purpose, I understand that. I know why you do it. But the program won't stop bad things from happening. You have to see that."

"I was working too much," Marus said. "I should've spent more time with you and with…Cade." He found it hard to say his son's name. As though it had taken on some alternative meaning. Pain. Loss. Failure. He swallowed hard. "It was wrong to put the work first for so long, I know that. But we were so close. Another month or so and it would have been ready. This never would have happened."

"You don't know that."

"*I do*. That's what I'm saying. The improvements we've made, they're substantial. I3 could end all crime."

The trees outside bowed in a sudden gust of wind. The leaves had already begun to turn. Reds and oranges. A yellow that seemed too bright for the day. He watched a woman chase her hat all the way to the corner until it scooted to a standstill on the sidewalk. She scooped it up, planted it firmly on her head, and spun on her heels.

"It doesn't matter. Even if you've made improvements, even if it was live, the program wouldn't have protected Cade."

"Why do you say that?"

Shey moved in closer. "The abduction wasn't random, Marus. Someone targeted us. They planned to take him."

He shook his head. "If that was the case, the system would have predicted it."

"What if it didn't?"

"It would. Don't you think I would know? When people are plotting to commit a crime, they scope things out. They pick a target and follow them. Every detail is mapped out. If there are multiple perpetrators involved, they have to have a way of communicating the plan. And the Protectors can see all of that. The program looks at everything."

"Just think about it for a second. The man never showed his face. We never saw which car was his. He knew where the cameras were and how to avoid them. He missed every single scanner, Marus. *How?* He knew we weren't there watching Cade, and he knew what to say to get Cade to go with him."

Her eyes began to water. She let them pool at the corners and roll. There was no use trying to stop it.

A man glanced up from his hash browns and then quickly away.

Marus leaned in a little closer. "Why would someone target us?"

Shey didn't answer.

"Why?"

She hesitated, twirling the band on her left hand as she often did when she was unsure about something. "I've spoken with some people. They think it was planned, that he was taken hostage."

"*People?* What people?"

"They think he could still be alive."

"Who, Shey?"

"Just people!" her voice rose above the morning chatter, and several diners turned their heads. "*Jesus,*" she said, wiping at her eyes. "Does it really matter *who*? If there was even a chance that your son was still alive wouldn't that be enough?"

He didn't say anything.

Now it was Shey who put a hand on his. Her face softened. "I'm sorry," she said. "If you want to go back to work, you should."

"What will you do?"

"I'll go visit Reagan."

Shey's older sister, Reagan, had been the voice of reason in many of their disagreements. She'd seen Marus's side when Shey couldn't. But more than that, she cared enough to communicate it, to help Shey understand.

"Maybe you could go see my dad, too."

"You haven't called him?"

"It's not really a conversation for the phone."

"Okay. I'll visit Reagan and your dad. But if you're going to go back to work, maybe you could look at Cade's Lifewatch. Just one more time."

Each time he looked, he was putting himself at risk. Eventually, someone would see that he was dipping into the data. But after everything they'd been through, how could he deny his wife?

"All right."

3

MORNING CREPT ABOVE rooftops and in through the window like a spirit stirring him from sleep. He lay naked, sideways and tangled in sheets that dripped from the edges of the bed. He turned to face his wife. The soft light made her skin all the more delicate. In sleep, even the anguished looked peaceful and whole.

The first few nights, eyes raw, and exhausted by emotion, they'd plunged violently into a desperate sleep. Last night had been different. Numb and silent, both laid awake in wait of sleep's release. But it didn't come. For hours they writhed there in the dark. Sometimes together and sometimes apart. Then, without a word, Shey rolled over. Lying on his back, Marus could see the gray shape of her body beneath the thin sheet. With fingertips that dug into the flesh at his shoulder, she pulled herself on top of him. Her thighs gripped the edges of his body as she bent his neck toward hers and worked the shirt up and over his head. He met her forceful kiss and slid her underwear off. Her lips held the salt of silent tears.

Gliding up the gradual slope of her frame, his hands stroked its peaks and valleys. Resting at that most perfect ascent from thigh to back, he pulled her hard against him. Her breath, warm and wet and trembling, crept from ear to neck to chest as the shadowed form of their fusion rose and fell, a tide of longing in the silvery hue of moonlight.

But the longing was for more than the body entwined in their own. They yearned for the normalcy that once was. Days filled with work and soccer practice, tummy aches and cartoons, exaggerated eye rolls and messes. Everywhere they'd looked, a breathtaking mess. It was unspoken but felt in each shiver of pleasure. Heard in every moan. And as they were brought into the fullness of the other, they exposed the emptiness growing inside.

■ ■ ■

At 7:00 a.m. Marus tried to eat breakfast. His daily Lifewatch report waited on the table screen for analysis. It confirmed what he already knew. He'd only achieved twenty percent of his nightly sleep goal. A severe lack in both the quantity and quality of his sleep was negatively affecting his ability to recover, process, and thrive. *Had he tried chamomile tea before bed?* the application asked. *Blackout shades? A lavender bath?* It gave him the opportunity to order all three from the screen. But he didn't like chamomile tea or taking baths. The blackest of blackout shades wouldn't be enough to block out the reality awaiting him each morning.

He took two long gulps from his steaming mug and closed the application. The morning's headlines appeared in its place. Cade's gap-toothed first-grade portrait stared back from the glass. Above it, the headline: POLICE STILL LOOKING FOR SUSPECT IN MURDER OF PROTECTOR'S SON.

Marus read through, scanning the details. A soccer game, the ball left in the parking lot. Surveillance footage, the marina, a jersey. *His* jersey. Marus clicked on a link to the surveillance footage from the school. Watching it for what had to be the hundredth time, he felt the heat beneath his collar build as soon as the man in the brown jacket entered the frame. He scanned the length of the article. Its author stated that police were asking the public to come forward with any information they might have on the boy's abduction. "The Intelligence Annex has been slow to share its progress regarding I3, a Protector Program update that will prevent random crimes like last week's kidnapping and murder of the son of prominent State employee, Marus Winde."

He shot back the remaining coffee in his ceramic mug and rinsed it in the sink. Outside the kitchen window, sanitation service men were already picking up garbage from the alley below. A sweeper truck noisily followed their route.

He went to his wife's side of the bed. Kissing her forehead, he whispered goodbye and closed the bedroom door behind him. He put on his jacket and shoes, retrieved his briefcase, and stepped onto the landing outside of the apartment.

How many people had been killed while he took his time with I3? How many more would have to die before it was ready?

The scanner chirped as the door clunked behind him, locking automatically.

■ ■ ■

Marus set out to walk the seven blocks from his apartment to the Protective Services Center, as he had every other morning before Cade's abduction, to do his duty. To keep the people safe.

It was colder than normal for the time of year. Commuters bundled in heavy coats ducked the wind as they stepped from the concrete boxes that held their homes. If the meteorologists were right, the harshest winter the city had seen in fifty years would come knocking in another month or so. And then—then it'd almost be Christmas, and everywhere he and Shey looked, there'd be something to remind them of the boy-shaped hole in their hearts.

Passing a scanner at a lamppost, Marus spotted a screen fixed to the back of a bench that displayed an advertisement for a sleeping aid. *Seize the day, every day.* An image of a man walking with a briefcase in one hand, a coffee in the other, smiled back. He looked like a slightly younger version of Marus, in better shape. The aim of every marketer. To get the consumer to see himself in the ad, using and benefitting from the product. Two capsules hovered in the corner. *Restin Sleeping Aid. The rest you need.*

As if it were that simple.

Though exhaustion weighed like a mask, the chilly morning air felt fresh against his face. He opened his eyes a little wider, watching as his neighbors hurried to meet autonomous sedans and coupes at the curb. He and Shey could get through this, he thought. *One day at a time.* Isn't that what people told each other? When Christmas came, they'd deal with it. Together. Maybe they'd finally take a vacation, go somewhere warm.

He remembered their wedding day, a small service at the Gardens. Reagan and her husband were there with their kids. His father, misty eyed and proud, held Cade, just over a year old, as he and Shey exchanged vows in front of a multicolored tapestry of crocus, foxglove, and salvia. With the bees as their witnesses.

I promise to cherish you and trust you, to love you with all of my heart, in good times and bad.

Across the street, he heard a car door slam. A woman wielding a microphone yelled, "Marus Winde!" Flanked by a camera man, she ran to meet him. "Valerie Finch, Channel Two News."

He kept walking.

"It's been nine days since your son was taken." The woman was only a couple steps behind him now. "How are you and your family coping?"

Marus continued on, head bowed. One foot in front of the other.

"Do you have anything you'd like to say to your son's killer?"

Say? No. Actions spoke so much louder than words.

Ms. Finch followed him for another two blocks and then tired.

As Marus crossed Third Street, a scanner read his iD, triggering the display of a targeted ad on the screen at the other side of the intersection. Every day as he walked to and from work, the screen displayed something his iD had identified him as needing. Virtual vacations, financial planning, health supplements, sleep aids, massages. Even the occasional ad for simulated sex or sexual enhancement made its way to the screen. The ads were often fodder for pillow talk, and in the occasion of a sex-related marketing campaign, something more.

Advertisers think it's been too long since we made love, he'd tell Shey, grinning.

I tend to agree with them, she'd respond, unbuttoning his shirt.

He walked toward the screen as he had a thousand times before, glancing at its message out of habit, in simultaneous annoyance and curiosity. What was it that he needed today?

This time, he wasn't ready for the ad it served. Vibrant yellow, red, and blue flowers surrounded a white building. In the right-hand corner, the ad copy. The single sentence that was supposed to convert Marus into a paying customer. A call to action so strong, so relevant, that it stung.

Where your wishes become meaningful memories. Redcliff Funeral Services.

■ ■ ■

The Protective Services Center was comprised of four annexes, towers that clung to the sides of the colossal Watchtower. An octagonal fortress encased in concrete and steel, the PSC housed all government agencies for the State's West Region.

The glass tower pierced the sky as it twisted upward, refracting and radiating the sun's beams onto the body of stainless steel skyscrapers below. A liquid flame at the heart of the Isle, it illuminated everything.

Struck by the totality of the structure, Marus would often stop after rounding that final corner on his walk to work. It was one of the most beautiful sights he'd ever seen. On sunny days, the glass, more brilliant than the sun itself, was blinding. He wanted to look, but he couldn't for long. The afterimage floated behind his eyelids long after he blinked and turned away.

Marus longed to be a Watchtower resident. Looking out their floor-to-ceiling windows, they could see people, people like him, scurry across the pavement below. High-ranking officials, celebrities, and multibillionaires were the only ones who could afford to live on the tower's residential floors. Here on the street, he'd be nothing more than a speck from their vantage point. But if they truly wanted to watch, they could look to the glass in their palms or the screens on their walls and see, in high definition, any public part of the city, or the State for that matter. Another perk on a luxe list of many for the elite who dwelled there.

The Watchtower was deemed the safest, most luxurious place to live in the world, but it afforded its residents more than guaranteed safety and awe-inspiring views. The tower also contained the world's tallest shopping mall, a handful of five-star restaurants, a theater, and a world-renowned spa. There was an aquarium and a museum, bowling lanes, and a virtual amusement park. The best of anything anyone could possibly desire was an elevator ride away, and completely secure. Only residents, their guests, and PSC employees, like Marus, were allowed access. Taking Cade on the weekends was one of his favorite perks.

Once Cade even spotted Luca Valdetti, a Watchtower resident. They'd been in the mall, coincidentally close to a sporting goods store. Cade approached Valdetti, wide eyed. He tapped him on the back to tell him he wanted to grow up and be just like him. *Well then*, Valdetti had said, *you'll need a ball. And you'll have to practice a whole lot.*

■ ■ ■

Marus had worked for the last five years in the Intelligence Annex, or IA, the PSC's north wing, as senior algorithm architect of the predictive policing program, what was known to the public as the Protector Program. It was his responsibility to develop, integrate, and optimize the predictive behavioral algorithm, aiding the region's police force and ensuring the safety of the State and its citizens. Without his work, the countless behaviors, actions, and communications collected by his surveillance-specialized counterparts at the IA would be useless.

Physical access points had been established and concealed decades ago, splitting cable lines and duplicating the data even before the New Era took hold. Back doors provided the State access to every bit of data produced in the years since. Phone calls, emails, browser history, the metadata, and the content. All of it was scraped, analyzed, and tagged to individual user profiles. The iDs collected offline data, behaviors, actions, and communications, even biometrics. It didn't matter the classification: direct, indirect, overt, or private. It was all observed. It had to be. The slightest oversight or break in the chain would render the entire system useless. Citizens didn't want uncertainty in the system. They needed guarantees, and that's what the State offered. There was no room for doubt.

The Protectors analyzed individuals' social circles, purchases, media consumption, utility usage, employment status, and routine, in real time. Each data point was scored individually and evaluated against additional data points to establish relevance and determine individual intent. The data points were grouped to create datasets, which were then classified, sorted, and paired to predict, without question, a specific and well-defined level of risk, zero to one hundred. A color scale served as a form of shorthand that designated the appropriate response. Threat indicators added up, increasing the individual's total, quantified risk. The higher the level, the greater the threat, the most dangerous of which required immediate, classified action.

Marus had only heard of one Red-Level threat. A crime lord who met justice only after subjecting the State to mass terror in the years leading up to the New Era. Assassinations, political hostages, bombings, shootings. Nothing was out of scope. Maybe now he was conspiring with other detainees in the yard of the detention camp where he was being held. Maybe he was being tortured. Maybe he'd already died there. No one knew. All Marus cared about was that he was no longer a threat.

Marus's work had helped bring peace to the streets, ending more than a decade of increased crime and terrorist activity, bombings, kidnappings, murders, chaos, and a State that succumbed to the rule of organized crime. He had worked with a skilled team of technologists and policymakers to create the infrastructure that enabled the birth of the New Era, providing a future free from fear for the State and its people.

His latest work with I3, the Internal Indicator Initiative, furthered the goal of the New Era. He and his colleagues were programming the future. Working toward a world where no one would have to endure a deprivation of human rights or the senseless loss of a loved one. I3 would change everything. It would be his legacy.

The only one he had left.

■ ■ ■

Three flights of concrete steps led to the entrance of the PSC's north wing, the IA. Marus ascended with downcast eyes, scanning the names etched beneath his feet. Casualties of the not-so-distant past. Their deaths had paved the way to the New Era just as their names now paved the way to the work that made the New Era so. What was in a name? Could a string of characters carved in stone really harbor the being who borrowed them? Would he see his son's face in the tracing of a *C* or an *A*, a *D*, or an *E*? Deep hazel eyes he'd so loved, a whisper of freckles bridging the familiar button of his nose? Or would they simply be letters, loops, and lines that became more foreign, as most words do, the longer Marus looked?

He scanned his wrist for entry at the main door, and once inside, again for an agent who verified his identity on a screen. Marus didn't know his name. He didn't recall ever looking at the man but glanced now at a wide, purple scar above his right eye. Had it been knife? Or a shard of glass? Had he narrowly escaped becoming another name stamped on a slab outside? Who had he lost? Much easier to contemplate the pain of others than to consider one's own. The man appeared to notice the questions forming on Marus's face and watched with distrust as he retrieved his briefcase from the conveyor.

The north elevator took him to the ninth floor of the IA, matching his voice to his profile so it could clock his time. A screen on the wall thanked him for being early, the fifteenth time that month. He nodded at the camera in receipt of the notification. The report faded, replaced by a message. *I am in charge of how I feel, and today I am choosing happiness.*

If there was one downside to a transparent world, this was it. He missed the days when he could be miserable and angry and no one, not even a computer program, had to know about it.

The doors dinged open and spat him out into a swarm of people headed to the conference room. He zigzagged his way through the crowd, head down, eyes fixed on the screen in his hands, bumping shoulders as he went. He'd almost reached the collaboration area when he ran directly into another person. Their phones clattered to the floor.

He picked his up and then the other. Righting himself, he saw that it was only Anj. She pushed her stringy blonde hair back behind her ear and rubbed at a red mark on her forehead.

"Oh good, it's you." He handed her phone over.

"*Marus*? What are you doing here?"

Under normal circumstances she would've made some smart remark. Punched him in the arm. Told him to *fuck off,* even. He would have preferred that to her wide eyes. The ill-matched tone of compassion in her voice.

"I work here."

"Yeah, but, I thought you'd be out for a while."

He turned to watch the speed-walking stragglers casually cut one another off, vying for the last of the seats in the conference room.

"There's a lot of work to do." His head dipped definitively, as if that explained everything. As if his presence—*at a time like this*—was normal. Admirable, not negligent.

He made his way through the café-like collaboration area and game room to the individual cubes along the back wall. His was a corner desk with a tall partition. He'd never done much for decor. Only two items were pinned beside his multiscreen configuration. One was an early rendering of the Protective Services Center, an image that had driven him during his years in college. The other was a photo of Shey and Cade. In it, Shey was laughing, her head thrown back, and Cade stared in awe at something off to the side. Marus looked at it now, pausing at the silhouette of Cade's nose, his severe eyes, not quite his mother's green, not his own glossy brown.

Each person's iris was as unique as their fingerprint. Never to be reproduced naturally. Never to be seen again in the whole human race. Upon a person's death, the eyes would sink back into the skull. Undertakers glued the eyelids shut for this reason. Marus shuddered at the thought.

"Does this have anything to do with that promotion?" Anj said, poking her head around the partition.

He waved on the screens.

"You know that Devlin would understand if you took a few more days, hell, a couple weeks off. Plus, you're a shoo-in. Everyone knows the promotion is yours. I'm sure Devlin's told you that himself."

Marus didn't want to talk about the promotion or why he was there. If he was honest with himself, it was because he didn't know how *not to be*.

"You know that billboard on Third?" he said instead. "The big one at the corner?"

She nodded.

"Today it targeted me for a funeral services ad."

"Oh shit, Marus." She put her hand on his arm. "I can't even fathom what you and Shey are going through."

"It makes sense though. I was identified as the target audience for that ad given this *life event*, or whatever advertisers call it. It was displayed because I need their service. That's the reality." The corners of his eyes began to water. "That is, if they can recover his body."

Anj looked away, allowing him the small courtesy.

"That's the beauty of the system," he said, wiping his eyes. "It works. It tells us where to live and what to eat and who to date, and it makes life more efficient. It predicts crime, prevents accidents, protects people. So why didn't it work this time? Why didn't it protect *my son*?"

Anj didn't say anything. She looked at the data overlay, the code active on the wall screens behind them. The answer was there, somewhere.

"It's because I3 isn't live. Because the system, as is, isn't good enough," he said. "It's my fault. My failure. As his father and as a Protector. That's why I'm here. I owe it to my son and to every parent out there to make sure nothing like this happens again."

■ ■ ■

The first step to solving a problem was identifying what the problem was.

He needed more than Cade's Lifewatch data. He needed all of it. It didn't take him long to write the script. Pulling back the geotags and other data was a matter of stringing together several database queries, nothing more. The trick of it, though, was masking the request. *Misattribution.* With the right adjustments, the script would appear automatic; the origin, unknown. He wondered how soon the algorithms would notice the pull, against protocol and unlike the rest. If he was as good as he thought he was, they never would.

The lengthy report waited in queue with hundreds of other legitimate ones. Algorithm engineering was more than design and implementation. It dealt in analysis and optimization. Experimental evaluation. A never-ending process of testing that involved scraping data to systematically analyze what was being collected, how it was sorted, and whether improvements could be made. *There was always room for improvement.*

Under normal circumstances, the work was daunting at best. Before the launch of a new initiative, when a major system update was in beta, it bordered impossible. Cade's data formed one report among hundreds Marus would have to sift through, but it was the only one that mattered. It was all he could think about.

He stood to stretch and peer above the partition. The floor hummed with the sound of the machine and pockets of muffled conversation. As long as Anj and Gene weren't around, he wouldn't be bothered. No one else had the gall to venture to his corner. He returned to his seat and clicked on the report. There was Cade's name. Their address. His son's State-issued photo. Though rudimentary and available to the public, the information in this context was decreed private. In the dozens of other reports, it was obscured by the system to prevent State employees from personally identifying individual datasets. A comical concession to put the public at ease. *We know you, everything about you, but don't worry, we can't see your name.*

This, of course, was not an ill-intentioned breach of citizen privacy. This was his son. This was his right. That flat line across the screen, sharp and straight as a scalpel, had cut his own heart in two. *Time heals all things.* He'd heard his father whisper the words to himself after his mother's death. What was closure if not a clock? Not an end as everyone imagined, but a beginning. *A reset.* He had seen it for himself, had pinpointed the exact moment his son's heart stopped. Now he needed to show it to Shey. Only then would she understand. Only then could time begin again for both of them.

The only thing left of Cade's life, the bit of code that represented his final interactions, illuminated the screen in front of him. The report showed the information Muñoz delivered the day Cade had gone missing. He saw the tag at St. Xavier Prep and, later, at the marina. That line, the ultimate symbol of life itself, a boundless plain from 2:14 p.m. on. Marus took a screenshot, then deleted it. Shey would have to take him at his word.

■ ■ ■

The lunch hour came and went, and still Marus remained in front of the screens. He wasn't hungry, anyway. It wasn't that he was averse to food; he'd simply forget to eat. Forget to shower. Forget to sleep. Grief did that.

Sometimes, he'd forget to breathe.

He hadn't accomplished much. Ten reports. That's all he'd been able to get through. Not even a fraction of what he was supposed to do to keep I3 on track. But he was here, wasn't he? Wasn't that enough for today, *given the circumstances*?

His colleagues were emboldened. Previously, no one but Gene or Anj would step near his cubicle, but several made their way over now, one after the other, to offer their own commentary on *what happened to Cade*. Had they known his name or age before? Marus doubted it. Tragedy was a window, a way to look in on other people's lives. To be present, but unaffected. After all, you didn't have to walk through the door.

Marus kept his head down, trying to appear as busy and focused as possible to deter his colleagues and their assortment of obligatory condolences. Often it's more challenging to appear to be something than to actually *be* it. *Authenticity* had been a buzzword during his coming of age at Newbold. Now he understood it had nothing to do with virtue; it was a matter of efficiency. It was too exhausting otherwise.

In addition to the others, Anj had already checked in on him three times. In his peripheral vision, he'd see her forehead, her eyes, then mouth, appear slowly from behind the wall. *Did he want to go for a walk? Had he had lunch? Could he join her for lunch? Had Gene stopped by?*

No, thanks. No. Sorry, no. Nope.

He kept returning to that thin, black line on the screen. Here one day. Gone the next.

Maybe he should've stayed home with Shey after all. He wondered what she was doing. If she'd eaten. How much she'd cried. If she'd gotten any rest. He picked up the phone to call, but a notification flashed across his screen. It was from Commissioner Jack Devlin by way of his admin.

Devlin wanted to see him, *immediately*, it read.

■ ■ ■

Commissioner Devlin waited in one of the small meeting rooms on the second floor. Marus had always thought of them as closets, but they were a necessity of the open-concept office. A place to gather your thoughts or have a "private" conversation. The setting for performance reviews, promotions, and warnings. And firings.

"Please, take a seat," Devlin said.

Marus closed the door, activating the privacy glass. He walked toward the empty chair opposite Devlin and sat.

Sit straight. Maintain eye contact. Nod and appear engaged.

He didn't have to feign interest. Marus's heart throbbed with it.

"Thank you for meeting with me. I know you're busy up there," the commissioner said, smiling.

Marus shifted in the chair. Impromptu meetings meant an increased likelihood of one of two things. Promotion or demotion. Plain and simple.

The last time he'd spoken to the commissioner had been some months prior. Devlin had come unannounced. He'd actually sought Marus out to cite several improvements Marus had made to the Protector algorithm and discuss his efforts with I3. Devlin had complemented Marus's work and dangled a carrot.

There's a new initiative on the tenth floor, he'd said. *I'm recommending you for it. We need a mind like yours up there.*

Another rung in the right direction.

Marus crossed and then uncrossed his legs. This meeting was either about the promotion, or the unauthorized data pulls. Either way, it was a move up or a step down. *You're a shoo-in,* Anj had said. He wasn't sure.

"I wanted to offer you my condolences," Devlin said.

"Thank you, sir."

"I also wanted to see how you're doing." The commissioner's brown eyes blinked with sincerity, and yet Marus could tell Devlin was studying him. Weighing him, even now. A test of some sort.

"It's a difficult time."

"How is your wife holding up?"

"She's trying to keep busy. We both are. She was very supportive of me coming in today."

"What a patriot." There was something about the way he said it that set Marus on edge. "I don't think my own wife would be that supportive," Devlin said and smiled. "But she wouldn't be wrong to want me home. It's important to be with family during times like these. The Protectors understand if you need more time off."

"I appreciate that, sir. But I3 is almost ready, and I'd like to see that through."

Devlin leaned forward. The wax run through his salt-and-pepper hair gleamed, a halo in the cylindrical glow of the recessed lights above. "Your dedication is commendable, Marus. Still, it's a matter of quality control. Of efficiency. The Internal Indicator Initiative should have gone live over a year ago. We keep pushing deadlines—"

"It wasn't ready!" Marus said, surprised by his own interruption and the volume of his voice.

Devlin raised an eyebrow.

"It wasn't ready then," Marus continued carefully, "but we're almost finished. Just a few weeks out now."

"We can't miss this deadline. Too many lives hang in the balance. There are plenty of capable people who can lead the launch if you feel you can't focus on the work. Your *position*, well, it's understandable."

"I assure you, sir, it won't be an issue. If anything, I appreciate now more than ever how delicate the system is. I'm committed to I3, and committed to resolving the program's deficiencies, for my son and for the State."

The commissioner tilted his round, clean-shaven chin toward the light. "Well, I'm pleased to hear that. No one knows the program like you." He smiled, blinking at Marus in approximation. "Handpicked from Newbold itself. Employee number three, weren't you?"

"That's right, sir."

"And you were responsible for calibrating and implementing the individual risk algorithm in its earliest forms?"

"I worked with a team."

He recalled the first day on the job, the breathtaking tour of the Protective Services Center with a handful of other Newbold Corp. recruits, Anj and his old friend Gene among them.

"There's no need to be modest, Marus. It's an impressive legacy you've built."

"Thank you, sir."

A little over a week ago, Marus had wanted the promotion more than anything else. From the moment Devlin mentioned it, his first waking thoughts and last conscious moments before sleep had been filled with notions of its possibility. Numerous perks would present themselves. An entire world of opportunity would open its doors the moment he stepped foot on the tenth floor. The salary and personal pride that would come with it were part of its appeal, but there was a greater pull. The promotion would afford them a larger, more secure apartment in one of the best complexes outside of the Watchtower, itself. He'd already found a floor plan Shey would love.

"I understand you've dodged all of the media's requests for comment on your son's death."

Death. Marus tried not to fixate on the word.

"We felt we needed some privacy."

"Understandable, of course. I do hope you'll reconsider, though. It'd be good for you. And good for the public to hear from the boy's father. People are feeling very unsettled right now, especially given the recent fearist threats against the PSC. I assume you heard about Li Syun?"

Marus remembered the video that was made. The slash, a deep-red smile carved across Li Syun's throat.

"Yes," he said. "I saw it on the news."

"If we can't protect our own, how are we expected to keep the public safe? That's what those bastards want people thinking."

"But as an isolated incident—"

"Don't underestimate them, Marus. A little doubt can go a long way. People begin to mistrust the system, mistrust the government. Their uncertainty blinds them. It makes them vulnerable. As Protectors, we must ensure the security of the State and citizen safety, at all costs. The only way to do that is to safeguard the system. If we waiver, if the deficiencies aren't resolved, we risk everything. Everything you've built. It's all the fearists need to sabotage the Protector Program and throw us back into a frenzy of chaos and fear. Some good news regarding I3 will ease their doubt. And the quarterly crime report ought to help. It's due out later this week. The decline should be significant, don't you think?"

Marus nodded.

Devlin was right. All indications pointed to a declining crime rate, the lowest it had been in his lifetime. Maybe in all of history. And yet, to Marus, the world felt more dangerous than ever before.

"Of course, stats only go so far," Devlin went on. "There's nothing like a story to rally the people. That's what they need. That's why I'd like you to make a statement. The public should hear from you. Your impressive background and commitment to the program should be celebrated. Cade should be celebrated. The people need to know how we're progressing. When I3 goes live, it will be dedicated to him."

Marus found himself nodding.

"Good. I'll have our PR team prep you." Devlin smiled triumphantly.

A politician's smile, Shey once commented.

4

CLOTHES WERE STREWN across the apartment. Several books and sheets of paper had been stacked atop the kitchen table. Marus closed the door and set his briefcase down. He plucked a book from the top of the stack. Creased and worn, it was a collection of essays and poems. A faded yellow note stuck out from the middle. He went to the marked spot, an essay, "Self-Reliance" by Ralph Waldo Emerson, and saw the words underlined there.

Speak your latent conviction and it shall be the universal sense; for always the inmost becomes the outmost...

He followed the pencil marks and dog-ears. Yellow strokes that bled from one page to another.

Trust thyself: every heart vibrates to that iron string. Accept the place the divine Providence has found for you, the society of your contemporaries, the connection of events.

He closed the book and returned it to its perch, scanning the crumpled papers stacked to the side. Shey's small, slanted handwriting crammed the lines.

"Hon?" he called, walking into the living room.

No one answered.

He reached into his pocket and turned off his phone. Shrugging out of his coat, he tossed it over the back of the couch. He walked down the hallway and into the master bedroom. The closet door was open. Several naked hangers littered the floor, but the room was empty.

Walking back toward the living room, Marus paused outside of Cade's closed door. He knocked and turned the knob. Shey was standing by the dresser, looking at the soccer ball sitting atop a mess of blankets draped across the bed. Neither of them had touched the ball since the night Muñoz had come to tell them their lives would never be the same.

"Hey," he said.

Shey turned to look at him. Her face was white. Her eyes, tired and heavy. *Empty.* A small duffel bag hung limp in her right hand.

"What are you doing?"

"I'm leaving."

"What do you mean?"

She ducked under his arm and went out into the living room. She set the duffel bag in front of his coat on the couch. "There are people who can help me," she said, reaching for a pair of pants on the coffee table. She folded them in thirds and set them inside the bag.

"Don't start on the *people* again."

Shey ignored him.

"Help you how, Shey?"

"Help me find him."

"Hon," he said, following her to the next piece of clothing, a sweater on the arm of the chair. He hesitated. "I looked at Lifewatch and the rest of it. He—he's gone."

If she heard him, she didn't acknowledge it. She moved back toward the bag and tucked the sweater inside.

"We need to face this, Shey. *Together.* We can't run away from it."

At this, she turned. Her voice was sharp. "I'm not running away." She stuffed several more sweaters and pairs of pants inside the bag and went to the kitchen table.

"Well, what are you doing?" Marus said, one step behind her.

"I'm doing *something*. I have questions I need answered. If I'm running, I'm running toward it. Toward the truth."

"There's a right way to do this."

"What? *The program*?" She folded the papers and slid them inside. "You know what Cade is to the program? Eight characters, bolded red text: DECEASED."

"They'll find who did it, Shey. They always do."

"They'll find *somebody*. I know how the legal system works, Marus. It's about numbers. Maintaining their goddamned solve rate."

"Shey!" He brought his voice to a whisper. "You can't say things like that."

She ignored him. One by one, she placed each of the books into the bag. "They'll look to the WatchList and find a man who meets the criteria and pin it on him. Someone who was in the wrong place at the wrong time. Some poor guy who rubbed them the wrong way. I've seen it before. I don't want that. That won't bring us peace. You're lying to yourself if you think it will."

"You can't just leave."

"Why should I stay? I won't make a difference here. There's nothing for me to do." She slung the bag around her shoulder and zippered it shut. "Besides, I don't feel safe here anymore."

He tried not to flinch at her words. She'd known this last comment would cut him.

"Let me ask Devlin for a security detail then. I'm sure he'd give us one. He wants to help."

"I'm sure he would," Shey said, her voice thick with sarcasm. She shook her head. "You don't get it."

"Then help me *get it*."

"Nothing can be done here. These people I'm going with, they can fix this. You don't have to worry. They'll keep me safe."

"These people! These people! Do you even know them? Do you know what their motivations are? Maybe they're manipulating you! Maybe they're..." he lowered his voice, "*fearists*. You don't know, Shey. Think about it. You aren't being rational."

"Why should I be *rational* after what's happened!" She began to cry.

He moved toward her slowly and took her in his arms. A truce.

"And we let it happen," she said. The words were muffled and warm at his collar.

"We'll get through this. We will," he said. He held her tighter, but she broke away.

"That's just it," she said, studying him. "This *isn't* something to get through."

"Leaving won't do any good. People will make their own conclusions about why you've gone. And the media will think—"

"What, that I was responsible? That I was negligent? Well, I was negligent. I am responsible. That's why I have to go. I have to do something about it."

"It's too dangerous, Shey."

She was quiet a moment. He could see the calculation in her eyes. Her lip quivered with the question she was asking herself. Then, the faintest exhalation. He'd learned to look for that. *Resolution.*

"I'm going, Marus," she said. "I've made up my mind."

So that was it, then. There would be no dissuading her.

Her face registered his disappointment, the hurt. But it wouldn't change anything.

"I know you don't understand, but—I just have this feeling."

"What feeling?"

"That Cade's out there. That he's waiting to be found."

"Jesus, Shey. I saw the line." Regretting his tone, he reached out for the back of her arms, to reel her in. To hold her. To help her understand. "I saw Cade's Lifewatch data. I saw his pulse. It was there and then it wasn't. Just like Muñoz said. He's dead."

It struck him then, this knowledge that somehow seemed new. As though he'd just learned it himself. *My son is dead.* The sharp certainty of it.

"Cade is dead," he said again.

His voice wavered, his lips trembled, and now it was Shey who inched closer to comfort him. Not in an embrace, but a nearness. She held his gaze for a moment. Her eyes were the same green but looked hollow now. *Dead*, he thought. She dropped her head, and he knew then that this was goodbye. On lifted toes she moved forward, craning her neck halfheartedly to kiss his cheek. Her lips were cracked and cold.

"I love you," she said.

She didn't wait for him to say it back; she didn't need to. The body of the duffel bag banged against the frame as she stepped through. The door clunked shut, and the locks reengaged. A mechanical whirring sound.

The incredible weight of silence.

He went to the window, searching for the shape of her along the sidewalk. Long, brown strands of hair flew sideways as the wind whipped into her. She clutched the strap at her shoulder and quickened her pace. She was almost to the corner and out of sight when she turned and tipped her head up at their building. She couldn't see him through the privacy glass, but she knew he was there just as he'd known she'd look back.

A gray sedan crept to a stop near the curb behind her. Shey lingered a moment. Her eyes scanned the shiny, black windows that were their home, seeking his.

Then she turned, stepped into the car, and was gone.

■ ■ ■

The apartment, once warm, even small for the voices and life that had filled it, became cold and cavernous the moment Shey stepped outside. Not knowing where she was headed or when she'd return made the accompanying quiet unbearable. Who was inside the gray sedan?

Marus went to the study and closed the door. A hundred items waited, arranged on the desktop screen. A to-do list that trickled far below what was visible.

Thirty minutes passed and then sixty, his fingers barely brushing the keyboard. A guttural snarl of stomach snapped him out of his trance. It was almost 9:00 p.m., and he hadn't eaten all day. He went into the kitchen, avoiding the empty table.

Dinnertime was his favorite part of the day. A time to be with family, to nourish the body and recharge. He enjoyed cooking, the methodical combination of elements to produce a desired result. Around the table, he'd ask Shey and Cade if they could list the ingredients. Cade would analyze the colors and give his guess. Shey would purse her lips and smack her tongue in an exaggerated display of detection that always made Cade giggle. There were very few ingredients she had trouble identifying.

He pulled a Ready-Made meal from the freezer—hearty chili and cornbread—and, once it was ready, hovered over the counter to choke down the slurry. The cornbread was hard and tasted of cardboard. He threw it out.

He glanced at his watch. It had been a birthday present, the first gift Shey had ever given him. He preferred its leather strap, the gold buckle, and its broad but understated white face to the Watch everyone at work wore.

The Watch was sleek, square faced, and embedded in thermoplastic rubber. Like Shey's gift, the Watch told the time, but it also displayed physiological signs. As with the Lifewatch app, it provided the information collected from the iD chip in its user's wrist, reading back heart rate, blood pressure, hydration levels, and chemical signs of stress. An exchangeable band would flash the wearer's "hue of wellbeing" with a two-finger squeeze.

The Watch and its maker, his previous employer, Newbold Corp., were certainly capitalizing on the New Era and the ubiquity of iD technology, but they were also empowering people in real time with the data their bodies produced. His old boss, Newbold's founder and CEO, theorized that regular wear and adherence to the recommendations and warnings it displayed would extend its owner's life by five to ten years. It was a bold claim but was marketed brilliantly and endorsed by dozens of doctors. Newbold sent him one before it was available to the public. He wore it for five months. The constant chirping for his lack of sleep and general *un*wellness almost drove him mad.

It was 9:45 p.m., more than two hours since Shey had gone. How far could one get in that time? What distance would she have to travel to feel safe?

He would find out. He had to.

Marus returned to the study and waved on the screens.

■ ■ ■

He awoke six hours later, covered in sweat and cramped in the reading chair beside his desk. He didn't remember lying down. The screens, in sleep mode, emanated a green glow. Three blurry, white digits glared at him from the screens' center. It was 4:17 a.m.

Scenes from a dream floated to the forefront of his consciousness. In it, his bedroom door creaked open and Cade's small, shadowy figure moved to his side of the bed. He was crying.

"They're gonna get me, Daddy."

It was too dark. Marus couldn't see his face.

"No one's going to get you. It was just a bad dream."

"They're gonna get me."

"You're safe. I promise." Marus tried to reach out to touch him, but his hand couldn't find his son's edges.

There was a pause. Cade's shadowed profile turned and began to walk away, stopping just inside the bedroom's open door.

"You're lying."

Had the dream ended then? Or had he simply forgotten the rest? He forced himself from the chair, making his way down the hall to the master bathroom, where he drank his fill directly from the faucet before splashing his face. His eyes burned bloodshot in the mirror in front of him.

Sheets of rain drove down on the quiet world outside the bedroom window. Out of the corner of his eye, he noticed something floating. The tiny orange object seemed to glow in contrast to the bleak sky behind it, swaying back and forth as it climbed higher. At eye level it became discernible. A large spider struggling up an invisible strand to shelter itself from the night's storm. How simple life was for such a creature. Survival was success, and death, the only failure that counted.

Marus had survived, but what did it matter if he failed to keep his family safe?

He pressed his forehead to the cold glass, applying the weight of his entire body. With his back arched, he pushed down harder, fantasizing the metamorphosis of a hairline fracture, the sound of cracking glass, the impetus of his own body moving through the jagged vertical plane. Shrouded in crystal as he tumbled toward nothingness.

How long would he live? It was a question he hadn't considered since childhood, during those uncertain years that followed his mother's death. It seemed more relevant now than it had then. Would he spend the next forty years with this hollow feeling of loss pressing upon his chest? Or would it be fifty? He tried to picture himself as an old man. Would he be alone like his father, in a home under the care of strangers? Lifewatch served to ensure that his death wouldn't be untimely. Genetic decoding and self-quantification would tell the doctors when he was ready.

He wondered if Shey would be there as he slipped into a comfortable bedchamber to close his eyes for the last time.

5

THE ROSE CAFÉ was four quick blocks from the PSC. At 12:30 p.m. Marus walked over. He avoided the billboards and sidewalk screens. Suggestions that seemed amusing before were cruel now. He didn't want to see what he needed. He already knew what he lacked.

Sitting at their table, he drank his third cup of coffee. The café was much busier than when he and Shey had come Sunday. People gathered at small tables around him with eyes glued to the screens in their hands. He scanned their faces looking for green eyes, freckles, and a familiar nose, but Shey was not among them.

He knew from the last tag he'd scraped back that she wouldn't be here. The night before, she'd been tagged at the entrance of Reagan's apartment building across the bridge, though the car hadn't appended her route there. Either it'd never been retrofitted, or the GPS had been disabled. He'd hacked into the security footage to get a better look. An old Buick LeSabre. Gray, as he'd thought. Rusted. But he couldn't make out the license plate. There hadn't been any other activity as of this morning. According to her geodata, she was still at Reagan's, in good hands. A small mercy.

Sitting in the café, some illogical part of Marus hoped the data was wrong. That she'd come back to the Isle and somehow slipped the scanners. Maybe she'd know to find him here, just as she'd known he'd be watching from the windows. How many times had they read each other's minds?

Wishful thinking. He drew back on the mug. Even as the ceramic touched his lips, he heard her words.

It's okay to think with your heart instead of your head once in a while.

That was what he was doing. He'd looked at Cade's data against protocol. The program he'd written last night was illegally pulling back Shey's activity so he could make sure she was safe. These behaviors were not the result of rational thinking. A rational act would be to notify the police. To tell Devlin. But he didn't want the commissioner to see his failure. He didn't want the media catching wind. And Shey was right; he didn't trust the police. Real detectives were hard to come by in an age of algorithmic absolutism, where everything was spelled out. But Marus knew what to look for. If there were clues, he'd uncover them. If the police couldn't track down Cade's killer and exact justice, Marus would. Somehow, he would find a way to piece his family back together. He and Shey could begin again.

An older couple sitting several tables away squinted up at the news report on the screen mounted on the wall behind him. A large-breasted redhead was interviewing Commissioner Devlin.

"Thanks to the enormous success of the Protector Program and the commitment and support of so many citizens, criminal activity has been cut eighty percent since the New Era began. While this quarterly crime report affirms that we are moving in the right direction, tragedies like the one our community saw earlier this month are a painful reminder that we are not doing enough."

Cade's soccer player portrait replaced Devlin's talking head. In it, he exposed a toothy grin. The rounds of his cheeks and the slope of his nose were dotted with small, late-summer freckles. He wore the same blue jersey now tainted with his blood.

"We must remain vigilant to avoid this kind of senseless loss of life," Devlin continued. "New improvements like I3 are crucial to the security and wellbeing of the nation."

The redhead nodded. "Thank you for your time, Commissioner. I'm sure everyone will agree that it's better to be safe than sorry." She smiled at the camera, but she was really smiling at the viewers at home, at work, in cafés across the city. At Marus.

He turned away.

From the corner, the grandfather clock coiled its spring in anticipation of the hour, chiming only once. In front of it, a man drank tea alone. It was the same man in the hat he'd seen sitting there Sunday. His sharp-cornered limbs jutted out from his tall, thin frame as he hunched over the wooden table to return his spoon to its saucer. He didn't speak to anyone, and no one spoke to him. Though Marus couldn't see the man's eyes for the hat he wore, Marus was certain he was watching him.

Then, as if in a trance suddenly broken, the man, *The Hat*, as Marus thought of him, set aside his tea to retrieve a pair of leather gloves from his coat pocket. He placed the napkin in the cup, centered it at the edge of the table beside a small plate containing the remnants of a croissant, and left.

■ ■ ■

Marus's coworkers had always acknowledged him when he passed by. A slight nod of the head, an upturned grin, even a nervous glance. They knew who he was, where he'd been recruited from, and about his quick ascent to the top of the IA. He was accustomed to the attention. The inability to walk down a hallway without being recognized had become a form of validation.

But the attention had never been quite like this. Men and women he didn't know frowned in his direction as he walked through the lobby, across the common spaces, and along the aisles to his workstation at the back wall. Their eyes were full of pity and, for once, Marus sensed, gratitude that they weren't in his shoes.

Gene's round figure was idling awkwardly at Marus's desk when he returned. His friend rested a chubby hand against the partition as he watched the data feed scroll. Marus looked on with amusement as Gene's head pivoted back and forth like a dog waiting for a ball to be thrown. It had been weeks since he'd seen him last, and Marus missed the ungainly sight of his friend tottering down the halls.

Gene worked more than Marus did. Without a family of his own, he hadn't risked being an absent father or husband. He could often be found at his desk, accompanied by an experimental health drink on a good day, and a doughnut every other. His penchant for yo-yo dieting, as well as the wildly distorted content of his online dating profile, made excellent fodder for email chains between him, Marus, and Anj. Mostly Marus and Anj. But Gene laughed along, never taking himself too seriously. It was one of his most endearing qualities.

"Where have you been?" Marus called as he approached the partition. "Don't tell me one of those diet pills made you sick again."

Gene swung around, revealing an expression at odds with itself. "I saw the news," he said. "I'm sorry about Cadien."

Marus hung his coat on the peg behind his chair. "Thanks."

Unsure what to do, Gene moved closer to Marus. His short arms extended slowly over his paunch as he went in for a hug.

In all of their years of friendship, Marus couldn't recall them ever embracing, and the oddity of it, the way Gene's fat fingers patted his back and his friend's round stomach thumped against him, provided Marus an unusual sense of comfort.

"Thanks," Marus said again.

Gene gave him a squeeze and a final pat before pulling away. "Do the police have any leads?"

"They don't have anything. I don't know what to do."

"What can you do?" Gene said.

"Investigate it myself. Look at the data, figure out who is behind this."

"Be careful with that, Marus. You know what Devlin would say."

He did know. Devlin would say it was understandable but not defensible. To Devlin, there was a difference.

"If someone found out that analysts—*Protectors*—could bypass the privacy blocks and access personal data, people would be beside themselves. And with the launch coming up, it might not be such a good idea."

The launch was crucial. Not just for public safety or the program, but for the analysts, the engineers. Everybody. It was job security. I3 was the next phase. Without it, they'd all be assigned to routine maintenance. And the problem with routine maintenance was just that. It was routine. New programs could easily be written to address the workload. Many of them would be reassigned. Many more would become obsolete.

"Speaking of the launch, how are things on your end? I haven't seen you in a while. Do you need help catching up with anything?"

Gene may have worked harder, but Marus was smarter and faster. It was an unspoken understanding between them. Gene was there when Marus needed additional manpower, and Marus was there for Gene when he couldn't quite wrap his head around something or was working on a deadline.

"No, no. I think I'll be good. Thanks though." Gene's flabby face ripened. Red pinpricks dotted his jawline, an absence of facial hair that sometimes flared up in response to stressful situations. His lips were darker purple now. His hands glistened.

"Are you okay? You don't look well," Marus said.

"Oh, uh, yeah. I'm on a cleanse."

"A cleanse?"

"Yeah, tea. All natural. The first few days you feel like you're dying, but once the toxins are flushed you can run a marathon in your sleep. So they say."

"How long has it been?"

"A week and a half," Gene said. "Apparently, I'm more toxic than the average person." The corner of his mouth lifted into a halfhearted grin.

"I could've told you that," Marus said.

Gene bobbed with a chuckle.

"It's good to see you." Marus smiled.

"Yeah, you too." He fidgeted as Marus took his seat behind the desk. "Say, you up for grabbing a bite after work?"

Marus swiveled in the chair. "I'd love to but I can't tonight."

"Right, you probably have to get home to Shey."

"Actually, I'm going to go visit my dad at Edenbrook."

"Does he—does he know?"

"He hates watching the news, and I haven't called."

Gene frowned, trying to think of something to say.

"Well, I better get back to work," Marus said. "Thanks for coming by. It means a lot."

"Okay, yeah. Of course." Gene said, straightening. He looked relieved, as though he'd been let off the hook. "Let's get together soon. We should talk." He leaned forward to pat Marus's arm and walked away.

Gene was reliably awkward, but there was something off about him. He seemed nervous, like he knew something that Marus didn't.

■ ■ ■

The Edenbrook Care Center was the nicest senior facility on the Isle. Surrounded by gardens and nestled among cliffs, it had a clear view of the ocean. Serpentine paths wound across expertly manicured lawns, around fountains and reflection pools, before ending at various observation points scattered atop the rocks.

Despite excellent health, Marus's father, Vic, had been a resident for five years.

It wasn't a matter of medical care. If Marus was honest, it was so he didn't have to worry about his dad.

Vic shuffled out into the lobby. The white shock of hair that hugged the base of his scalp stuck out from one side, as though he'd slept on it.

"What a nice surprise." He walked over and hugged his son. "I thought you already met your quota for visits this month," he said, winking at him. "Where's your prettier half? And our all-star?"

"Can we go outside? Take a walk?"

"I already had my exercise for the day. The nurses around here, let me tell you..." He looked to Marus for a reaction. "I guess it'd be good to take advantage of the fresh air while I'm still alive." He laughed at himself. "Let me get my jacket."

■ ■ ■

As they walked along the path, Marus tried to think of how to tell his father that his only grandson was dead. Was it better to soften the blow or just come out with it? He spotted a bench at the observation point ahead. It was best if they were seated, he decided. If not for Vic's well-being, for his own.

"You know, I am glad you are here," Vic said. "I've been meaning to ask you about Cade."

Marus stopped and turned to face his father, but his dad kept walking.

"I know his birthday is coming up, and I wanted to talk to you about a present."

"Dad—"

"Don't say it. We both know I'm getting him something. Actually, it's already in the works."

"Dad—"

"Just listen to me. I'm pretty well taken care of here, thanks to you, and I have a bit of savings. There's no point in holding onto it. God knows how much the government will take when I'm dead. No offense. Anyway, I was thinking, for his birthday, we could go on a trip, the four of us. I'd like to take him to a fútbol game. I know he thinks that Luke guy is hot stuff, but I bet he'd get a kick out of the European league."

They reached the observation point. Though the Watchtower rose up among a crowd of skyscrapers behind them, there was nothing ahead. Nothing but the setting sun and the sea. Marus went to the railing, leaning hard against it as he watched the fiery globe slip in the sky.

"So what do you think?" Vic said, turning to face his son.

"I need to tell you something, Dad, but I—I don't really know how."

Vic glanced over at him. "Well, I suppose you should just start with what you know."

"I think we ought to sit."

"All right," Vic said and shuffled over and took a seat.

Marus joined him on the bench. "You haven't seen the news have you?"

"You know I hate half-truths," he said, grinning.

What was the truth? The program had failed. Marus had failed. He'd never see Cade again. And Shey?

Marus looked out to the horizon.

"What is it, Marus? What's going on?"

Start with what you know. This was what he knew.

"Cade was kidnapped. He's—he's dead, Dad."

Vic was silent. His eyes glistened as he faced the sinking sun. The wind moved through the trees, shaking leaves from their branches. They fluttered to the ground like fallen birds. He turned and took Marus in his arms, and the reservoir that had run dry overflowed once more, filling and falling from Marus's eyes into the crook of Vic's collarbone.

It would have seemed that they sat there in silent mourning for hours, were it not for the colors that washed upon the waves in those last moments of light. When the sun had vanished and the lamps blinked on, Vic turned to study his son's face.

Marus expected a dozen questions about the circumstances. When it happened, how it happened, who did it, and why. They were questions for which he was supposed to have answers.

"How is Shey?" Vic asked instead.

"I don't know. Not good. Neither of us knows what to do. Doing things, even basic things—eating, sleeping—it all seems *dishonest*. Like we're pretending Cade was never a part of our lives. But sitting around doesn't feel right, either. I want to honor him somehow, give his death meaning."

"Don't place more importance on his death than his life, Marus. The best way to pay homage to a loved one is to fight for the things that mattered to them while they were here." Vic's muddy brown eyes blinked away tears as they searched his son's. "You remind me so much of your mother," he said. "You're just as passionate and strong-willed as she was. You have the same fire, the same expressions. After she died, it was hard for me to look at you, because all I saw was her. It was wrong of me to distance myself the way I did."

"Dad, you've been a good father, and a wonderful grand-father," Marus said, blinking away the tears welling at the corners of his eyes.

Vic shook his head. "I dwelled too much on Mom's death, instead of celebrating her life. You were her greatest joy, Marus. I wish she could be here to see everything you've accomplished. She would have adored Cade." He lifted his chin to the graying sky above and took a deep breath. He took Marus's hand and squeezed it. "Don't make my mistake. Don't let your grief alienate you. Family is the most important thing. It's the only thing that matters."

■ ■ ■

Menacing clouds rolled low overhead, encasing the world in a moonless sky as Marus drove from Edenbrook toward the apartment. Vic was right. Marus let Cade's death matter more than his life. He'd been so focused on work that he'd forgotten that the most significant difference he could make was the one at home. Cade's birth had sparked conversations of deeper commitment, ultimately leading Shey and Marus to the altar. But the vows they made that day were not null in his absence.

For better or worse, they were bound to one another. They couldn't allow tragedy, even as horrific as it was, to turn them into strangers.

He picked up his phone and dialed Shey.

The line was disconnected.

He called Reagan, but it rang to voicemail. "Reagan, it's Marus. I need to speak to Shey. Please have her call me."

6

A PATROL CAR waited at the curb in front of Marus's building. A tall African-American man stepped from the driver-side door as Marus slowed the coupe. Young and muscular, his sharp eyes that leapt from the darkness. He waited for Marus to roll down the window.

"Marus Winde?" he said.

"Yes."

"I'm Detective James Ballo. I have some questions for you."

"Okay," Marus said. "Let me park. I'll be right up."

The detective nodded.

Marus pulled away and around to the gate in the alley. What kinds of questions? he wondered. Would he be asked to identify a piece of clothing? A suspect? *A body?*

Was he ready for that? Maybe it was good Shey had left. Imagining what had happened to their son was bad enough. Physically seeing its aftermath was unfathomable.

He parked in the underground stall and took the stairs to the building's entrance.

"It's nice to meet you," Marus said, opening the door to meet the detective's handshake.

"Likewise," Ballo said.

"What happened to Detective Muñoz?"

"She's still investigating your son's homicide."

"What have you found? Were you able to identify the man from the marina?"

"Why don't we go up to your apartment?" Ballo said, gesturing toward the door.

Marus waved his wrist in front of the sensor. The elevator read Marus's iD and preselected the tenth floor as they stepped inside.

"Have you recovered anything else in the bay?" Marus asked trying to make eye contact.

The detective didn't respond. His eyes and mouth were set, straight ahead. Statuesque. Military.

The elevator doors dinged open.

"Welcome home, Mr. Winde," the automatic elevator attendant said.

The men stepped out and started toward the first door. Marus scanned his iD and pushed the heavy door open for the detective. The apartment bloomed with light as they entered.

Pulling out a kitchen chair, Ballo sat down and gestured that Marus do the same.

"Did you find more clothing?" He tried not to sound impatient. Desperate.

"I'm not here to discuss your son's case, Mr. Winde."

"Oh," Marus said, surprised by the echo of relief in his own voice. "Then why are you here?"

"I'd like to ask you a few questions about your wife." He retrieved a tablet from his messenger bag and placed it on the table between them.

"Okay." Marus glanced at the pinprick of yellow light pulsing at the top of the black screen. A sign that their conversation was being recorded. "Can I ask why?"

"The program has identified her as a threat. To herself and to society."

"That's absurd. That has to be some kind of mistake."

"A mistake?" Ballo's eyes narrowed. "Are you saying the Protector Program is inaccurate in its classifications?"

"No. I mean, yes. It *can* be."

"How so?"

"It might not be weighting contextual information the way it should. Behavior it classifies as peculiar or threatening could, in actuality, be an emotional response to loss. A sort of coping mechanism. But instead of analyzing the cause, the system is looking only at the effect."

"So, the program is incomplete?"

"There's always room for improvement, officer."

"*Detective*," Ballo corrected. "And how do you recommend we correct for such shortcomings?"

"Soon we'll be able to identify the signs of stress and analyze them in real time. The Internal Indicator Initiative will fill in the gaps; it will eliminate some of the guesswork."

"*Guesswork*," Ballo said with a smile. "You mean, police work."

"I mean it will better equip you to make arrests."

"Do you know the difference between a detective and an officer, Mr. Winde? Officers patrol; they make arrests. But it's my job to *solve* a crime. Facts and figures are only part of the picture."

"How do you mean?"

"Anyone can read a report. Sometimes you have to look beyond the data and see the unseen."

The problem was that everyone saw something different. The program wasn't susceptible to confirmation bias. Racism, sexism, casteism. Prejudice of any kind. It only looked at the facts. That was the point.

Ballo shifted in the chair. "Do you know where your wife is, Mr. Winde?"

"She's with her sister, Reagan Meyers who lives in the Wells District."

"How do you know your wife is there?" Ballo asked.

He knew because he'd hacked the system and found a geo-tag at Reagan's address.

"She told me," he said, trying to keep his heart rate steady. If analysts were watching his Lifewatch data, they might be able to determine that he was lying.

"When did she tell you?"

"Yesterday, before she left."

"Did Ms. Meyers pick her up?"

"I don't know." Reagan could have been the driver. But to Marus's knowledge, she didn't own a LeSabre. "Have you checked Reagan's iD? What does her data say?" Marus asked.

"To be frank, I don't care much what the data says, Mr. Winde. I'm asking you."

"I don't know if Reagan picked her up."

The detective's eyes fell to the tablet as if for confirmation. Maybe he was analyzing Marus's physiological functions on his own.

"Did Shey leave in a vehicle?"

Breathe. Fifteen to thirty breaths per minute. Anything outside of that range looked abnormal.

"I don't know," Marus lied again.

"Has she been in contact with you since?"

"No," Marus said. "I tried calling this evening. Her phone is disconnected. I called her sister, but it went to voicemail."

"Why did Shey leave in the first place?"

"I've been very focused on work. With new updates and the upcoming I3 launch, I couldn't take time off. My hours are all over the place, and with everything we're going through, it was hard for her to be here alone."

"Were you fighting?" Ballo asked.

"No."

"Are you angry with her?"

"What? No. Not at all. Why?"

"For not being at the school when your son was taken."

Marus didn't like his tone. "It's not her fault. She had to work. So did I."

The detective tapped at the tablet's screen, bringing it to life. "Shey was tagged at the Rose Café that morning." He swiped a finger across the glass, reading what was displayed there. "She ordered a black coffee and a croissant." He slid the tablet forward. Checkmate.

Shey hadn't told Marus that Joey's mom was taking him to the game. All she'd said that morning was that she would meet him there after he finished up at the Protective Services Center. She was working, she'd told Muñoz. She needed to run errands, she'd said later to Marus at the police station. But she hadn't said anything about the Rose. Why would she have kept that from him? Why would she have gone?

"She didn't tell you she was there?"

"No, she didn't." Marus saw the intrigue in Ballo's expression. The judgment. He pursed his large lips as he made his conclusions about Shey. About their marriage. "But where my wife goes and what she does is her business," Marus interjected.

Whatever reason Shey had for going to the Rose, for asking Joey's mom to take Cade to the game, and for keeping it from Marus must've been justified. Theirs was a happy marriage. An honest one. It always had been.

"And what about money?" Ballo said. "Do you feel the same in regard to how she spends it?"

"What are you talking about?"

"Twelve hundred and fifty dollars." He didn't look at the tablet to verify Marus's physiological response. He didn't need to. The detective assessed him straight on. His naked eye saw all there was to see. "Does that ring any bells for you?"

"No. But again, detective, what she does with her money—"

"Is her business. Right. I got that part." Ballo leaned back in the chair and glanced around the apartment as though in search of something. "So weekly transfers of twelve hundred and fifty dollars are of no concern to you?"

"No—well, *yes*. They would be. I didn't know about them, if that's what you mean."

"Do you have any idea where or to whom she'd be sending that kind of money?"

"No, I don't."

Another glance at the tablet. But this time, Marus was telling the truth.

"I paid a visit to the Prosecutor's Office. It seems there have been some problems with Shey at work," Ballo said.

"Yes, I know about that. She was a public defender before the New Era, then repurposed for this job. It's very different work. She doesn't feel as fulfilled as she once was, but she's working through it."

"That's interesting," Ballo said, rubbing the pale of his palms together. "Because one of her coworkers said Shey mentioned she wouldn't be there much longer, that she was planning on leaving. Shey would quit her job without at least discussing it with her husband?"

"She knows I'd support whatever decision she made."

"She's lucky to have such a great support system."

Marus couldn't tell if the detective was being sincere.

Ballo pressed the small black button on the side of his Lifewatch for the time and showed it to Marus. Large, yellow numbers flashed across the screen. 9:33 p.m.

"Shey's iD went offline approximately four hours ago. We have no idea where she is, who she's with, or what state she's in. We don't have Lifewatch data, geotag data, comms, anything."

Marus felt his heart hammering. The last he'd checked, Shey was at Reagan's, and all was fine. That had been just over four hours ago, before he'd gone to visit his father.

"We think her iD was extracted," Ballo said.

He grimaced at the thought. The inside of his shirt felt damp. Removing an iD was a federal offense, and a daunting surgical task. Inserted by a needle, the chip was delicately placed between the radial artery and the ulnar nerve. Damage to the artery could cause the host to bleed out, while damage to the nerve could render the hand useless.

"Do you have any idea why your wife would want to go offline?"

Marus knew what the detective was getting at. It was in the same vein as what the reporters were hinting. The same thing he'd warned Shey about. *Negligence of the mother.* A wicked lack of responsibility of some sort. Was she running from the police? They were wrong, of course. And yet, Marus didn't know how to answer the detective's question.

"Are you sure the iD was removed? Were there any indicators to give your analysts that impression?" Marus asked. "Lifewatch would have captured physiological signs of stress before going offline. There'd be a second before the iD was destroyed where Lifewatch would register the disconnect and capture a flatlined heart rate. Was that the case?"

"Please answer the question," Ballo said, his dark eyes gleaming in evaluation. "Why would your wife go offline?"

There were only two explanations that made any sense. Knowing Marus would track her, she might have had the iD removed so he couldn't come after her. He didn't like what it suggested—that she was being dishonest, or didn't trust him—but it was better than the alternative: that she was in danger.

"Right before she left, she said she didn't feel safe anymore."

Ballo looked at him with disbelief. "And so she went to the Wells District?"

He knew how it sounded and what it implied. He was an inadequate husband. Here, near the center of the safest city in the world, with *him*, a Protector, Shey didn't feel safe. And so she'd gone to Wells to take refuge in a tenement building with Reagan and Reagan's two young children.

What had he been thinking? He never should have let Shey go, especially not alone.

Another oversight. Another failure.

"If someone got ahold of her, they could have forced extraction," he said, finally.

"Who?"

"I don't know. *People*," Marus said. "Maybe fearists."

"You said Shey mentioned she didn't feel safe. Had someone threatened her?"

"Not that I know of."

"Did she have enemies?"

"No, she didn't."

"Was she engaging with anyone of questionable character?"

"What do you mean?"

"You mentioned fearists. What makes you think they're involved?"

"I don't know. Maybe they targeted me like they did Li Syun."

"You think fearists are behind your son's murder?"

"You tell me. I haven't heard anything from anyone about my son's case in days. When I call, all anyone ever says is that I'll be notified when there's a new development. How does a child go missing, post-New Era, in the heart of the safest city in the country—in the world—and no one knows a thing about it? Ten days have passed, and I still don't know who did this or why. That *man* is out there somewhere and you're here, sitting in the same seat Muñoz was when she told me my son was murdered. And you're implying that my wife—" Marus stood. "What is it that you're implying, Detective?"

"I'm not implying anything," Ballo said. He pulled the sleeve across the tablet and tucked it back into his bag. "I'm doing my job, just as, I'm sure, Muñoz is doing hers." Ballo stood and gathered his things. "I am sorry for your loss, Mr. Winde. You have our sympathy."

Marus didn't want sympathy. He wanted answers. "Thank you."

Detective Ballo went to the door. "I trust you'll let me know if Shey, or anyone else, contacts you. I appreciate your cooperation," he said and let himself out.

■ ■ ■

Marus awoke three hours later in front of the screens with a twinge in his neck. The bottle of whiskey he'd purchased once Ballo had gone remained unopened on the desk beside an empty glass. He'd dreamt of Cade again.

The dream had been more vivid than the first, and in it his son was older. He saw Cade among a sea of strangers. Cade's head was shaved, and his face seemed different, but it was him. They looked at each other from opposite sides of the street. Marus tried to get to him. He crossed the road but got caught in a wave of people. His legs felt like lead against the tide. By the time he stepped up to the curb, Cade was gone. Panic thudded in his chest. He tried to call his son's name, but his voice was little more than a whisper, no matter how hard he tried to shout. Empty faces floated all around, but none belonged to his child.

Then, through the crowd, he saw the back of Cade's head, his dark cropped hair, just before it vanished around a corner. He ran after him, turning into a narrow alleyway paved with cobblestone. Walls towered on either side, their tops unseen in the clouds above. There were no doors, no windows, no exits. Weaving through the maze in search of his son, he finally arrived at the end. A small square. Cade was nowhere to be found, as though he'd taken a secret door Marus hadn't seen, or had never been there at all. The square was empty. A couple numbers were etched into the stone wall in front of him. An address? They'd dissolved as soon as he regained consciousness.

He waved on the screens. His illicit export of Shey's data was complete. He clicked on the file and Shey's State-issued photo stared back from the glass. It had been taken three years prior, but he didn't remember seeing it before. In it, her eyes, always so full of life, were vacant. She looked bored and unhappy. He scrolled down to her Lifewatch data. Her heart rate had been steady. Blood pressure and oxygen levels were fine. And then, at 5:30 p.m., the feed ended. There weren't any spikes or fluctuations. Nothing to indicate iD extraction. The data had simply, inexplicably, disappeared.

He scrolled back up to the top of her profile. Next to the picture, her threat status was listed: Orange. In a live environment, he'd be able to click the status and view the collective data points that resulted in her elevated risk classification. A list of flagged tags, correspondence, actions, and interactions would appear chronologically. But the script hadn't reproduced her profile. It had merely scraped the information, pulling back the data and exporting it into a PDF. He scrolled through the pages searching for an account of the behavior and the associated flagging criteria.

Emotional instability. Civic unrest. Fearist influence. Psychosis. Her media consumption was labeled as both *Progressive* and *Fanatical*.

A list of Shey's influencers were bolded in red. Marus knew that bolded red text elements signified inclusion on the WatchList. State researchers had spent decades determining the recurrence of specific media and celebrity influence across individual terrorist and criminal profiles. The New Era put that research into effect. Seemingly isolated instances of devotion to a particular influencer could, with other criteria, prove indicative of a fixed political leaning or tendency toward violence.

The name at the top of Shey's influencer list, Christopher Axtell, was associated with the majority of the bolded articles in her reading list. The name was unfamiliar, even though her reading log showed that Shey was an obsessive consumer of Axtell's work. Especially over the past two years.

Marus opened a new window and typed the name into the search bar. Scanning a few articles revealed that Christopher Axtell had been the poster child for an ethical media. He'd covered everything from the economic collapse across Europe and

Asia to domestic policy and was lauded for his humanistic and transparent approach. Axtell sought the truth and reported it, even when it jeopardized his career and, occasionally, his life.

In a bio, Marus read that the journalist had spent his first years as a reporter overseas, mostly in China, writing about the trade embargo. In more recent years, he'd joined *The Sentinel* and wrote about cyber security and privacy. This was the work Shey clung to, even idolized, it seemed. It was controversial, especially at its end. Bordering on what seemed to be the disillusioned drivel of pure conspiracy theory, Axtell laid preposterous claims, muddling words and souring his reputation.

Then, almost overnight, all record of him disappeared. He left *The Sentinel*. Stopped writing and stopped being written about.

Marus clicked out of the search and returned to the scraped results. He scrolled through the pages until he found Shey's tag log. There, an account of every physical location she'd visited, accompanied by date, time, and relevant receipts, was arranged chronologically. He fished a retired pen out of the desk drawer and grabbed an old envelope. The query had scraped three months' worth of geodata. He scrolled through routine trips to coffee shops, namely the Rose, stops at the grocery store, the library, Shey's work, their apartment, and, to his surprise, the park. Near the bottom of the results, he saw the tag Ballo had mentioned, a trip to the Rose the morning Cade disappeared. Several results beneath, he recognized the tag he'd seen the night before, the one that put her in front of Reagan's apartment building. It was her last tag. Under it, he noticed a bit of code that had been scraped back with the results.

He copied it and threw it into his test environment. It was a ghost state developed to hide the data it encapsulated. Scrolling back up to Shey's Lifewatch feed, he understood the implications. A ghost state could mask the data that would otherwise indicate iD extraction. Someone was deliberately concealing the data and, as a result, altering the system's predictions.

But who?

PART TWO

they are dull because they have been
made dull and they are
vicious because they are
fearful of losing what they have.

—Charles Bukowski, *People*

7

WHERE IS SHEY Vanguard? Why did she leave her husband, State employee, Marus Winde, just days after their son's murder? Why has she gone offline? What is she hiding?

Shey's grim State-issued photograph inhabited every screen. He saw her at the kitchen table, on his way to work, in the palm of his hand. Everywhere he turned, there she was. But it wasn't the Shey he knew, the one with a broad smile and spirited eyes. There were dozens of photographs the media could have used, but none supported their portrayal of her quite like this one. *Smile baby*, he wanted to whisper. *Show them who you really are.*

There wasn't a news outlet or media personality who wasn't talking about his wife. Ignorant postulations and blatant accusations dominated every outlet. Each day brought another source to the stage, someone who was "close to the family." They regurgitated information anyone with a computer could have pieced together and layered in their own opinion.

Cade was unplanned, so he must have been unwanted. Shey's career was rendered obsolete with the birth of the New

Era, so she must have resented the system. She was a woman with liberal leanings, so she must have been an extremist.

An editorial titled *Vanguard of Deceit* went as far as claiming Shey was at the helm of the western fearist faction.

Her marriage to senior algorithm engineer Marus Winde served her as a cover and a form of infiltration, the conspiracy theorist wrote. The author suggested that Shey had engaged in a relationship with Marus only after the fearists had identified him as a potential candidate for the State's Protector Program and that she'd intentionally become pregnant. Somehow, the author had obtained Shey's reading list, the controversial articles she'd read over and over again, and published it as a means of proof.

Marus parsed through sound bites, social media comments, and blog entries looking for anything that could point him in her direction. Reagan hadn't returned any of his calls, and he had no way of knowing if either of them was safe. The thought of Shey in the company of fearists terrified him. If she was with them, she was either an accomplice or a victim.

As a capable individual with a wealth of experience in the strategic portrayal and manipulation of circumstance, is it implausible to believe Vanguard is simply doing what she does best to evade the law? Is it possible she is spinning a story of victimization to cover up her convenient escape from motherhood, family life, and her duty as a citizen of the State?

One unnamed source cited a recent conversation with Shey in which she'd mentioned leaving the city and her marriage behind. *I can't do it anymore,* the source quoted her as saying. The woman Shey worked with at the Prosecutor's Office also came forth, telling reporters Shey had been planning to leave for several weeks.

Was she having an affair? Was Cade's abduction and murder a way to shirk her parental responsibility? Why don't we know more? Is the State protecting her husband, Marus Winde?

A mommy blogger's post saying she sympathized with Shey's plight went viral. *How many of us are one tantrum away from unraveling? One sidelong glance from a husband who doesn't get it? Who among us doesn't dream about turning back time? We were young and beautiful once, with the entire world ahead of us and hardly a care in the world. Now, between career and motherhood, many of us are overworked and gravely undervalued. Shey Vanguard's disappearance is not indicative of her incompetence as a mother and wife, but rather demonstrates the fundamental inequity of gender-based roles at home and in the workplace. Can we blame her for doing what many of us dream of: escaping?*

A million eyes appeared to be looking from all angles. But mainstream media only had one: Shey was dangerous. Reporters cited her threat level, urging citizens to call the police if they spotted her.

■ ■ ■

On Friday, Marus woke early and got dressed. Somehow, he'd managed to sleep. According to the Lifewatch report waiting on his phone, he'd attained nearly seventy-five percent of his sleep goal, though he felt no better rested for it. His head throbbed, and his stomach felt uneasy. He'd dreamt something terrible but couldn't remember what it was.

It was almost 6:00 a.m., more than an hour until sunrise, but he was already running late. The lamps outside beamed down on the pavement below, moonlike.

He slid on his shoes, zipped up his jacket, and grabbed his briefcase. Descending the stairs, he entered the address into the car app on his phone. The coupe was idling silently at the curb by the time he walked out. He scanned his wrist at the passenger door. A light on the dash blinked green and the lock popped up. He opened the door and slid inside.

It was a forty-five-minute ride to Reagan's apartment. She lived in one of the reinforced tenements in the Wells District across Mid Bridge. The building was older, and the apartment was small. But she was a widow with two children, and it was all she could afford.

The light-rail above was packed with people shuttling into Safety's Center. Marus could see the stark silhouette of their blurred mass against the fluorescent tubes that hung above them. A steady line of headlights pulsed in the same direction. He'd forgotten how many made this commute each morning. There'd been a time when he'd sat on the dirty seats beside them on the train, or later, when he could afford to call a car, in the traffic among them. But that was a long time ago, before he'd become an *islander*, as his friends used to say in mockery. Things were bad all over in the years before the New Era, but the urban isle he called home truly did become Safety's Center when the nation's crime rate exploded. Isolated from the rest of the country by a heavily patrolled border and two bascule bridges, crime wasn't as prevalent on the Isle as it was elsewhere. At least, not at first.

A handful of coupes and sedans sped alongside him as he raced over the water, away from the Isle, toward Reagan's. A few surged ahead, in manual drive mode, no doubt. He wondered how many were returning to their beds after a nightlong security shift in one of the glass or steel skyscrapers on the Isle.

By the time the coupe wound its way through the streets and turned toward the outlying districts, the edges of the clouds were beginning to turn blue and pink with the coming of dawn. The sun would be up within a half hour, and he would have to turn around and fight the traffic back to work.

The car stopped at the curb in front of one of the buildings. Dark stains wept from opaque and crusted windows, streaking the building's brownish stone facade. An old fire escape bisected the building in rusty zigzags.

He counted, four stories up, third and fourth window on the right. Unremarkable as windows come. The lights were off. The glass panes, intact. What had he expected? Caution tape? Ghostlike drapes sagged in the first window. Yellowed blinds in the second were drawn shut except for a slit where one plastic blade bent upward. He imagined a pair of eyes looking out to scan the street below.

Marus got out and watched as the car pulled away to park. Across the street, a black SUV with tinted windows idled. The windows were too dark to see a driver or any passengers, but Marus got the sense that he and the building were being watched.

A small set of iron steps, flanked by a liquor store and barber shop, led up to the building's entrance. With an eye over his shoulder, he ascended and pressed Reagan's call button.

Someone's forgotten pet, a gray tabby, bounded up after him, rubbing against his pant leg and mewling to be let in. The door remained locked, and no one answered on the speaker. He took out his phone and dialed Reagan, pacing back and forth on the small landing while it rang. The cat followed, arching its back as it skirted around each of his legs, cutting him off. The other line clicked on.

"Hello?" Marus waited. Nothing. "Hello, Reagan?"

The line was silent, but alive. Someone was there.

"Reagan, it's Marus."

There was another click. He took the phone from his ear to look at the screen. The call ended. Whoever answered had hung up.

He called again, but the call went straight to voicemail. "It's me, Marus. What the hell is going on? I need to talk to you. Please call me as soon as you can."

He dropped the phone into his pocket and began pressing each of the buttons on the panel. The cat meowed at his feet, lifting one of its front legs to claw at his khakis. He kicked it away. Apartments one through eleven ignored his call. He would have thought everyone would, but apartment twelve buzzed him inside. No wonder crime was more prevalent here, he thought. He grabbed for the door and yanked it open. The cat ran back up the steps and slid past him, disappearing up the stairwell.

There was a strange odor that became more pungent the higher he climbed. A mix of cat litter, mold, and meat that had been left in the freezer too long. He reached her apartment on the fourth floor and knocked on the door.

"Reagan! Open up. It's Marus."

He knocked harder.

"Reagan!"

A door at the other end of the hall creaked open, revealing a wary nose. He turned toward it.

"Hey," he called, walking over. "Have you seen—"

The nose retreated.

"Wait," Marus said.

But the door slammed shut as soon as he approached it, the bolt snapping quickly into place.

"I'm looking for Reagan Meyers. Have you seen her?" He asked as innocuously as he could.

Though he could hear the creaking of boards and shifting of feet at the entry, there was no answer.

"If you see her, tell her Marus Winde needs to speak to her." He turned away, adding a "please" before he reached the stairwell.

Across the hall, sitting squarely in front of Reagan's door, the tabby was studying him. It flicked its tail back and forth and stared with green eyes.

The black SUV was gone by the time he returned to the curb for his car. He looked up and down the street, but it had vanished.

8

ANJ AND GENE were talking near the elevators when Marus entered the lobby. Anj was leaning forward, shaking her head at Gene, whose head was retracted, pushing forth several chins. Marus couldn't hear what was being said but, as he approached, he detected a certain sharpness at the edge of Anj's words. Gene cleared his throat, and Anj swiveled on her heels.

"Hey, Marus," she said turning toward him. She lifted an eyebrow at Gene. "Well, I've got to run. Catch up with you guys later."

Gene wiped at his sweat-dabbled brow. "How are you doing? How was the visit with your dad the other day?" His voice seemed strained.

"As good as could be expected," Marus said.

"I've been thinking about you."

"Thanks," Marus said. "Everything okay between you and Anj?"

"Oh, yeah. Everything's fine."

Marus waved his wrist in front of the sensor at the elevator door and gestured that Gene go ahead.

"Actually, there's something I need to tell you." Gene wiped at his brow again and moved away from the elevator. "You see, I've, uh, been in training. That's why I wasn't around."

Marus stepped away from the elevator door. "Did I miss an email? Was I supposed to go?"

"Oh no. You didn't miss anything. It's just that I was," he forced a little cough, "I was, uh, recruited." Gene leaned in closer. "The tenth floor," he said, his voice was no more than a whisper.

Marus was too stunned to speak. In the fifteen years Marus and Gene had worked together, first at Newbold Corp. and then at the IA on the eighth and ninth floors, they'd aspired to employment on the tenth floor. It was the most prestigious work in the annex, and highly classified. Not even those on the ninth floor fully knew what their counterparts on the tenth did. It was a matter of national security.

"The tenth?" Marus asked.

"The tenth," Gene confirmed.

"I don't understand."

Devlin hadn't recommended Gene. If the commissioner had, he would have told Gene, and Gene would have made it known to everyone, especially Marus. That's just how he was.

Besides, Devlin *wouldn't* have recommended Gene. Not, at least, if project completion and success rate were key considerations. Marus knew his own stats, and they were far better than Gene's.

A matter of seniority, then? He couldn't recall who'd started working there first. They had worked together, since the beginning. They were promoted to the ninth floor on the same day, two or so years ago. In many aspects, they were equals. But Marus possessed the stronger intellect. He was *an effortless innovator and an apt problem solver with a penchant for pushing capabilities.* At least, those were the words Devlin had used the day he told him he was recommending him.

"I didn't know how to tell you with, uh, everything that's been going on. I know you had your eye on it and things have been really tough lately, and—"

"Congratulations."

Gene grabbed Marus's arm and squeezed. His flustered look of constipation was gone. "It's our time. What we've always talked about." His eyes shimmered. "They need people up there. They've got a new project. A doozy. You're next. I know it. So do you, so buck up buddy."

A doozy. Who said stuff like that? Marus nodded, forcing a smile.

"Well, I've got to get going. Duty calls," Gene said patting him on the back before skirting around him toward the elevator door.

■ ■ ■

At 7:00 p.m., the ninth floor, still brightly lit, was empty. The data feed continued to crawl, an overlay on the glittering evening sky rendered by the wall screens. Alerts triggered overnight would be processed automatically and assigned as necessary to the patrols. Marus shut down his workstation and packed the laptop away in his briefcase. The slender necks on the ceiling pivoted silently as he strode past. Dozens of tiny cyclopes, staring.

He rode the elevator down to the main floor alone. The bustle of the day had dissipated, leaving only pockets of quiet conversation here and there.

Anj spotted him from the other side of the vaulted lobby and waved. She trotted over as quietly as she could, the clacking of her shoes echoing all the way.

"I thought you might still be here, hiding on the other side of the Great Wall of China over there in your corner," she said with an uneasy smile. "I'm glad I caught you. We were just about to head to Mickey's for a celebratory drink."

Marus looked up in confusion. "What are you celebrating?"

"Gene did tell you, didn't he?"

"Oh right, *that*. Yeah, he told me."

"Look, it's shit. We all know it should have been you. Doesn't make the damnedest bit of sense, but what can we do?"

"You know I don't drink."

"I guess I thought maybe you'd started," she said. "Shit, that was the wrong thing to say. I'm sorry." She lifted her hand to his arm. "I heard about Shey. I'm sorry you're going through this. All of it. Please, just come out with us. Just for a little while."

He looked down at his watch. "I should be getting back. It's been a long week."

"Come on. You know how Gene gets when he drinks." She opened and closed her hand. A talking mouth. "I'm sure you're just as curious as we are."

■ ■ ■

Various shades of night swirled ominously in a sea of unstable air above as Marus and Anj reached the curb. For the first time in a long time, he felt hungry. His stomach growled in agreement. He'd grab a bite and a soda, clink glasses with Gene. Then get the hell out of there.

"Wait here," Anj said. "I'll be right back."

Moments later, she pulled up in her red Mustang and whistled through the open window.

"Going my way?" she called.

He got in, eyeing her hands at the wheel. "Manual override, huh?"

"What's the point of having a Mustang if you don't actually drive it?"

■ ■ ■

Mickey's was a small, privately owned, back-corner business. The pours were heavy and the bartenders friendly. Its customers were a faithful group who liked to keep to themselves. Anj was the one who found it, though Marus wasn't sure how. It was the only place you could go for a drink without running into someone from the Security Annex. Everyone knew SAs— strong arms, as they were called at the IA—were angry drunks. An excess of testosterone and tequila that didn't mix well.

Marus ordered chicken wings and a club soda. He was almost through the wings when Anj set a shot glass in front of him.

"Here's to Genie," she said, raising the glass in the air. "May you never forget the lowly lives of those who worked with you, even though we're below you now, you son of a bitch." She threw it back, and everyone cheered.

Gene was smiling like a moron.

"I want to give a toast," Gene said, picking up several glasses from the line of freshly poured shots and divvying them out. He walked over to Marus and set one beside the other before raising his own. "To Marus Winde, my long-time friend and colleague. He probably deserves this a lot more than I do, but I'm sure he'll be joining me soon. Maybe you too, Anj. *Maybe.*"

"Hey!" she yelled, lurching forward to punch his arm.

"To Marus and Anj!" Gene shouted, lifting the glass higher and splashing a few drops onto Marus's shoulder.

"To Marus and Anj," everyone yelled back, downing their drinks.

Marus forced a smile but hung on the word *probably.*

Fuck it. He took the first shot. The alcohol burned at the back of his throat and surged down deep into his gut. It was a burn that beckoned to burn again, and so he took the second shot, and then a few more. He drank until he could feel the load in his limbs. From mouth, to spine, to head, he was numb.

■ ■ ■

Even though Gene and the others had long been gone, Marus and Anj remained at the bar. Every time Marus got up to leave, Anj grabbed his jacket and said, "just one more." He'd lost count of how many times she'd said that.

Marus palmed his phone on three different occasions with the intention of calling a car, but changed his mind when he envisioned the empty apartment that waited. *Just a little bit longer,* he told himself. Anything was better than that terrible silence.

"To self-driving cars," Anj said in a garbled voice, raising another glass. Her face stretched into two and bobbled a little; though he was sure she wasn't moving.

"Do you think it's worth it, what we do?" Marus asked.

"How do ya mean?"

"All the time away, all the work we do. The things we miss."

"You're askin' the divorcée?" She put the glass to her lips, but there was nothing in it.

"Oh yeah, I forgot. Sorry."

"No, it's okay," she said. "After Jim, I wondered that myself. And you know what? I do. I mean, the work matters, you know? We're making a difference in people's lives."

"What about the people in our own lives? I kept telling myself it'd get better, that things would slow down. I missed so much of Cade growing up, and now what do I have?" He threw the drink back and let it burn.

"You can't blame yourself. When I found out about Jim, I thought it was my fault because I wasn't there for him. I neglected our marriage, or whatever. Then I realized, whoa, that's fucked up. 'Cause it wasn't me; it was him. I was the one doing something that mattered, and he was fucking some girl." Anj put her hand on Marus's thigh. "You just gotta remember why we do what we do."

Behind her, in the corner, Marus noticed a woman with long brown hair. He couldn't see her face, but her upright posture, slack shoulders, and arced neck looked exactly like Shey's. He slid off the barstool and stumbled toward her.

"Where you going?" Anj asked, the empty shot glass still in her hand.

He dragged a hand along the bar to steady himself and arrived directly behind the woman. The man sitting in front of her looked up, startled.

Marus plopped down on the chair beside her.

"Shey."

He reached a hand toward her shoulder, brushing her hair aside to see her face. It was too dark. He couldn't make out the rest of her features, but the slope of nose was familiar.

"Hey!" The man said, setting his own drink down and standing. "What the hell do you think you're doing?"

"I'm sorry," Marus said in stilted speech. He squinted his eyes in the darkness, but everything looked blurry. "I been looking for you everywhere."

"Leave her alone."

The man was at his side now, pulling on his arm to get him up off the chair. But Marus was lead. He was heavier than lead. He was plutonium.

"Come back home," Marus said reaching out for her once more. His fingers brushed her face.

She pulled away, dodging his touch.

A woman called his name. "Mar-us! Marus!" He turned to see where the voice was coming from and realized he was being lifted from the chair. The man clutched the front of his shirt and hoisted him up before shoving him backward.

"Get outta here!" the man shouted.

Marus stumbled back, tripping over his own feet and falling hard to the floor. His head hit a barstool on the way down, and everything went black.

■ ■ ■

The Mustang pulled curbside, and they got in. The ride seemed to last only a few minutes. Marus thought it the wrong address at first, but, when he looked out the window and saw a blurred version of his building, he knew he was home. His head throbbed where the stool had struck it, though he knew the alcohol had been a contributing factor as well.

He rested against the frame of the open window and took a sip from the water bottle Anj had given him. The cool air helped slow the spinning.

"Do you think there was a mix-up?" he asked.

"With what?"

"With the promotion. You think maybe they made a mistake, somehow?" Even as he said it, he knew it was a ridiculous question. The State didn't make mistakes.

Anj didn't respond.

"Forget I said that."

"No," she said after a while. "You're right. I've been wracking my brain around it, and I don't get it. You were a shoo-in, like I said before. Everyone knew it. Even Gene knew it. The pudgy bastard didn't even tell me until this week. He knew what I was thinking." She turned in her seat to face him. "Don't get me wrong. I'm happy for him, but you—you're a fucking genius, Marus."

She reached over the center console, wrapped her arm around his neck, and kissed him.

It was wet and sloppy and entirely out of character, but, to his surprise, he kissed her back. When he pulled away, the gin from her breath now on his own, he realized what he'd done.

"That was wrong," he said.

"Gee, you sure know how to make a woman feel good." Anj turned away from him.

"I'm sorry, I'm not being myself," Marus said, unfastening the seatbelt. "I don't drink. I don't do this. It's not me." He opened the car door.

"Well, who are you, then?"

He staggered out onto the pavement. "I'm a—a husband. A father," he said, closing the door.

"And I'm the corner whore."

He bent toward the window, resting his fingertips against its edge. "You know that's not what I meant, it's just—"

"Don't worry about it," she said, and the Mustang drove away.

Across the street, another car started up and pulled out. It was Detective Ballo.

9

A FIST POUNDED at the door. Three loud knocks, mimicking the pounding in his head.

Marus rolled over. Light from outside washed the bedroom walls a bright white. The clock glared the time from the table. 10:46 a.m.

He closed his eyes in defiance. For a moment, he thought he smelled bacon. In the sharp silence, he swore he could hear the sound of cartoons. The clanking of pans. Shey making breakfast. Cade sitting cross-legged on the carpet. It was easy to see them that way.

The ringing of the doorbell. Another knock.

He opened his eyes. Took a breath. The sheets beside him were undisturbed. Creased and tucked with care. A subtle truth confronting him.

His son was dead, and his wife, gone.

Slowly, he sat up. His head was spinning. He had the urge to vomit. To lie back down. Whoever was on the other side of the door was insistent. Shey? But she'd be able to let herself in.

Not without her iD, he remembered.

He slid his jeans on. Grabbed a shirt and shuffled out into the hallway. He heard the voice.

"Mr. Winde? Please answer, sir." Another knock. "I need to speak with you."

He opened the door. A rush of heat from the hall made him dizzy. He closed his eyes, staggered backward, his hand on the knob, the only thing steadying him.

"Mr. Winde? Are you okay?" Detective Muñoz stepped inside. She lifted an uncertain hand, touched it to his arm, and then retracted it. "Here," she said, pulling out a chair. "Why don't you sit?"

She opened a cabinet and retrieved a glass. She seemed to know exactly where everything was. Dipping it quickly under the faucet, she filled it and returned to his side. She set the glass down and frowned. "Maybe I should come back another time."

Marus shook his head. "Now's fine." His mind was foggy. There were questions he knew he wanted to ask. Questions that escaped him. "Did you find," he took a drink, "a body? Did you find Cade?"

Muñoz sat across the table. The same seat she'd sat in the night she'd come to tell him his son was dead.

"No. But we got the man who did it."

Marus straightened. Blinked hard. "You're sure?"

"He confessed earlier this morning."

She removed the tablet from its leather case. Held her thumbprint against the circular button. The screen came to life. She tapped the glass and slid it toward him.

"His name is Anthony Jennings," she said.

The man was Caucasian. Similar in skin tone to Marus. A slight stubble dotted his jawline. He had dark brown hair. His eyes were honey brown. Friendly.

"This is him?"

Muñoz nodded.

"How?" Marus looked up from the glass. "Why'd he do it?"

The detective lowered her head in disgust. "He said he was walking by."

"*Walking by?* What, he just happened to be passing through and decided to murder an innocent child?"

"He saw the boys practicing and went over to watch. It turns out he had a son who was kidnapped six years ago."

"That doesn't make any sense."

"Cases like this never do. He said Cade reminded him of his son. He went over to talk to your boy and thought it up from there. That's why the system wasn't able to predict it. Anyway, it turns out, a friend of Jennings has a boat. It was at the marina that day. We've got a forensic team on it now."

"How did you find him?"

The detective shifted uncomfortably. "Actually, he came to us. He's a very troubled man." The detective took the tablet back. She slid it into the leather case and snapped it shut. "We're putting him through a lengthy interrogation process. Our priority now is to find Cade's body. Jennings will be brought to justice, I assure you. I want nothing more than for you and your family to have closure."

He'd wanted closure, too. But not like this. Not if it felt wrong.

Facts over feelings. That had been one of the early slogans for the Protector Program. A mantra he'd wholeheartedly agreed with.

Until now.

■ ■ ■

Anthony Jennings was an electrician. A father. He had two kids. Ages eight and six. One ex-wife. The divorce went through seven months after his firstborn, who would have been ten, was kidnapped. There was nothing to suggest criminal tendency. Nothing to indicate homicidal thirst. A violent streak. A fixation with little boys. Not even misconduct.

If there had been, the system would have issued an alert the second he stepped near a school, a playground, a first-grade soccer game. The Protectors would have swooped in, taken Jennings through the crime prevention program. A reeducation followed by an extensive evaluation. Maybe he'd be released. Maybe he wouldn't. Either way, Marus and Shey would be sitting in the sun at St. Xavier's field, cheering Cade on from the bleachers. This very minute, they'd be watching as his blue jersey wove through shirts of another color—maybe green today—his wide eyes fixed on the goal.

But they weren't. And not because the program had missed indicators or overlooked clues. There simply wasn't a threat to identify. The crime was random. Motiveless. At least, according to Muñoz and now, the media.

Marus didn't know what he was looking for, but he searched anyway. Another infraction. The risk of being written up. Or worse. *So be it.* He had to see Jennings for himself.

There was a lot to be learned from where a person went. What he did. Didn't do. Even without I3, one could gauge character, mindset, motive.

Marus scraped back Jennings's profile. Conversations and geotags. Purchases and service routes. App and utility usage. Media consumption. Lifewatch stats. Hospital records. Notes from his marriage counselor. Five years' worth of information. Plenty to know a man, to get a glimpse of his psyche.

But there was little to see. A blue-collar man trying to make ends meet. He was depressed. In recent years, his health had deteriorated; his marriage, disintegrated.

Jennings rarely ventured from his home across Mid Bridge to the Isle. In fact, Marus's query pulled back twelve trips in five years. One, just two weeks before. The day Cade was taken.

Define patterns. Isolate singularities.

Marus scanned the data. But there wasn't much else. Nothing to make a man want to take a young boy and kill him. Cast his body out into the sea. Nothing to push him over the brink but his own loss: Ashton Jennings, age four. Kidnapped in the self-checkout at a grocery store. *There one moment; gone the next.*

Had some switch flipped when Jennings's son was taken? Maybe Jennings wanted to replicate the fear, the pain he'd endured. Or maybe Cade was a spitting image of Ashton, and, during his unprecedented stroll near St. Xavier, the sun had caught just right, and for a moment he thought he saw his own boy working the ball through the grass, and decided then and there that if he couldn't have him, no one could.

Marus searched the database for a photo of Ashton. Would he be able to grasp Anthony Jennings's actions if he saw Cade's hazel eyes, his button nose, and dark brown hair looking back from Ashton's image?

He'd never know because, rather than a boy resembling Cade, the photo of four-year-old Ashton revealed dark eyes, brown skin, and braided hair. A purple bow. Ashton Jennings wasn't a boy at all. She was a beautiful, little black girl.

10

THE SCULPTURE SAT on a concrete disk at the center of a circular plot of fine, white sand. Quartz, actually. A man in a cone-shaped hat was busy combing ripples into the grains. He wasn't Japanese. Or Asian, for that matter. But the straw cone atop his head bestowed the kind of tranquil assurance to rival a Zen master. Marus wondered whether it was the man's choice to wear it or simply a part of his uniform.

The park's manicured lawn yielded beneath his boots, forming to his soles like a luxurious carpet, as Marus crossed over to the sculpture's circumference. Lime green, purple, and blue poles twisted in on themselves and up toward the sky. Chains from several swings zigzagged through a flight of monkey bars flecked with rust. Or was it blood? He'd seen an interview with the sculptor, a tiny woman with round glasses and wine-colored lips, shortly after the memorial was installed. She hadn't painted or altered the materials, she'd said. Everything used in the sculpture had been sourced from the rubble. She'd only cut and welded the pieces together. But had she cleaned them? Had she needed to? Where did blood go in an explosion?

Everywhere, he thought.

■ ■ ■

It had been the start of a Saturday like any other, unmemorable in its perfect simplicity. Marus could still see the light, the way it filtered in through the copper-colored drapes at the bedroom window, tinting everything orange. Among the tangled sheets of their sleepy sanctuary, Shey peered up at him from her pillow. Her green eyes smiling as they reveled in the warm, midmorning quiet. He kissed the back of her hand and slid out from under her arm to make breakfast. French toast for Cade and eggs for Shey and him.

Cade was sitting squarely on the rug watching cartoons in the living room when Marus emerged from the hall. The rich aroma of ground coffee beans wafted through the apartment as Marus prepared breakfast, whisking batter and clanking bowls and pans to Cade's dismay. *Can you louder it?* When Marus didn't jump to, Cade grabbed for the remote. Situating himself on the loveseat, he clicked the volume up until the living room was booming with the animated sounds of explosions, horns, and nasal cartoon voices.

He didn't hear it, but he felt it. The floor trembled beneath him as he flipped the omelet. A demolition? When Shey, draped in her robe, came to the kitchen ten minutes later with a twisted look of incomprehension on her face, Marus had thought it was because of the noise from the TV. She padded over to him in slippered feet as he set breakfast on the table.

Did you hear that? she asked. *Someone just bombed the park.*

Cade ate his French toast and powdered sugar with the enthusiasm of a four-year-old, requesting additional syrup twice, but his parents sat, silently pushing their food around as they snuck glances at the news on the tablet.

Five adults and eleven children were instantly killed, a dozen more critically injured by the homemade explosive that blew from an inconspicuous canvas backpack left by the swings. As an isolated incident, it would have been enough to linger in the community's consciousness forever. But several weeks later, during the last days of summer, the terror was magnified. Forty-two middle-school students and four faculty members were killed in the bombing of a school on the other side of the country. People flocked from the far reaches of the city for a candlelight vigil at the center of the park. Pictures of the victims, those from the park as well as the middle school, leaned against the chain-link safety perimeter, looking back at those mourning them through the flickering light of candles at dusk.

Marus and Shey had watched the State address from the refuge of their apartment as Cade played with Matchbox cars on his bedroom floor.

These are our children, our future. Any grievance against them is an assault on innocence and an intolerable threat to humanity. We will stop at nothing until those responsible for these heinous crimes are brought to justice, President Orlane said in a speech peppered with condolences and promises he couldn't keep.

Though the school in Redmond had been torn down so it could be rebuilt, the park on the Isle remained as it was, collecting prayers and memorabilia, teddy bears and flowers that became soggy with time. Three months after the bombing, the city held a ceremony dedicating the park as a memorial. Families, friends, and the larger community brought colorful ribbons they carefully chose as a tribute to those lost. Mothers and fathers, sisters and brothers, their eyes full of tears and their hearts filled with grief, came forward to fasten them to the same fence that kept them from the wreckage. Together, they formed the words, *YOU LIVE ON IN LOVE.*

As time passed, the number of colorful knots grew, simultaneously obscuring the confetti-colored message and fortifying it in the minds of those who had furnished the fence with their own love and loss. Eventually, the sculpture was commissioned, and the chain-link fence came down, replaced by a permanent and sturdy substitute. The knots were retied and, soon, joined by even more ribbon. The park immortalized lives lost too young, commemorating, not only the victims of the bombings, but also those of the kidnappings proliferating across the country, the savage and inexplicable shootings, and tragic acts of recklessness that pervaded the nightly news.

■ ■ ■

Now, two weeks after Cade's murder, Marus came with his own piece of ribbon, a dark green, his son's favorite color. He slid several knots up and several down to make space near the middle. He tied it tight beside a weathered purple ribbon and watched as the colors caught in a cool breeze. They fluttered from the fence like spirits trying to break free. He wondered how many had received a proper burial. Was this as good a grave as his son would ever get? He rubbed the ribbon between his fingers and closed his eyes.

He heard a faint padding of feet approach somewhere behind him, but didn't turn. Privacy may have been an unnecessary luxury to everyone else, but, to those grieving, it was one of few comforts.

"Walk with me," a quiet voice called.

His heart leapt as he let go of the ribbon and wheeled around to face its source. The man from the café, *The Hat*, stood there, draped in his heavy black overcoat. He didn't look at Marus, but pulled a thin cigarette, hand rolled, from his right breast pocket and placed it tightly between his lips. Then he set off toward the cover of a few tall trees at the western edge of the park. Marus followed.

"Want one?" he mumbled, keeping his lips pressed together as he fetched a lighter from the same pocket.

"I don't smoke," Marus said.

The Hat looked unimpressed. He took a drag, a question of Marus's character forming on his face.

"Let me see your phone," he said.

Marus took account of the surroundings. A few pine trees blocked his view of the memorial, and the road was completely obscured. As far as he could tell, there weren't any cameras or scanners here. Nothing attached to the trunks of trees that might record their conversation or provide immediate protection to Marus, should he need it. A resident squirrel and several busy song sparrows served as the only witnesses. He took the phone from his pocket and switched it off. "It's off," Marus said, lifting it to show the black screen. "What do you want?"

The Hat puffed on the cigarette, ignoring him. He exhaled pleasurably, letting the smoke billow from a gap at the side of his mouth. The wind carried it away, filtering it through the trees.

"I've seen you twice now at the café," Marus said.

The Hat stopped, turned toward him, and took the cigarette from his lips. He chuckled. "I like it there. Don't you?"

"You were watching me, weren't you?"

The stranger was several inches taller than Marus and looked about fifteen pounds lighter. His large, gray eyes were barely visible, and yet Marus felt the chill of his stare.

"How many people do you watch in your position?" He smiled this time, a twisted and unnatural grin.

"What do you mean?"

"You're a Protector, aren't you?"

"How do you know that?"

The Hat tilted his chin in amusement. "It was on the news." He exhaled a tendril of smoke.

"You were at the Rose that day, watching us. Why?"

The Hat ignored the question. "It must be awful business, playing God the way you do," he said, tapping a bit of ash to the ground. "People used to live by a moral code; now they live by the code you created." He held the cigarette inches from his lips. "Salvation for some, condemnation for others."

The wind shifted, caressing Marus's face with a veil of smoke.

"Who are you?" Marus asked.

"*Who* is unimportant. All that matters is what I know."

Marus moved closer. "Where is she?"

The Hat tossed his cigarette and toed the butt firmly into the ground.

"You know where Shey is, don't you?" Marus said.

"Meet me here tomorrow at ten p.m. I presume you know how to avoid the scanners."

"Yes," Marus said, though he'd never tried before.

"Turn your phone off or leave it at home."

"Okay."

"Oh, and Marus? If you really want to help her, I'd make sure our secret meeting stays secret." He kicked the butt away and tipped his hat.

Then he was gone.

11

THE BLACK SUV was following him. Marus had seen it three times since his trip to Reagan's apartment. And here it was again. It hung back but made every turn he did, disappearing when he parked and reappearing each time he got into his car again. The vehicle didn't have government plates, but it looked like something State personnel would drive. He wondered if it was Detective Ballo behind the black glass, taking surveillance into his own hands. What had he called it? *Police work.*

Or maybe they were journalists? Paparazzi? Certainly it was plausible. Almost a week had passed since Shey vanished, and well-intentioned public curiosity and concern regarding his son's disappearance had erupted into a full-blown media spectacle encumbered with accusation and alarm. The people wanted, demanded, to know. Marus couldn't fault them for it either. Information, disclosure, transparency. That was the trade-off. Those were their rights. Without answers, the media and its audience came to their own conclusions. Networks began to mention Marus. If Shey was a fearist, how did he not know? If she wasn't, and had been lured and taken, how come he couldn't stop it? He was a Protector, after all.

A clean-shaven man in a gray suit sat at a crescent-shaped table on the evening news. "Let's talk about Marus Winde for a moment," he said. "What does his lack of knowledge regarding Ms. Vanguard's activities suggest about the stability of the Protector Program? As one of the engineers responsible for developing the program's first predictive risk algorithm, is it possible that he overlooked key behavioral triggers that are necessary to identify potential risks?"

The camera panned. One of the women, a security consultant in a coral blazer seated to his left, responded, "It seems that, while the system succeeded in identifying the threat, the man failed." Several people nodded.

A glimpse of Marus on camera warranted at least a ten-minute conversation about his son's murder and Shey's disappearance. The reporters waited out in the open, never shying from the opportunity to stick a lens in his face.

One woman had gone so far as to follow him into the elevator at his apartment building. She smiled and nodded in a familiar way, so at first Marus thought she was another tenant. They exchanged hellos.

"Marus," she said, retrieving a pen recorder from her pocket. She thrust its tiny eye in his face. "Is your wife a fearist?"

He didn't want to answer, but an involuntary spasm of the lips and tongue overtook him. The video that would later be the subject of so much speculation showed him looking wounded, staring directly into her eyes as he muttered a defeated response. "I'm not sure."

Another journalist slipped into the Protective Services Center and began questioning him as he placed his briefcase onto the conveyer. "This is obviously very close to home for you. As an engineer, what are you doing to address the deficiencies in the program? Do you believe I3 would have prevented your son's murder? Why wasn't the update made sooner?"

For the first time in his life, Marus felt unqualified for the job. If he'd worked a little faster, if he'd listened to Devlin to push the update sooner, maybe his son would still be alive. And if he still had Cade, he'd have Shey, too. His family, safe. Whole.

If he hadn't felt the sense of accountability and inadequacy on his own, the media was there to ensure he made the connection.

This is your life's work. This was your family. How many times and in how many ways can one person fail?

Marus didn't answer. He passed through security refusing to look back, as the guard with the curious scar ushered the reporter out. But the questions couldn't go unanswered forever.

■ ■ ■

The door was slightly ajar when Marus reached the entrance to the small condo at Edenbrook.

"Dad?" He said, pushing it open. But there was no response. He crossed the small entry into the combined kitchen and living room. The TV was on but muted. A brunette mouthed the news. A special report. The news ticker scrolled.

POLICE CONTINUE SEARCH FOR THE BODY OF SEVEN-YEAR-OLD CADIEN VANGUARD-WINDE. ABDUCTOR ANTHONY JENNINGS CONFESSED AND IS BEHIND BARS THANKS TO PROTECTOR PROGRAM.

"Dad?"

Marus heard a small gasp of air come from the bedroom. Rushing to the door, he saw his father sitting on the edge of the bed. Photographs sprawled out on all sides, covering the comforter. Marus watched from the doorframe as Vic carefully turned the pages of a thick album in his lap. His fingers brushed a couple of the photos as he brought his head close to the page to get a better look. He was crying.

"Dad, what are you doing?"

Startled, Vic looked up and wiped at his eyes. "Oh. I wasn't expecting you."

"Your front door was open."

"Was it?" he said, sliding the album from his lap. "Well, it doesn't make a bit of difference. They can get in even if it's locked."

"It's so they can get to you if you need help, Dad."

"I was on the toilet the other day, and this gal let herself in. Probably thinking I was asleep or dead. She walked right up to the open bathroom door, looking like she'd seen a ghost. I don't know who I feel sorrier for, her for coming upon a wrinkly old man with his trousers at his ankles, or that wrinkly old man who can't even defecate in peace."

"What are you doing with all this stuff?" Marus lifted an old photograph from the bed. It was a picture of a very young girl with a kitten in her lap.

"Remembering."

"Who's this?" He turned the photograph so Vic could see.

"That's your mother. Most of this is hers."

"I've never seen these. Where have you kept them all these years?"

"In boxes, in attics and garages. I never could throw it all out, but I never could look at it, either."

Marus set the photo down on the bureau.

"You know, after all these years, I still miss her," Vic said. "When I look at her picture, it feels like I've barely lost her, and I grieve all over again." He took a picture from the bed and held it up. It was of the three of them, when Marus was no more than five years old. He handed it to his son. "Do you remember much about her?"

"Yeah," he said, examining the photo. He smiled at his dad's thick black glasses, his mother's shoulder-length bob. "I do. She used to tell me stories before bed. She never had to read from a book. She just made them up as she went along." He looked at his own boyish face in the picture. He'd always thought Cade was a spitting image of Shey, but now he could see that the slant of chin and roundness of cheeks had come from him. They even had the same long, sweeping eyelashes. Shey had always envied Cade for those. "Mom used to move her hands in front of the lamp to create shadow puppets on the wall. She was really good at it. I remember there being a dog, or something."

Vic nodded and chuckled. "Pip, the plucky Pekingese," he said.

"That's right, and his many adventures. I remember that."

"How on earth she was able to make her shadow look like a Pekingese, I haven't the faintest."

Marus set the family photo atop the other.

"Why do you think people take pictures?" Vic asked.

"To remember, like you said."

Vic shook his head, gathered the scattered photos. "If they really wanted to commit a moment to memory, they'd be present in it. They'd think about what was going on, how things looked, what they felt like in that moment. Photographs can't capture all of that, not even video, but we take them anyway because we like the idea of permanence."

Marus had tried not to watch Cade's childhood through a camera. He and Shey would take turns capturing his first steps, first haircut, first day of school. Mostly, they'd snap quick pictures and then put their phones away to watch for themselves.

Now, he wished he'd taken advantage of every single photo op. If only he'd kept the video rolling.

It wasn't permanence he sought. Just life. The rightful length. Parents were supposed to be able to watch their children grow up. And if he couldn't do that, he'd settle for Cade's childhood. He'd replay it again and again until he died.

Marus helped Vic gather the loose photographs and tucked them back into the box.

"I'm sorry. I'm sure you're not here to listen to all of this."

"It's fine, Dad."

"Shall I grab my coat?"

"Yeah." Marus set his cellphone on the bureau beside the box.

■ ■ ■

The afternoon sun set the waves ablaze with its blinding re-flection. A few seagulls cawed as they struggled over a sand crab on the beach below. Some distance up the shoreline, a couple walked hand in hand, leaving the stamp of their soles behind in the sand.

"How are you holding up?" Vic asked, taking hold of the guardrail.

"Not very well. I'm trying to keep busy."

"I can understand that. Just don't forget to allow yourself time to grieve, too. It's important."

"They found the guy who did it," Marus said.

Vic turned. "They did?"

"That's what they're saying, but I don't know."

"What do you mean you don't know?"

"The news is saying the Protector Program found him, but he came to them. That's what the detective told me. He willingly confessed. Some electrician, a middle-aged guy named Anthony Jennings. He lives over in Wells. Not far from Reagan, actually. One of his kids was kidnapped prior to the New Era. I saw his picture. He doesn't look like a murderer."

"I've seen plenty of things that don't look how they ought to, but that doesn't mean anything. Sounds to me like a sicko exacting his own perverted justice on someone else. But then the guilt got to him. That's why he came forward."

"It was a daughter he lost. Not a son."

"That doesn't matter. Guys like that—they're messed up in the head," Vic shivered. "How's Shey?"

Marus squinted at the water's surface. "Shey's gone," he said.

"What?"

"She left after Cade was taken."

"*What?* What do you mean?"

"I didn't say anything because I didn't want to worry you. I thought she'd be back. But now the State's looking for her. The system identified her as a threat."

"Why?"

"She's offline. Her iD was extracted."

"No, I mean why did she leave?"

"Someone gave her the notion that we were targeted, that Cade's abduction was planned. She thought she could find out who was responsible."

"Now that they've got the guy, will she come back?"

"I don't know. She doesn't even believe Cade is dead. At least that's what she said before she left."

"And what do you think?"

"Cade's Lifewatch feed showed that his heart stopped beating. They found his soccer jersey, with his blood on it."

"Why does Shey think he might still be alive?"

"She said she had a feeling, that she couldn't explain it."

Vic nodded, considering this. "You know, there was this one time, when you were a little boy, maybe three years old, and we called a babysitter over so we could go to a party. One of my work functions. The sitter had watched you a number of times, and we really liked her. She was responsible, and very good with you. We'd been at the party maybe thirty minutes when your mother said we had to go. She had a feeling something was wrong. I told her everything was fine and that she should try to enjoy herself. Five minutes later she told me she was leaving with or without me. She demanded the car keys. I think part of me worried she was right and that I'd be the schmuck for staying at the party, so I went with her. Fifteen minutes later, we pulled up to the house, and I swear to God I was stunned stupid. You were tottering around on the grass in your pajamas, maybe a foot from the street. It was dark out, and cold. If we hadn't come right then...Lord only knows what would have happened to you."

"I never heard that story."

"You were a sneaky little fellow. It turned out the sitter had invited her boyfriend over, and somehow you'd managed to get outside without them noticing. From that point on, I never questioned your mom whenever she got a funny feeling. They don't call it a mother's intuition for nothing," Vic said, squeezing Marus's arm.

"So you're saying Shey could be right? That Cade's still alive and this Jennings guy is a phony? Why would he come forward? Why put his life on the line like that?"

"It doesn't matter what I think, or even what you think. If Shey believes it, you need to support her. You can't let her do this on her own, Marus."

"I don't know where she is, or whether she's all right."

"What about her microchip? Can't you trace it?"

"You can't trace them, Dad. They're passive. They have to be scanned by something. But, like I said, she's offline anyway."

"Do you think she's in danger?"

"I don't know." He leaned in close to his dad. "A man's been following me. I think he can tell me where she is. I saw him at the café the day after Cade disappeared. The way she watched him, it looked like she knew him. Anyway, he wants to meet tonight at the park."

"Are you going?"

"I have to. It's the only lead I have."

12

MARUS HAD NEVER visited the park at dark. The memorial, powerful and haunting during the day, became sinister in the impenetrable vastness of night. Beyond the iron fence and the fluttering of ribbons in the wind, several lone spotlights cast harsh, white light on the sculpture's stylized pieces of wreckage, transforming art into what looked more like the remnants of an otherworldly war zone.

Pines and hemlocks broke free of the hard ground and slithered up toward the sky, creating a natural fence that kept the park's contents concealed from the street. There were few scanners in the park. Fewer than Marus would have liked under different circumstances. They were attached to benches and lampposts at the perimeter but became scarce the deeper one walked into the park. The patrols watched but preferred to do so from the warmth and safety of their vehicles. A less-than-exacting view.

To evade the scanners along the sidewalks, Marus had taken the motorcycle. It was Reagan's late husband's: a 2006 Yamaha Virago he'd converted into a Café Racer. One day,

Reagan would give it to her son, something to remember his father by. In the meantime, Shey and Marus kept it in the storage closet near their parking stalls in the garage. It wasn't registered or insured, but Shey made sure it was meticulously maintained. Now he wondered if her efforts were less nostalgic and more strategic than she'd initially let on.

A scanner affixed to a post near the garage's exit blinked green as Marus drove past, but he was almost certain he'd slipped every scanner since. The bike, however, was incredibly loud. He parked it across the street, in an alley near the Rose Café, and sprinted toward the park. Two patrol cars circled the park regularly, creeping down side streets before looping back to the parkway. The taillights of the first signaled Marus to move fast. There was a gap, but the other would be shortly behind. He ducked as he ran straight into the heart of the park, only slowing his stride once the road was out of view.

He made a point of entering the same way he had when he'd come with the ribbon hours before. Otherwise, he thought, it'd be impossible to find the same grouping of trees again. A flashlight would have given him away in the shallow darkness between the pile of twisted metal and the sidewalk, so he'd left home without one.

The patchwork of dirt and sand underfoot was damp, molding to the tread of his boots as he ambled cautiously closer to the trees. The sky was clear and the breeze crisp. He caught a whiff of an earthy, ashy scent hanging in the air.

"Are you here?" Marus whispered among the trunks.

No one answered. He continued walking westward, criss-crossing through the trees and calling out in sharp whispers until he reached the last of them on the western edge of the park. There, from the cover of the foliage, he watched as the patrol made another pass.

The brake lights burned as the car came to a halt. Its reverse lights flashed white, and the car inched backward. Marus felt the fear lodge in his chest. He wasn't doing anything illegal. Curfew wasn't for another two hours, and the park was a public place. He had every right to be here, he reminded himself. But having the right didn't always warrant its exercise, not if you wanted to be left alone. In any case, it wouldn't look good and would certainly raise questions with Ballo, maybe even Devlin. Questions he wouldn't know how to answer. Not yet.

The car continued to back up until it was parallel to a spot in the park only several yards in front of him. He reversed into the cover of a few more trees, but tripped on a root and fell backward, landing hard on his tailbone. From a low crouch, he could see the exhaust billowing in the red glow of brake lights. The rest of the car was obstructed by several tree trunks and bushes. Eventually, the driver released the brake and turned the car around, driving in the direction from which it had just come.

He was brushing the dirt from his pants when a cloud of cigarette smoke blew past him.

"Nice bike," The Hat said, puffing on his cigarette.

"Just tell me she's okay."

"I haven't seen her in a few days."

"But you know where she is."

"On her way to the colony, I assume."

"The colony?"

"It's a settlement, their home base."

"Whose?"

"They call themselves the Patriots."

"Who are they?"

"Disgruntled citizens. People like you and me. Like Shey."

"What do they want?"

"Same as what we all want, I suppose: life, liberty, and the pursuit of happiness." He flicked the cigarette to the ground. "They fight for the rights this country was founded on, those that can no longer be guaranteed, at least, not under the Protector Program."

"*Fearists*," Marus said. "They aren't fighting for rights. They're fighting for chaos. Without the program, what are we left with?" School shootings and bombings, Marus thought. A racist and corrupt police force.

"Fearists," The Hat said, "an appropriate designation, however gravely misattributed. You wouldn't consider Shey a fearist, would you?"

Marus squinted in the dark, trying to read his face. "She's... *one of them*?"

"There are two kinds of people," The Hat said, reaching into his pocket to retrieve another rolled cigarette. "Those who wish to know and those who don't. Each of us has our reasons, but most are just afraid of something. We either fear the unknown or fear the truth. It's as simple as that." He lit the cigarette. "People like to think they're a certain way. They romanticize one notion or another. But sometimes the truth is more terrifying than the unknown, and, by the time they know it, it's too late. If you go looking for the truth and you find it, it becomes part of you. And from then on, you'll live either trying to change it or learning to accept it. There's no unknowing." He lowered his head, bringing it closer to Marus's. "Only fools seek the truth before knowing what kind of man they are."

"Well, I'm no fool."

"No, I didn't think you were," he said with a smile. "All these patriots—*fearists*, whatever you want to call them—want is to expose the truth. So does Shey. So do I."

"And what's the truth?"

"The answer is as simple as a question. How do you achieve total power and preserve democracy?" The Hat waited, but Marus didn't answer. "You give the people a reason to give up their rights. *Fear.* With it, the State can legislate away liberties as easily as tyrants seize power. The Protector Program never would have garnered public support if the people weren't afraid of what was happening and what *might* happen. Ten years of progressive bombings, shootings, and kidnappings were made to look isolated and random, when really they were all connected. A massive fear campaign, bankrolled by the State in an effort to obtain total control."

He took another drag.

Marus watched the ember as it burned. "What evidence do you have?"

"You remember that woman, Li, the State systems administrator who was murdered a couple months ago? Well, she came across a misfiled document after a data migration. It had the Secretary of Treasury's signature on it and distribution instructions for more than five million dollars, payable to members of crime boss Xander Novak's family."

"What?"

"A week after the document was signed, Novak miraculously escaped the maximum security facility where he was being held. He killed three guards in the process. Right after that, the IA pushed a new initiative."

"The Prison Patch," Marus said. "I worked on it. It was designed to automatically suppress unruly inmates."

"That's right, and the SA tightened security and increased patrols, but they never found Novak."

"What about the video made for Li? There were two men in masks who took credit for her death. The PSC received a number of threats that week. Those men claimed to be fearists."

"If you look at every fearist attack close enough, you'll see it's actually the State cleaning up after itself. Every cover-up is another opportunity to frighten the public and strengthen their position. Even the Prison Patch update ensured that anyone who knew anything in Novak's facility wouldn't speak out," The Hat said.

"No, the Prison Patch employs the most basic I3 technology to look for adrenaline and an influx of testosterone, indicating that a prisoner will act out. Only then will it trigger the timed release of a tranquilizer."

"Maybe that's how it was *designed*, but a couple tweaks here and there, and you've got a very effective tool for mind control. Intention and application are two very different things, Marus. I'm sure you know that." The Hat drew on the cigarette and let the smoke out in one long, ghostlike wisp.

Marus watched it lean into the wind. "So what's your plan then?"

"Like I said, all we want is to expose the truth. The people deserve that much, don't you think?"

"And you think a single document proves that this happened?"

"Not that it *happened*, Marus. That it's *happening*, even now. The document Li uncovered barely scratched the surface. We believe there are hundreds of other documents—execution orders, commissioned attacks—contracts between high-ranking officials and known criminals. Novak, and others. People like the men responsible for your son's death."

"That's what Shey meant when she said we were targeted."

The Hat nodded. "The point is to give the people the facts and let them decide." He flicked a bit of ash to the ground. "Shey wants that, too."

"She never told me outright. She never said a word of what you're saying."

"She was trying to protect you, and Cade. You should know that."

"Before she left, she said she thought he was out there, waiting to be found."

"It's possible they've kept hostages. We'd expect, for the most part, that they'd be political, but I suppose your son could be among them. You've heard of Black Mine Bunker?"

"The State's subterranean data repository?"

"Theorized to be hidden in an abandoned mine, yes, though we can't yet confirm its existence, let alone its location. Still, if they were keeping hostages, they might keep them there."

Marus tried to imagine it, a barracks-like facility in the ground. Cold hallways, flickering lights. Cade in a cell beside the senator thought to be dead.

"I don't suppose you know where it is?" The Hat asked.

"No. No one does."

"No one?"

"No one," Marus said. "Except maybe those who work on the tenth floor."

"Shey mentioned you were up for that. Now, at least, you know that it wasn't for lack of merit."

"How did she get involved in all this?"

The Hat looked at the cigarette thoughtfully. "In truth," he said, "I suppose it's my fault."

Somewhere behind them a branch snapped. The sound of careful footsteps in the grass.

"I'll be in touch soon." The Hat stamped out his cigarette and slipped his hand into the overcoat's interior breast pocket. He retrieved a folded piece of paper and held it up between a gloved thumb and forefinger. "In the meantime, a letter for you," he whispered, placing the paper delicately in Marus's outstretched hand. "From Shey."

■ ■ ■

Marus smoothed the paper out on the kitchen table and studied the distinct slant of Shey's words. He knew her handwriting much like he knew her face.

Shey had always preferred a handwritten note to an email or text when the situation allowed for it. It was common for her to leave him notes on the kitchen table or bedroom bureau. He'd leave them for her, too, often tucking them into her pocket before she dressed, or setting them beside the coffee maker. Pen on paper, it was their love language, the way they expressed their gratitude as well as their anger.

Because of this, he was able to decipher uncertainty in the pooling of ink, the same way he could read it in her eyes. Excitement or affection shaped each letter. Her every word altered just so, allowing him a glimpse between the lines.

The ink was blue instead of the usual black, and the paper not as crisp or clean. He could see she'd been in a hurry. There were tiny indentations, loops where the pen had faltered and come to life again. Each word gave chase to the next, leaping and reaching for those that followed. Her signature was sloppy and smudged at the bottom. It had bled upside down onto the middle of the page after being folded while the ink was still wet.

> *Dear Marus,*
>
> *By now you know there are things I've kept from you. These secrets were meant to protect our family, but I see they've only caused harm. We are well past danger now.*
>
> *This is a difficult letter for me to write because I can't predict the circumstances under which you shall receive it. I don't know what monster the media will make of me, or what lies you'll be told. I don't even know if I'll still be alive by the time these words reach you. I can only hope you will hear me, your wife, in these lines and see the truth in what I have to say.*
>
> *Over the past few months, I've come across information that implicates the government in numerous crimes in the years before and since the New Era. A group of activists and I have successfully linked numerous acts of terrorism to the State, with the understanding that these attacks were carried out to strike*

fear into the heart of the nation, turning neighbors against each other. The Protector Program was not the solution, but the goal all along. Every update gives the State greater power. Increases its control. We've created a glass box that future generations will never be able to escape.

13 will only further this. Regardless of your due diligence and how hard you've worked, it can't go live. You have to trust me on this, Marus. It must be dismantled.

I know fear to be a powerful motivator. Someone was following me in the days before Cade's abduction. Our home was being watched. I should have told you, but I thought I could protect you and Cade by leaving. I didn't know how far they'd go or how quickly they would act. Please forgive me.

If they find me, they'll kill me. Maybe the media will say I was a fearist, or maybe they'll say I died in fearist hands. It won't matter. Either way, they'll use it to fuel their cause, just as they did with Cade. He could still be alive. I know you think I'm crazy. Maybe I am.

To evade the State, I've taken certain precautionary measures. The system can't see me, but I'm no longer safe in the city, either. The people I'm with have a plan. They can help you, help us, but they need your help first. They are good people. You can trust them.

The thought of the three of us together again keeps me going. It gives me hope, and hope is the greatest defiance, the only force that can overcome fear.

I love you, now and always,
Shey

■ ■ ■

He was dreaming, again. They were laughing together. The sunlight splashed her face, and her freckles came alive. She smiled. He could always see it in her wild, green eyes before her lips parted and bore a perfectly pale grin. He put her hand in his and squeezed, trying to absorb the warmth of her flesh. At this moment, the world was whole. Absolute.

And then something strange happened. Blood began to drip from her mouth. Shey wiped it away with her fingers, but there was too much. Her attempts only smeared it across her face. He didn't know what to do. He tried to call for help, but no sound came from his mouth. And then she started to fall. His hand still clutched hers, but she was too heavy, and he was too slow. She reeled backward in slow motion until she hit the ground unmoving, eyes like glass, open and staring. Marus didn't bend down to shake or revive her. He knew she was dead.

"You let them do this."

The voice came from inside his head, but it wasn't his.

It was The Hat's.

■ ■ ■

Marus's eyes flew open. It was dark and cold. He looked around, shivering, stunned to realize that he wasn't at the kitchen table, in the study, or in his bedroom. He wasn't at his apartment at all. He was outside.

He lay cramped on a hard, cold surface, a park bench, but couldn't remember how he'd gotten there. His throat burned, and his eyes wouldn't focus. He felt the sting of a cut along his left shin, and the back of his other leg throbbed, as though he'd run into something. He sat up slowly. The wind howled as he searched his memory. A scanner attached to the wooden backrest detected Marus's iD and blinked green.

A whisper of wind met his ear.

"Marusss…" it hissed.

It came again, more audibly this time, tangible. *Human.* Ahead in the darkness, he made out the slender figure of a man. The Hat? The musty scent of cigarettes hung faintly in the air. Marus stood up.

"Marus Winde, stay where you are!" the man yelled.

It wasn't The Hat's temperate voice calling out to him. It was Detective Ballo's. The detective shot a beam of light squarely at Marus, blinding him. He stammered backward in attempt to shield his vision and fell to rest once more on the bench. Ballo's quick steps crunched the leaves beneath his boots as he rushed at Marus. A moment later, Marus was on the ground, Ballo's knee in his back.

The yellowing grass scraped against his face as the detective cuffed him. Beneath the bench among the weeds, he caught sight of the shredded butt of a cigarette. Ballo yanked him up off of the ground.

"I'm taking you in."

"That's unnecessary. I was sleeping. I woke up out here. Look." Marus held out his cuffed wrists so Ballo could scan his iD to confirm with Lifewatch.

"I don't give a rat's ass what the data says. It's after twelve o'clock, and I'm looking at you with my own eyes, aren't I? That warrants an arrest."

Marus's head spun. He stumbled several times as they walked to the patrol car at the curb. Ballo opened the back door.

"Wait, I'm going to be sick." Marus grabbed the top of the car door and retched into the gutter just as the detective's phone began to ring.

"Oh, come on!" Ballo jumped back to avoid the deluge.

Marus spat and straightened. He didn't resist as Ballo pushed him into the back of the vehicle.

From inside the car, Marus watched the detective pace back and forth on the phone. Though muffled, Ballo's voice seemed to have changed. It was slower, softer. The detective nodded several times. "Yes. Yes, sir," Marus thought he heard him say. Then Ballo hung up.

Neither of them said a word as the car pulled away from the curb. Trees and buildings streaked by in a blur. The world outside was silent and still. Marus rested his forehead against the cold glass of the window, peering out into the blackness. Somewhere among shadows, The Hat moved slowly, quietly, like a predator in the night. Marus could feel it.

■ ■ ■

The car turned onto Second Street, throwing even more light down a corridor of neatly lined lamps and clean entries to buildings that looked almost identical to his. Concrete boxes, several stories high.

"Commissioner Devlin will be in touch," Ballo said as he parked in front of Marus's building. He walked around to the rear door and let Marus out onto the curb.

"Thank you, detective."

"I know it was you," he said, turning Marus around so he could remove his cuffs.

"Excuse me?"

"You were at the park earlier tonight, meeting somebody."

Marus rubbed at his wrists. "I don't know what you're talking about."

"No one is above the law. You might be able to work around the system, Winde, but you don't fool me." He opened his car door. "You're not the man everyone thinks you are."

"Good night, detective."

13

FOUR RED FINGERTIPS slipped through the narrowing space just in time. The metal doors threw themselves wide to allow the blonde woman entry.

"Sorry," Marus said, stepping aside to make room. "I didn't see you."

"That's all right," she said in a throaty voice. "It's my fault for being impatient."

The automatic elevator attendant weighed the superiority of each of its passengers and prioritized Marus's floor.

"Good morning, Mr. Winde. Ninth floor. Going up."

"Can I have the seventh first?" he said.

The elevator confirmed his access. "Seventh floor. Going up."

"That's where I work," the woman said.

"Then you won't have to wait."

The doors opened, and the woman smiled and exited.

A receptionist at the large, horseshoe-shaped counter greeted him. "How can I help you, Mr. Winde?" he said, looking up from his screen.

"I'm working on a project and need to speak with someone who specializes in sleep monitoring."

"All right," he said, entering the request to see what the computer pulled up. "Ms. Roth. She's available now. Down the center hall, take your third left. She is in the fifth cube to the right. Will that be all?"

"Yes, thank you."

He followed the receptionist's directions and arrived at a cubicle with "ROTH" embedded plainly in a metal plaque on the gray, carpeted wall. Her desk was empty.

Several minutes passed as he lingered in the walkway waiting for Roth to return. He was about to leave when a blue shoe caught his eye down the opposite end of the hall. A half inch of its pointed, suede toe jutted out from behind the carpeted divider of another cubicle. *Mazarine blue*, he'd been told, named after a type of blue butterfly. He'd first seen it on a pair of very similar-looking suede heels on Shey's side of the closet. He'd never seen another pair like them. Until now.

He turned, walking slowly past the sixth and seventh cubicle to get a better look.

"Hello again," the throaty voice called from the other end of the hall. Wisps of blonde hair fluttered around the woman's flushed face as she hurried toward him with a full cup of coffee. "I'm sorry, I didn't realize you wanted to speak with me."

"Ms. Roth?"

"Please, call me Roz."

He hesitated, looking back at the blue shoe, still barely visible ten feet in the other direction.

Roz stood, resting briefly against the high wall of her cubicle, waiting for him. "Shall we?" She nodded toward the cubicle, raising a brow.

The shoe slid behind the wall.

Marus joined Roz at her desk.

"I didn't want to say anything earlier, but you look different than you do on television," she said.

He shifted, not knowing how to respond. "Well, they say the camera adds five pounds."

She laughed. "That's not what I meant."

"The receptionist said you had time to meet with me."

"I do. Please," she said, gesturing toward the chair beside hers.

The screen blinked on in their presence. It was filled with a dozen black windows and documents. "You're working on a project?" Her eyes were large and childlike. A bright, inquisitive blue. She cleared the screen and turned toward Marus.

"Actually, I had a question about the sleep clock," he said. "It logged something peculiar, and I was wondering if you could help me understand it."

At this, she grinned. "You're wondering about your own data."

He nodded. "I won't take up too much of your time."

"Go ahead," she said.

"Last night, I woke up in the park and have no recollection of how I got there."

"It sounds like somnambulism. Do you have a history of sleepwalking?"

"No," Marus said.

"Mind if I pull up your sleep clock?"

"You can do that? You have access to individual user data?"

She nodded. "As it pertains to wellness. Doctors get it, and so do we. I guess they figure studying sleep cycles and physiological response isn't an invasion of privacy. What's your iD?"

"328541."

She entered it into the search window and pressed *enter*. "Okay, let's see here." She studied the screen, placing markers along several trend lines. "Ah, see this line?" She pointed to a black line that arced up, leveled, and then dropped off.

He nodded.

"That's your blood alcohol content, which might explain the unprecedented bout of sleepwalking. Alcohol, sedatives, and other medications can trigger it."

"I was disoriented when I woke up, and a little sick, but I didn't have anything to drink."

"From the look of this line, you cleaned out the bar," she said.

"Really, I don't drink. At all. I haven't since...my son was born."

She scrolled the timeline backward looking for fluctuations. "At all?" she asked, pointing to Friday's line.

"That was a very rare exception. The data there is accurate, but I know for a fact that I didn't have anything to drink last night."

"I'm not judging," she said.

"What is this graph?" Marus asked, pointing to several bars in varying shades of blue.

"That's your sleep stage analysis," Roz said. "It maps your cycle to show when you entered which stage of sleep, and the duration you remained there."

"The x-axis is the length of time?"

Roz nodded.

"Can you scroll forward again, to last night's data?"

She did.

"I woke in the park, here," he pointed to the three thirty a.m. hash mark. "I have no idea when I got there."

"What does your tag log show?"

"I was tagged leaving my apartment around one thirty a.m. There's not another tag until the park. Somehow, I missed every single scanner on my way there."

She moved closer to the screen. "That's interesting. Right here," she said, pointing to the blue bar graph, "it says you were in REM at the time you were tagged leaving your apartment."

"Why is that interesting?"

"Sleepwalking usually occurs during deep, non-REM sleep, stage three or stage four, unless it's part of an REM disorder, in which case, it'd be recurring. According to this, after REM, you go into stage one and two. Which is normal, but you stay there until the time you said you woke at the park. That's impossible. People usually spend five minutes in stage one and ten to twenty-five minutes in stage two."

"Is there a medical explanation for something like this? Are there precedents I could research?"

"Not that I know of, but you could check with the Wellness Annex. If this has happened before, they would know about it."

He could feel her hot breath in the small space between them, the smell of peppermint under her tongue.

"Could it be misattribution? Or a problem with the hardware?"

She shook her head, looking at the screen. "It doesn't appear to be either."

He stood, suddenly feeling claustrophobic in the close quarters. "Is it possible that someone could have changed the data?"

She hesitated and stood to meet his gaze. "Maybe," she said. "But why would someone do that?"

Marus thought about it for a moment. "I don't know."

He thanked her for her help, despite her insistence that she hadn't actually done anything, and turned to leave.

"Marus, let me know if you have any other questions. I'll be around." She smiled, taking her seat once more.

"Thanks." He wasn't looking at her. The blue shoe had reappeared with its mate, at the feet of a brunette strolling down the end of the long corridor of cubicles. The woman turned around a corner and disappeared.

Marus ran after her, past men and women at their desks in the cubes bordering the narrow hall.

Roz poked her head around the wall. "Are you okay?" she called after him, but he was already gone, turning sharply at the corner to meet another long row of high-walled cubicles.

The shoes and their owner had vanished, taking refuge in one of the twenty workspaces before him, if not down another hall. It was already past 9:00 a.m. As quietly and quickly as he could, he strolled past cubicle after cubicle, peeking briefly into each in search of the woman in the blue shoes. Men and women paused from their work to watch. Even Roth had left her desk to see what was going on.

He had nearly searched the entire floor by the time he saw them again. The brunette was filling her coffee with her back to him.

Marus cleared his throat. "Excuse me," he said.

The woman turned around. She looked nothing like Shey. "I'm sorry, I thought you were someone else."

■ ■ ■

The ninth floor was already humming with conversation by the time the elevator released him. A manufactured sunrise of prolonged oranges, reds, and pinks on the wall screens was beginning to fade into a powdery blue. Another beautiful day, expertly rendered. Marus took his seat at the corner cubicle, foregoing his usual trip to the coffee machine. He waved on the screens.

Logging into the system, he pulled up his profile and isolated the *Lifewatch* tab. Roz was right. According to the data, he'd been completely sauced the night before. But he hadn't had a drop to drink. He'd watched the SUV tail him halfway to Edenbrook. He'd spoken with his father and gone back to the apartment to wait until it was time to meet The Hat in the park. When he returned with the letter, he'd sat at the kitchen table and read it again and again. He didn't remember falling asleep. One moment he was at the kitchen table, and the next he was horizontal on a park bench. Then Ballo was over him, pushing his face into the ground.

He stared at the lines and bar graphs that were supposed to represent his data and wondered. Was it a glitch? Was it intentional? Was the State behind it, or someone else? Why would the data be falsified in the first place?

"Marus? Are you back there?" It was Anj on the other side of the cubicle wall. She rounded the corner. "You know, if I was you, cheated out of a promotion like that, I'd be in later than usual, not earlier. But good for you, way to stick it to Devlin."

He didn't say anything.

She looked around, taking a few steps toward him, hands clasped reverently in front of her blazer. "Okay, look, I wanted to talk to you about Friday real quick. No need for either of us to feel awkward. We're two professionals, and we're friends. You were in a shitty spot, I'd forced a lot of liquor on you, and we were both really drunk. I just want you to know that it's not a big deal." She plucked a hangnail from her finger and sprinkled it to the floor. "It might as well never have happened."

He was quiet, still fixated on the screen when he saw the bar graph, his sleep cycle, change. Right before his eyes, the blue bars altered, reshaping the story. The bar graph that had indicated he was in REM when he left his apartment shortened to reflect stage three instead.

"What?" He clicked on the screen, backing out and reentering to see if the information changed again. But it didn't.

"Uh oh," Anj said. "I know that look. What is it? What's broken?" She walked over to his side to look at the screen, her long nose and big mouth level with his. "The sleep clock? Why are you looking at this?"

He didn't respond.

"If Davey fucked something up again, I swear, I'll have him fired. Just tell me." She straightened up, shifting her scrutiny from the screen to Marus. "Hello? A little acknowledgment over here," she said, waving a hand in front of his face.

"*Please*, Anj. Stop talking for a second. I'm trying to figure this out."

With her thumb and forefinger, she pretended to zip her lips. She let her hand fall from her mouth, her middle finger flexed.

"I know things are rough for you right now, Marus, but from one *friend* to another, you're being a bit of an asshole. Just thought you should know that." She spun on her heels and walked away.

■ ■ ■

All eyes were on him. He could hear the footfall on the other side of the cubicle wall. People seemed to go out of their way to walk past his desk. They lingered a little too long, and then shot past without a word. He couldn't see their faces, but he heard the hesitation in their steps. They were unsure about something. Unsure about him.

He'd been getting close with 13. Feeling he had something to prove, to Devlin, to the media, to himself, he'd worked faster than he'd anticipated. It could be ready in as little as two weeks. After so much time and doubt, it would have been his name they remembered. *Would have.*

Shey's letter changed all of that.

It must be dismantled.

Of course, he couldn't be certain that the letter was even from Shey. Someone might have copied her script. Someone could have forced her hand.

He considered what The Hat had said about Li and Novak. The document the Secretary of the Treasury had signed, a check cut to Novak's family. It could all be true. Or it could be a setup. He hadn't seen the document, and the Protector Program hadn't detected anything.

The Hat said the code could be tweaked to change the program, to prevent particular predictive outcomes. But Marus would have seen those changes in his analysis. The hundreds of reports he parsed through daily ought to have revealed something.

Unless it wasn't the program that was altered, but rather, the data. *No, not altered,* Marus thought, *concealed.* He remembered the string of code in Shey's data. A ghost state used to veil information. In her case, it concealed the iD extraction. Theoretically, it could hide a lot more.

He'd stored Shey's report in an encrypted folder on his laptop in case someone got hold of his machine. He took the laptop from his computer bag and placed it on the desk. Glancing over the partition, he powered it on and retrieved the file.

Marus woke the screens at his workstation and began querying the system for instances of the same code string. Depending on the number of occurrences, the scrape would take a while, but if it worked, he'd have a list of every user whose data had been modified by the string.

Returning his laptop to its bag, he tucked it under the desk, switched off the monitors, and grabbed his mug. As he emerged from his cube and made his way toward the coffee machine, Marus formed a wide wake. His coworkers moved around him, matching his gaze, they frowned. Their faces fell quickly to the floor.

Fucking Anj, he thought. She was a talker; he'd always known that. The whole floor probably knew about the drunken kiss. His coworkers' eyes seemed to hold him in estimation. Some even looked embarrassed on his behalf. He wondered what else Anj had said and to whom.

As he walked through the common area, a man Marus didn't like made eye contact. His name was Chirag, and he didn't like Marus much, either. That was the way it was. Coworkers either admired or abhorred him, and Chirag fell far at the latter end of that spectrum.

He shook his head, a complacent smile. "Women these days," he said.

Marus felt his face flush, the need for an explanation beginning to rise in his throat.

I was drunk. It didn't mean anything. I still love my wife.

Chirag interrupted the thought. "Sorry, man, but this is why there's a virtual dating market. Trust me, I know." He excused himself without clarification, leaving Marus in the common area alone with the screen.

BREAKING NEWS: NEW EVIDENCE SUGGESTS SHEY VANGUARD WAS BRAINWASHED BY FEARIST LEADER WITH WHOM SHE WAS HAVING AN AFFAIR. VIDEO SURVEILLANCE SHOWS VANGUARD

MEETING WITH A MAN PROTECTORS ARE SAYING IS "INVISIBLE" WHILE HER SON WAS LEFT ALONE AT ST. XAVIER'S THE MORNING HE WAS ABDUCT-ED. WHEN FOUND, VANGUARD WILL BE TRIED FOR TREASON AND CRIMINALLY NEGLIGENT MANSLAUGHTER IN SON'S DEATH.

Her face was blurry because of how far away she was, but it was her. His wife in her jeans and sweater, the same outfit she was wearing the day Cade disappeared, standing at the edge of the park. She looked both ways. A man walked up from behind her to meet her at the curb. He touched her shoulder. She turned to face him. They embraced. The video showed them cross the street and continue toward the Rose Café, closer to the camera. But even from afar, Marus knew the man immediately.

He recognized him by the hat he wore.

■ ■ ■

Marus didn't make it to the coffee machine. He'd left the wall screen in the common area, and his mug with it, and started back for his cubicle when he noticed a man in a suit, a strong arm, only a few steps behind him. He veered right for the men's room, but the man continued straight.

The bathroom was empty. Marus let himself into the far stall and latched the door. *An affair.* It couldn't be true.

Regardless of his affiliation with the fearists, The Hat couldn't be anything more than an acquaintance to Shey. Certainly not someone she'd be intimate with. *That*, he knew for sure.

But how did he know? *A feeling?*

They loved each other. They'd been happy.

Marus thought of his late nights at work. The weekends spent at the IA. Where was Shey while he was away? She'd been with Cade, of course. Theirs was a happy marriage. An honest one. And yet, Marus couldn't help but recall a shift. A distancing. He'd attributed it to work. She was dissatisfied with hers, and he was preoccupied with his. But maybe it'd been something else. Something more difficult to swallow.

By now you know there are things I've kept from you.

That Sunday at the café, he'd caught her looking at him, this strange man in the hat. There'd been something in her expression. Something Marus hadn't acknowledged until now. It surpassed recognition. She'd looked...wistful.

Whatever their relationship, she trusted The Hat. That much was clear. Enough to give him the letter, at least. And what must he have felt for her, to deliver it? To approach her husband, a Protector, and risk being found out. Hadn't he admitted to being the reason Shey was involved in the first place?

The Protectors thought he was offline. *Invisible.* But how could someone without an iD frequent a café? How could he transact? The times Marus had seen him there he'd had a mug, a croissant. He'd taken such care to tidy his table each time. He'd been showing off, Marus realized.

The bathroom door swung open. He heard footsteps across the tile, a zipper, and then a stream. A moment later, a flush and an exit.

There was no proof of an affair. The media didn't get to be the authority on a matter like that.

The door swung open again. A man called from the door. "Commissioner Devlin would like a word when you're done."

It was the man in the suit. Marus followed him into the elevator. Though the man didn't indicate which floor he wanted, the steel doors closed and the elevator lurched and fell. When the doors parted, they revealed a long, fluorescent-lit hallway Marus didn't recognize. The man guided him toward an open door at the far end of the corridor.

Devlin waited opposite a large, glass table in the small room. He gestured toward the chair across from him. "Take a seat."

The door closed with a hollow thud as the man in the suit exited.

Marus did as instructed, glancing periodically at the two-way mirror that comprised the right wall.

Shey's face was illuminated on the tabletop glass. Beneath her State-issued iD photo, Marus could see her network diagram. The diagram was a part of Marus's team's code at work, linking obvious connections, as well as imperceptible ones. Beneath an image of Reagan and the descriptor SISTER, was Marus, identified as SPOUSE.

A series of dashes originating from Marus's image led to a photograph of Cade. One bolded word, eight characters, was all that identified him: DECEASED. Marus's work had been a part of the greatest technological advancement of their time. But here, it was as flat as the pane of glass it illuminated.

A grainy screenshot from the surveillance video popped up on the screen below Marus's face. It was The Hat. The relation read CONSORT. There wasn't a name.

"I'd like you to take some time off."

"But sir—"

"This is a challenging time, Marus, and you have my sympathy, but your being here is doing more harm than good." The commissioner folded his hands. "The media is starting to point fingers. The public wants to know how an IA developer was blind to his wife's involvement with a fearist leader. It was bad enough that she took off, but this—how do you think this makes us all look?"

"Sir, with all due respect, I don't think that park surveillance footage warrants the assumption of an affair. There's no hard evidence to suggest—"

"And what about your surveillance footage?"

"Sir?"

"Antagonizing civilians at a bar? Getting thrown out of a public establishment? Imagine the story they'd run if they got hold of that. What the hell were you thinking?"

"I'm sorry, sir. Things got out of hand. I don't usually drink. I haven't since." He thought about what Roz had shown him and wondered if Devlin had looked.

"Several of your colleagues have approached me with concerns about your character."

"*Who?* Anj?"

"Your sprint through the halls this morning set quite a few people on edge. I think, up to this point, I've been very understanding of your situation, but a line has to be drawn. People are starting to doubt whether you're fit to lead. They're worried that the system is inadequate and wonder if, under your direction, the program will be sabotaged." Devlin looked briefly to the pane of glass on the wall, at the obscured observer on the other side. "Frankly, I'm beginning to wonder that myself." He exited out of Shey's profile and rolled the chair back. His hands grasped the edge of the glass. "Your leave of absence will go into effect as of this afternoon. The PR team has already prepared a statement for the media on your behalf."

"What about I3? Sir, I've been leading this project since the beginning, and I'm almost done."

"Anj and the others will take it from here."

"Sir, please reconsider."

"The system has deemed you unfit for the work. We have to follow protocol here, Marus. Maybe in a few months, once the dust has settled—"

"*Protocol?* What about the promotion? You recommended me and then gave it to Gene. What was the protocol there?"

"You aren't the man for the job," Devlin said flatly. He lifted a bag from the floor. It was Marus's computer bag. "Protocol also requires that the IA retain anything that may contain the State's intellectual property. This includes personal laptops. Your machine will be returned to you once it's been wiped." He pulled the laptop from its sleeve and slid the bag across the table. "Security will give you thirty minutes to collect the rest of your things."

PART THREE

A nation of sheep will beget a government of wolves.

—Edward R. Murrow

14

REAGAN MEYERS'S BODY *was discovered by a sanitation service worker this evening at a waste management facility twenty-six miles east of her home in the Wells District. Authorities say Meyers's murder resembles the brutal, execution-style killing of Li Syun, a State systems administrator. Shortly after Syun's death in late July, a video emerged crediting fearists with her murder and threatening other State employees. Though she was a teacher, Meyers's brother-in-law, Marus Winde, is the former algorithm architect for the State's Protector Program. In a statement, Winde announced that he was stepping down today to focus on his family. Winde's seven-year-old son was murdered September 14th. His wife, Shey Vanguard, disappeared a little more than a week later, after being tagged at Reagan Meyers's apartment.*

Meyers was last seen September 24th by a neighbor she'd charged with watching her two children. A video has not yet been released in conjunction with her murder.

Authorities encourage anyone with information to come forward. The Protectors are warning residents to exercise extreme caution until the Internal Indicator Initiative goes live October 14th.

■ ■ ■

So Devlin had known. He'd been watching Marus's progress and announced the launch. Two weeks then.

Watching the screen at home, he felt he might be sick. A picture of Reagan accompanied by video of the waste management facility was replaced with Shey's State-issued photograph. A news ticker scrolled below.

SHEY VANGUARD RESPONSIBLE FOR DEATH OF SISTER, REAGAN MEYERS? PETITION GOV. ROSEN TO INCREASE SURVEILLANCE IN LOW-INCOME NEIGHBORHOODS.

Sitting in his cold apartment, Marus recalled an early fight he and Shey once had. The details didn't come to mind, but he remembered Reagan acting as the mediator. She'd talked at length with each of them. Hearing their concerns and frustrations, she offered advice without taking sides. Practical, sincere, and straightforward, Reagan was his sister-in-law, but over the years, she had become one of his closest friends, too.

Now she was dead, and her children, orphans.

■ ■ ■

Fat, round raindrops detonated against the windshield as the coupe raced across the bridge toward Wells. Marus watched the surge and tallied his losses.

First his son and his wife. His friends. Then his job. Now, he'd even lost Reagan.

He wondered if Shey had heard the news yet. Would she come home now, to bury her sister? Would she come back for the kids? For him?

At the building's stoop, he pressed every button on the intercom. Even Reagan's. He went down the entire panel in order and then started again from the top. He'd continue until someone called the cops or let him inside. He'd wait all night if he had to.

Pulling his collar high against his neck, Marus leaned hard against the railing. The rain bled through his clothes, through his skin. All the way into his bones. Two headlights approached, pulling off toward the far curb a ways down the street. The lights went out. Several minutes passed, but no one left the vehicle. It was the SUV, Marus realized.

He tried the buttons again. There was no answer. The clapping of boots against wet concrete called his attention to the sidewalk. In the faint light of a flickering streetlamp, Marus could see a hooded figure approach, running in his direction.

Curfew wasn't for another hour and a half. Still, it could be someone in a hurry to get home, Marus reasoned. *Nothing to fear.* Down the street, the SUV was dark, stationary. He couldn't see inside.

Shivering, he pushed the buttons again. This time all at once. His breath formed a shallow cloud with each exhalation.

The hooded figure was at the bottom of the steps. Head down. Marus's heart hammered inside of his chest. A few steps were all that separated them, and then, a moment later, they were standing next to each other. The person in the hood faced away from Marus, so he couldn't see a face. A hand extended toward the scanner, and the door unlocked. It wasn't one of Novak's men, Marus realized. It was just a kid. A kid with a different curfew to meet.

Marus glanced back at the SUV and stepped inside.

The kid pulled at his sweatshirt, flinging rain from the fabric. Noticing Marus, he jumped.

"I'm a Protector," Marus said.

"Whatever man." He turned and ran up the stairs.

From the floor above, Marus heard a door open. A woman yelled. The kid yelled back. Then the door slammed shut.

Six stories above, Reagan's door was locked. Police tape hung limp across the frame. Marus knocked for sheer lack of another plan. The door across the hall opened with a squeak. A long nose jutted out.

"I thought that might be you at the buzzer," the voice said. "Damn near woke up the entire building."

A large woman in a nightgown and slippers appeared in the doorway. "You came for them kids, huh?" Her voice was hoarse. A chain-smoker's song.

"I did," Marus said, unmoving.

"Well, come on then." She moved from the door but left it wide. "Don't let the cat out."

The tabby raced through the door, bounding for the stairs, but Marus scooped it up in time. Its clawless paws tried to pull at his jacket.

Marus closed the door and set the cat down. It ran for the window and jumped up onto the sill. The woman put some hot water on. Her thin, gray hair was pulled tight into teal curlers, forming bald spots that exposed a mottled scalp.

"That's Reagan's cat. Don't know its name. Kids wouldn't tell me." She lit a cigarette. "Maybe it don't have a name. Either way, I 'spose it's mine now."

"Where are they?" Marus looked around.

Dirty plates and glasses were stacked high near the kitchen sink. The linoleum was crusted with dirt and hair. In the adjoining living room, the TV flickered, illuminating the silhouette of a bald man staring straight ahead at the screen. He didn't turn or say anything. There was no sign of the kids.

"Some lady came for 'em a couple hours ago. Said she was putting 'em in emergency protective custody. Whatever that means."

"It means the State has them." Marus moved toward the door, then hesitated. "Why did Reagan bring them to you in the first place?"

"She told me someone was after her sister. She had to help get her out. Said I had to keep quiet 'bout the whole thing. Poor kids kept asking when their ma was coming home, and I kept sayin', 'Any day now.' I didn't know I was lyin'."

15

MARUS HADN'T SEEN The Hat in days, though he walked around every corner in search of him. Though he felt watched.

Every moment he didn't have to be at home he spent at the café and in the park. He made himself as available to The Hat as possible, walking out of his way to be nearer to the tree line or barely beyond a building's edge. But The Hat never whispered his name or appeared momentarily to flash a "follow me" face before disappearing again. It seemed he'd vanished as quickly as he'd appeared.

September surrendered to October as though it'd merely been a dream. The air was crisper and smelled more of autumn. Rich, wet, and clean. The green that clung to the leaves of a few trees gave way to golds and deep reds. Other trees had already started to undress. Their leaves danced along the walkways, skipping behind the quick steps of thick boots along the pavement. Marus barely noticed.

He hadn't heard from Muñoz or Ballo, or Gene and Anj, for that matter. He would have thought they'd call, at least. Especially Gene. Marus's system access was revoked, and

Shey's friends hadn't returned any of his calls in regard to the alleged affair. He'd gone to visit his dad, but Vic hadn't quite been himself and kept dozing off in the armchair.

Without purpose, Marus idled aimlessly, ever aware of the black SUV lurking in the distance.

Sitting in the café or walking briskly to the park, Marus noticed people looking at him. The screens had made his face familiar. Theories were transformed into truths via the media, and he was now fully part of the story. The disillusioned husband who hadn't seen the signs. He was accused of being too incompetent to see a threat when it stared him in the face, and of keeping Shey's fearist plans secret, all in the same day. Sometimes on the same network.

But he'd amassed more than just critics. Somehow, on social media, he'd gained a following of female admirers as well. From the corner of his eye, he saw women of all ages sneak photos of him. Some, more brazen, stepped directly in front of him to snap his picture.

Around dinner, the Rose was all but deserted. A waiter cleared off nearby tables. Dirty ceramic cups clanked like piano keys breaking up the silence, as he set them inside themselves and carried them off for cleaning. A woman behind the counter packed away croissants that hadn't sold to save for the next day. When the display was empty, she shut off the lights and started wiping down the counters. They wouldn't close until 8:00 p.m., but they prepped and cleaned, hinting to Marus, as they had every night, that it was time to leave.

At first, Marus had given in, politely placing his cup in the bin near the counter at the sight of a broom or washcloth, nodding in silent appreciation of the waiter or waitress's company, and walking out into the cold. But the lonely hours at home, before an aching sort of half sleep took over, were too awful to face. The staff would have to wait until 7:59 p.m. Of course, they didn't know that, and so they continued to sweep, scrub, and tidy in vain, loudly pushing in stray chairs and casting each other looks.

He stood up a bit more forcefully than he'd intended, and his chair slid backward, crashing loudly against another. He pulled it back as gently as he could and grabbed for his cup. His hands fumbled for it clumsily and knocked it over. It was empty. The woman behind the counter looked up at the other café employee, hopeful.

But Marus didn't return it to the bin. He walked up to her instead, arm outstretched, the cup dangling loosely from his oversized thumb and forefinger.

"Can I get another?"

"Sure," she said taking it from him. She made no effort to conceal her disappointment. Quickly, carelessly, she filled up the cup, splashing excess over the rim. She set it on the counter and slid it back toward him.

He returned to his seat and pulled out his phone. His last text from Gene had been over a month ago, before he'd been handed Marus's promotion.

Hey, can we talk? Marus pressed *send*.

He saw that Gene read it and that he didn't respond.

Please. Marus wrote.

A moment later, Gene replied. *Not a good time for me. Maybe this weekend?*

It will take fifteen, maybe twenty minutes. I need a friend, Gene. I'm going crazy.

Gene took his time to respond. Marus watched the ellipses float on the screen as Gene crafted his reply. They disappeared and appeared three times before Marus finally received a response.

All right. Can you come here? Gene said.

I walked to the Rose from my apartment. Let me call a car. Fifteen minutes?

Actually, I'm down the street. First Ave. The Harbinger Building, twentieth floor.

The Harbinger Building was *his* building. The one he'd planned on moving to after receiving *his* promotion. It was breathtaking. Marus remembered the black granite that covered the lobby floor and the sculpture that looked as though it belonged in a museum. There was a garden and more glass than one would have thought possible. Everywhere, floor-to-ceiling windows. And that was just the lobby. He was the one who'd told Gene about in the first place. *Doesn't matter*, he tried to tell himself. But it did.

On my way.

As he got up to leave, he noticed something by the grandfather clock. The edge of a coatrack peeked out from the hall behind the corner. A worn, gray hat was all that hung there. He recognized it immediately. It was The Hat's hat.

The café employees were in the back. He could hear their mumbled conversation as the sink ran. Quietly, he set the cup down and slid from the chair. Soft on his feet, he made his way over to the rack. The gray felt was soft and dull in places from too much wear. A frayed black band hugged the base above the weak brim. The inside was lined with what looked to be a delicate cream silk protected beneath a layer of clear, shiny plastic that was nicked and scuffed in places. The initials *CA* were weakly stamped in gold on the inside of the band.

He returned it to the peg, and then, thinking better of it, placed it atop his head and walked out into the night.

■ ■ ■

Gene was reluctant to let him in. Marus heard him on the other side well before he turned the handle. When he finally pulled the door open, he tried to smile, but only ended up looking concerned.

"Hey, Marus. Uh, nice hat," he said.

"I didn't know you'd moved." Marus said, removing the hat. He eyed the foyer. From what he could tell, it was the exact floor plan he'd wanted for himself, on the same level, in the same building. Gene was unoriginal, at best. And at worst? A fucking thief.

"Yeah, about two weeks ago," Gene said. "The lobby's something, isn't it?"

"Sorry, I didn't notice," Marus lied.

The apartment was even better than it looked online. The vaulted ceilings would dwarf even the tallest of occupants. The carpet was lavishly plush, and the walls, like ironed eggshells, were painted in such complementary hues that Marus couldn't tell if the colors were actually varied or if the room's precise lighting was only fooling him.

Then he saw the view. He wished he hadn't looked, but the enormous windows beckoned, even from the entry. It was perfectly staged, employing the rule of thirds. In the foreground, the tower, an exotic-looking crystal stalagmite at this angle, was positioned to the right. Horizontally, the distant silhouette of the hills served as the backdrop. Marus looked away, his gaze falling instead on a picture frame resting atop the tediously carved credenza beside him. In the photo, Gene sat, rosy cheeked, his purple lips pursed neatly into a smile—a real one. A woman Marus had never seen before cuddled up to Gene, her chin rested affectionately on his shoulder. For a moment, she resembled Shey with her pretty, green eyes, freckled complexion, and shiny, reddish brown hair. But she was no Shey, Marus thought. They looked happy. Glowing, really, among the tiki torches that surrounded them, with umbrellas in their drinks.

"Who's this?" Marus asked, gesturing toward the photo.

"That's my girlfriend, Denise."

"Oh," Marus said. "Well, she looks nice. And your place is very nice, too."

"Thank you. Here, let me take your coat."

"No, that's all right. I won't be staying long."

Gene rested a hand atop the kitchen's enameled lava stone counter. He took a sip from his mug and winced at the temperature before setting it down. He was on a cleanse, he explained, and was drinking a lot of tea. Denise had introduced him to it. Marus had to admit he looked—*thin* wasn't the right word—livelier.

Marus continued through the kitchen toward the living room. The view was even more magnificent at this angle. The sun had just begun to sink, washing the hills in purple and pink. A reverse sunset like nothing he'd ever seen.

"It really is beautiful."

"Thanks," Gene said.

"No view of the water, though?"

Gene smiled. "Yes, actually, you get that on the other side, out of the office and the master suite."

"I bet it's spectacular," Marus said, taking a step down into the sitting area.

"Oh, uh, would you mind taking off your shoes?"

"Not at all," Marus said, transfixed by the floating fireplace above a console table in the living room. Tiny crystals glittering at its bottom subtly changed color. Soft, varied shades of blue mimicked the exact coloration of the sky.

Gene offered him tea and a seat in the living room after Marus set his shoes by the door. The couch looked rigid and imposing, a piece of art more than a piece of furniture, but, to Marus's dismay, it relaxed underneath his seat. Conforming to each curve and wrinkle, it embraced him.

Gene moved to the couch opposite Marus and took a seat. He pressed a button along the side of the table between them, and the extended work surface retracted automatically, transforming the lift-top into a regular coffee table. He glanced momentarily at the laptop, still open, shook his head, and closed it.

"Everywhere I look these days, I see you. The news, social media. It seems every camera is pointed in your direction." Gene laughed uncomfortably.

"But not here, right?" Marus said with a smile. "I read all Harbinger tenants are Privacy Privilege subscribers."

In other buildings, in other homes, the cameras could come on, whether or not the residents wanted them to, and often without them knowing. Speakers worked both ways. The intelligence of the devices people bought and brought home with them often superseded their own. But not here. Transmitters killed the signal, eliminating the possibility of a quiet eye. If Marus was honest with himself, it was one of the major draws for living here. Privacy was deemed unnecessary, and like anything unnecessary, it was a luxury, purchased for a price. The affluent couldn't buy their way out of being tagged by public scanners or cameras, but not having to worry about being watched in their homes was a comfort many—Gene now one of them—enjoyed.

"I heard Commissioner Devlin's given you some time off. That must be a relief."

Marus didn't answer. He drew the cup to his lips and took a sip. "Do you ever have doubts about what we're doing?" he asked, instead.

Gene set his tea on the coffee table beside the closed laptop and a book about sculpture. Marus was almost certain that the only kind of art Gene appreciated came in the form of comic books, action figures, and hideous T-shirts.

"Of course. I have doubts all the time. Am I good enough? Can we really make a difference? But it's only natural to—"

"No, I mean, doubts about why we're doing it. Do you ever wonder if the Protector Program really *protects*?"

"We don't have to wonder. You've seen the quarterly crime reports and heard testimony from would-be victims. We know it does."

"What if the program were meant to do something else?"

"Like what?"

"Subdue. Control."

"What are you talking about?"

Marus pulled Shey's letter from his jacket pocket and set it on the coffee table. "Read it," he said.

Gene raised a brow but didn't move. He looked concerned, unsure. As though the piece of paper were dangerous. "What is it?"

"It's from Shey. Read it."

He hesitated, looking to Marus for reassurance. Sighing, he took the letter from the table and unfolded it.

Marus watched his face as he read. Gene's expressions always betrayed his feelings. But this time, his face was blank. He folded the piece of paper, set it back on the table, and retrieved his tea. He took a sip and then another.

"What if Shey's right?" Marus said. "Remember that systems administrator who was murdered a couple months ago, Li Syun? Guess what she stumbled across during a data migration the day before she was murdered."

"You aren't thinking clearly, Marus."

"What if the State is behind all of it? All of those bombings and shootings, the protests, kidnappings. What if the government was feeding the fire all along, waiting for the tipping point?"

Gene shook his egg-shaped head. "How can you trust her?" he said. "After everything she's done."

"This is my wife we're talking about."

"Yes, *your wife*, the one who left you. Who committed a federal offense. Who's been fraternizing with a fearist leader, for God's sake. Even if she was coerced, something like this—it just can't be taken seriously. The fearists can't be trusted. The best thing to do is to take this to the police, or straight to Devlin."

"Don't you think it's strange that the system didn't predict Cade's abduction?"

"It was random," Gene said. "That guy, Jennings—"

"Cade was taken in broad daylight at a public outing in the middle of the Isle by some electrician, and no one saw it. You think that was chance?"

"I think this kind of speculation is dangerous. It's what the fearists want. They want the public to doubt the program. You know that. You know what's at stake."

Marus reached for the letter and tucked it back into his pocket. "Everything we've done," he said. "Everything we thought we were doing. We enabled it. And now what? I can't just pretend it never happened. You heard about Shey's sister being killed, right? Well, I went over to her apartment last Friday, and there was a black SUV parked in front of the building. Someone was watching her. That same SUV has been following me."

"That's exactly why you need to go to the police. You have no idea who it is."

"It looks like a government vehicle."

"Jesus, Marus. What's gotten into you?"

"It explains everything. Even the promotion."

"What?"

"Devlin promised me the job months ago." Marus waited for Gene's reaction but was met only with a stabbing silence. "They found out that Shey was onto them, so they ordered Devlin to give it you."

"I don't understand."

"They didn't want me to have that level of clearance, to have access to national secrets."

"National secrets?"

"Black Mine Bunker is their last resort. If the patriots were able to shut down the program, they could resurrect it from the repository."

"*Patriots?*" Gene pressed the mug to his purple lips and drank until the last of the tea was gone.

"The man in the hat says they might even be keeping hostages there."

"The man in the—" Gene cleared his throat. "Marus, I say this because you're my friend, all right? This is crazy talk."

"You're my friend?" Marus forced a laugh. "Some friend you've been. My son is murdered, and my wife is missing, possibly in danger, and I barely hear from you. You knew the promotion was mine, and you took it anyway, and then you kept it a secret." He stood up. "Congratulations, though, on," he made air quotes, "*earning* it and moving into the apartment I told you I was going to buy."

"You're an asshole, you know that?" Gene said, struggling to his feet.

"By the way, glad to see you finally found a girlfriend. Really happy it's all working out for you."

"Get out, before I call the police."

Marus put on his shoes and collected the hat. "With pleasure."

■ ■ ■

As Marus exited the Harbinger Building and walked out into the night, he noticed the black SUV at the corner and again when he looked back after turning onto his street. He no longer suspected Ballo behind the black glass. Whoever was watching him was far more dangerous than a detective.

Marus watched as the SUV pulled up behind a small car parked at the other end of the road. The streetlamp beside it illuminated the windshield, revealing the silhouette of the driver. The driver killed the headlights.

Another car slowed and pulled up to the curb in front of his building. Marus recognized the man who got out, a neighbor, and some of his friends. Their presence instilled new confidence in Marus, who left the building's entry and started toward the SUV. As he moved closer, he could see the man's dark jacket, his neck and chin. It wasn't Ballo; the man was white and thick necked. The stature of a bouncer. An enforcer.

Marus looked up at the corner of the building for its unblinking eye, though it didn't provide the reassurance it once did. If the man in the vehicle had ties to the State, it didn't matter what the cameras caught on tape. Turning to make sure the small crowd was still at the curb and within earshot, he retrieved his phone and turned on his own camera. He could see the man move in the driver's seat, perhaps questioning what to do next. Marus advanced, steadying the camera. The SUV's headlights came on, briefly blinding him. He was five feet away when the vehicle reversed out of its parking space. The man had put on a pair of sunglasses and turned to face Marus as he drove away.

Marus's hands were trembling. He could hear his heart thudding hard against his chest as he walked back toward the building. And then he heard footsteps. Before he could turn to look, a hand grabbed his arm. He wheeled around, ready to swing, when he saw Roz Roth, a beacon of color against the night sky in her red petticoat.

"I need to talk to you," she said. Her nose was pink, and her breath heavy. She looked over her shoulder to the empty space at the curb where the SUV had been. "It's about the sleep clock. Can we go up to your apartment? It'll take five minutes."

■ ■ ■

He scanned his wrist at the building's entry and pushed the heavy door open, allowing her to go first.

"What is it?"

"You were right. I didn't believe it at first myself, but the data has been altered."

Once inside the apartment, he held out his hand for her phone. She handed it to him, but it was already switched off. He placed both phones on the kitchen counter and led Roz down the hall toward Cade's bedroom. It was the only place inside the apartment out of range from a screen. The only room where they wouldn't be watched or heard. He tried to focus on Roz rather than the soccer ball on the bed or the toys spilling from the closet. It was evident that she, too, was trying not to look at them.

"Your data was definitely modified," she said. "If you look at it closely, there's a small bit of code missing. The data collected Monday morning when you awoke in the park is incomplete. It looks like the original sleep pattern was replaced with a new one."

"I saw it happen," Marus said. "Right after we spoke, I pulled it up, and I saw the data change right there on the screen."

"I saw that, too. But what you and I looked at wasn't even the original sleep pattern."

"The data was altered twice?"

"Yes. And there's something else." She glanced around the room nervously. Her eyes stopped at the soccer ball. "You were drugged."

"How do you know?"

"Your biometric input showed trace levels of ketamine up until today. Whoever altered your sleep pattern didn't select a broad enough range to completely conceal its presence in your system."

"Ketamine?"

"It's a tranquilizer, typically injected intravenously or intramuscularly. It would take an abnormally large dose to knock you out for as long as you were, but it would explain why trace amounts were detected so long after the dose was administered. It would also explain your behavior that day." At this,

she grinned, but not unkindly. "It can cause conscious seda-
tion, leaving you in a dreamlike state. Other common side
effects include double vision, confusion, and hallucinations.
With a large enough dose, you can feel sick, even hungover,
the next day."

Marus studied her a moment in the soft bedroom light. She
hadn't averted her eyes, a common indication that someone
was lying, but her blink rate had decreased, a sign of cognitive
overload. A story being spun. Her pupils were dilated. From
what he'd researched, that had nothing to do with whether or
not the truth was being told. It meant, instead, that she was
attracted to him.

It was he who averted his eyes. "It must be a glitch in the
system," he said finally. "Accidental transposition."

"They found that ball in the parking lot the day your son
was taken, right?"

Marus nodded. "He always had it with him."

"Look," she hesitated before placing her hand on his arm,
"I heard about Devlin telling you to take some time off, and I
saw the SUV out there. I know something's going on, Marus."

"I appreciate your help. But this isn't your responsibility,"
he said firmly. "I shouldn't have bothered you with it in the
first place."

"Whatever this is, it isn't something to take on alone. I can
help you."

His hesitation was obvious.

"You can trust me, Marus," she said.

"I don't know what to trust anymore."

16

Marus was first to the Rose the next morning. He had to be. The fewer witnesses, the better.

He approached the counter cautiously, waiting for the disinterested barista with a nose ring to look up. Her eyes were fixed to the screen she held just beneath the counter. Her thumbs rapped a reply. She hit *send* and looked up.

"What can I get you?"

The phone chimed with another message. Her two-toned neon fingernails made a metallic tapping sound against the hammered tin counter as she stole glances at the screen.

"A croissant, maybe?"

"Hey, you're that guy...aren't you?" She looked at the tablet to confirm his name with the customer tag log. "Holy shit. My roommate is gonna die. She watched some special on you the other day. I think she wants to have your babies." She lifted her phone from behind the counter and started texting. Bringing it eye level, she snapped a picture of him. *Click, click. Click.* She sent it.

The phone chimed again in response, and she laughed. "Oh man, she's freaking out. I'm glad I came in today." She set her phone on the counter. "So, what can I get you?"

"I'd love a croissant," he said.

She turned toward the display case and fished out a large, flaky roll.

"Let's do a cappuccino, as well."

She entered his order at the tablet. "That'll be five, seventy-five."

He held out his wrist, and she scanned his iD for payment.

"The cappuccino will take just a minute. I can bring it to you when it's ready."

He smiled and took the croissant. When she turned to begin making the cappuccino, he snatched the café's tablet, replacing it with his own, State-issued one.

He took a seat at The Hat's usual table in the corner by the grandfather clock, just out of view from the counter.

With access to the café's customer log, he'd be able to find out who The Hat really was. Marus isolated the dates and times he'd physically seen him at the Rose, bringing up a list of relevant patrons. Filtering them by purchase, a croissant and coffee, he narrowed the results. A chronological arrangement of faces and files lit up the tablet. He searched the list for The Hat's pointed chin and sunken eyes. A long, pale face, thin lips. But none of the photos were his.

He looked then for duplicates. The same picture and name tagged for the same order both days. There weren't any matches.

He hadn't actually seen The Hat order. By the time he'd gotten to the café, The Hat was almost finished. Ballo had said that Shey ordered a coffee and croissant the morning Cade was taken. The surveillance feed put both The Hat and Shey in the vicinity of the café. It was possible she'd purchased it for him. Other people might have done the same. People who knew him and could help Marus find him.

He looked through the list. Rand Harford had purchased a croissant and coffee that Sunday morning shortly before Marus and Shey had arrived. He clicked into the profile. Harford was bald with faint blue eyes and a blond mustache, pinched at the corners. The consumer account provided the Rose demographic information that would, in this case, help the café sell more coffee and croissants. Harford was fifty-five, divorced, a pilot and a father, who lived across the bridge, near Reagan, in the Helms. Cost was listed as his primary motivation for purchase. According to the data, he did not frequent the Rose and, per the system's recommendation engine, should be awarded a coupon to bring him back the next time he visited the Isle.

Marus exited Harford's profile and scrolled through the rest of the Rose's tag log. Only a handful of other people had purchased both a coffee and a croissant and nothing more. There was Ennis Bates, Vanessa Torres, and Michael Danos.

The barista brought the cappuccino and set it in front of him.

"Sorry about the wait. My roommate called." She laughed. "She totally wants to have your babies."

Two women walked in and made their way to the counter.

The barista went to meet them, and Marus jotted the names and addresses from the customer log onto his napkin.

"This is so weird," he heard the barista say around the corner. "I've never seen this screen before. I'm locked out."

He slipped the napkin inside his pocket and stood, leaving the tablet beside the cappuccino. He hadn't gotten exactly what he'd come for, but it would have to do.

■ ■ ■

The ribbons danced in the autumn wind, a flickering undulation of colorful tongues. Marus watched as they jerked and flapped from the iron bars that held them. Somewhere in the park, children were playing. The wind carried the sound of their shouting and laughter.

He told himself he'd come for The Hat. He'd intended to look at every square inch, behind every bush, but he'd only made it this far.

Taking the single dark green cloth between his thumb and forefinger, he halted its quivering and closed his eyes.

Prayer was for people with their backs to a wall. The ones who couldn't—or wouldn't—take matters into their own hands. So they put their hands together instead. There'd been times like that in his life, when circumstance reeled from his grasp, beyond his control. His mother's untimely death. Reagan's husband's illness. He'd prayed then. He'd begged.

Little good it did.

The phone buzzed in his pocket. An unidentified number. He answered. "Hello? This is Marus."

"Marus, hi, this is Leann from Edenbrook Care Center."

"Hi."

"I'm calling about your father, Victor. He's been transferred to urgent care. Would you come over?"

"What's going on? What's wrong with him?"

"It'd be best if you could come quickly," she said.

"Yes, of course. On my way." He hung up.

If prayer didn't bring you to your knees, life would.

■ ■ ■

"I don't understand. None of the risk factors apply to him. I was with him just the other day, and he was in perfectly good health," Marus said, pacing behind the nurse.

"Age and stress are contributors, as is a lack of physical activity. I'm sorry, Mr. Winde, I don't know what else to tell you. We're not sure what caused it, specifically."

"What do we do now?"

"We're still assessing the amount of damaged tissue. Heart failure can be a temporary problem that dissipates once the heart recovers, or, if the damage is extensive, it can become chronic. The best thing to do right now is to go in there and spend time with him."

"How is he?"

"He's resting, but he's responsive. I'll let the doctor know you're here."

Marus opened the door. "Hi Dad." He took a seat beside Vic.

"Hey," his father said. Vic's white hair stuck up from the pillow. He looked pale, more fragile than Marus had ever seen him. His papery skin was blue and purple where they'd stuck him for the IV. He smiled, exposing chipped and yellowed teeth.

Marus took his hand. "How are you feeling?"

Vic lifted his other hand and gave a thumbs-up.

"Good." He squeezed Vic's bony hand. "What happened?"

"I fell." His speech was labored, his voice scratchy.

"When? Where were you?"

"Outside, this morning, or the other day. I don't know. They brought me in to make sure I was okay."

"What did they do?"

"An x-ray. A nurse helped me back home and hooked me up to an IV. Nothing's broken."

Marus moved closer. "An IV? Why?"

"My fluids were low. Dehydration."

"And then?"

"I guess I had a heart attack. Someone must've come to check on me right then. I woke up here."

"That doesn't make any sense. They didn't tell me any of that."

Vic waved his other hand, as if to say don't worry about it. "Did you find Shey?" he asked.

Marus shook his head. "No, not yet."

"Then what the hell are you here for?"

"Dad, you almost died. And based on what you're saying, it seems like," he leaned in closer to whisper, "like it was *intentional*. You've never had problems with your heart, and suddenly, after being hooked up to an IV, you have a heart attack?"

"If it was intentional, why'd they resuscitate me?"

Marus was silent a moment.

"I don't know."

"They should have just let me go. I've lived long enough."

"Dad." He took a deep breath, not knowing what to say.

"I miss her, Marus," Vic said, his muddy brown eyes turning misty.

"I do, too."

"You know I love you. Even when things were—*difficult* between us, I still loved you. You know that."

"Yes, I do. I love you, too, Pop." He squeezed his father's hand again.

"Don't worry about me. Whatever happens, I'm ready now. Your mother is waiting for me. I believe that."

Marus forced a smile.

"And Shey's waiting for you. Do the right thing, Marus. Trust your gut; it will get you there."

17

WITHOUT THE SYSTEM, there was no way to find The Hat. Marus sat in front of the sleeping screens and tried to remember how it'd been before. The screens were black, *blank*, but far from empty. Through them he could do anything. There was no *before*, he realized. It'd been a quick progression, a nation's predilection. Connectivity was born from convenience—laziness, really—and it bred dependence. Going off the grid was impossible. Even before the advent of iDs and the New Era.

Use your gut.

Instinct made him a successful developer. But work was different. At the IA, he had all the data he needed. Here, he had nothing but a napkin, a few names, and addresses.

Rand Harford.

Ennis Bates.

Vanessa Torres.

Michael Danos.

One of them would lead him to The Hat and, as a result, to Shey. But without the system, they were useless. Clues he couldn't cash in.

If he had access, he'd pull back communications and activity for the last three months. He'd go back to the day Li was murdered and scrape anything and everything that could link these men and woman to each other, to The Hat, to Shey. He'd analyze their behaviors. Get to know them.

The screens contained everything. Without them, there was nothing.

Start with what you know.

He could hack in. It was a matter of exploiting weaknesses in the code. There were few, but they existed. And he knew what and where they were.

He moved the mouse to wake the machine.

The Protectors would be watching him even now. They'd know what he was up to long before he made any progress. They'd arrest him, prosecute him, jail him. If Shey was right, they'd do worse.

The proximity of the addresses to one another might tell him something. At the very least, it would give him a starting point, a place to go.

He opened up Maps in his browser and entered the first address, Rand Harford's home in the Helms on the other side of Mid Bridge: 479 E. Londale Street, apartment 115.

The satellite and roadside images showed a tenement building like Reagan's, but with more graffiti. Fat words in pink and purple appeared to drip beneath windows, in between fire escapes. It wasn't a great neighborhood. The images didn't tell Marus much else.

He moved on to the next address. Ennis Bates, the professor, lived on 146 Takara Place, a once-historic neighborhood nestled low on the south end of the peninsula, now forgotten. It had been charming in its day, Marus could tell. Now a freeway went over the top of it.

Vanessa Torres lived at 12400 S. Sego Way, apartment 306. Another erect cube. Squares for windows, a rectangle for a door. Nothing to be learned.

223 E. Banton Avenue, unit B. Michael Danos's small duplex. Some sad shrubs. More graffiti. Nothing to be learned.

Marus looked at the pins he'd dropped on the map. The addresses were miles and miles from each other. The Hat could be hiding in any one of them. Or none.

An effortless innovator, Devlin had called him. *An apt problem solver.* Ego allowed him to believe it. He'd created the technology; therefore, it couldn't exist without him. But without it, what was he?

Helpless.

He slammed a fist down on the keyboard. The keys compressed and the body bounced, but it didn't break.

He picked it up and whacked it against the surface of the desk. A pleasurable snapping sound. A couple keys popped out and scattered like broken teeth. Swinging hard, he struck the screens. One and then the other. Harder. The glass spiderwebbed. He struck again and again. Finally, the display shuddered black. Empty.

Only then was he satisfied. He dropped the remnants of the keyboard and walked out into the kitchen.

The old hat waited atop the table.

There was a weight to it, a palpable energy, much like that of Cade's ball. An inanimate object, alive with meaning.

It wouldn't simply have been forgotten at the café. It was left there for him, to communicate something. The CA stamped inside was a clue, a confession. But it wasn't enough. Surely The Hat would have known that.

Marus approached slowly, as though it might actually spring to life. He picked it up and examined its felt, the wear of the band, the delicate CA that seemed to have faded since the last time he looked. There was a small stain on the right side of the crown. The bow was frayed, and there was a bend in the brim. He placed his palm against the plastic liner, feeling each scuff and tear. And then he felt something sharp. A point.

When he turned the hat over, he noticed a small white triangle peeking out from a slit cut through the plastic and silk liners at the back, just above the sweatband. His smallest finger couldn't fit through the gap so he ran to the bathroom for a pair of tweezers. Carefully working its jaws inside, he retrieved the tiny, folded piece of paper.

The handwriting was childlike, shaky and abrupt.

Being followed. Come to me. 555 Estancia Blvd. Apt 3B.

■ ■ ■

Marus took the motorcycle. Crossing the bridge, he drove toward the outer boroughs, the small piece of paper with The Hat's address in his pocket, close to his chest. For the moment, the stretch of asphalt behind him was clear of the predatory lights he'd come to expect in the distance. He wondered how long it'd last.

Without the GPS, the route was uncertain, inefficient. It took him ten minutes longer than it should have. But after a few wrong turns, he found it. 555 Estancia Boulevard. From the street, Marus could see the lights on the third floor were off. A couple of young men sat laughing on the steps at the entry, sharing a cigarette. The door behind them was propped open.

Security was different in neighborhoods like this. Crime was worse, and yet, people couldn't be bothered to take certain precautions. Some entries had been fitted with off-the-shelf scanners, but most people still used keys, if they locked their doors at all. Doors were propped open and forgotten. Fire escapes were jungle gyms let down and left.

Marus went to the alleyway, hoping this would be the case here, but it wasn't. There was no way to reach the ladder. He'd have to go back around, past the young men, and through the open door.

Just act like you own the place.

That's what Vic had told him before his first day at Newbold Corp. *Fake it till you make it.* Confidence was key.

The men hardly looked at him as he passed. They were more preoccupied with the bottle in the paper bag that he'd almost kicked over.

He climbed the steps to the third floor as quietly as he could, the stairs creaking underfoot. Before reaching the landing, he could see that the retrofitted scanner affixed to the doorjamb at 3B had been smashed in. The door was pried open and left ajar. He crept to it and peered inside. Light from a large, neon billboard across the street illuminated the aftermath of invasion. As his eyes adjusted, he could see that a large bookshelf lay toppled in the middle of the room. The wall screen was shattered beside it. Papers and torn books were scattered across the floor like casualties.

Cautiously, he stepped inside, crunching pieces of glass underfoot as he edged around the destruction.

Drafts of articles and essays covered the dingy linoleum. He bent over to sort through the leaves of pulled paper.

Predictive Policing Widens Class Gap.

A childlike scrawl in red ink cluttered the margins. Words were crossed out and written over again.

Marus picked up a small, black notebook and leafed through it. Lists and notes in The Hat's cramped handwriting filled every page.

Qualities that Magnify Risk Perception:

Familiarity – Fear of the unknown increases perception of risk
Catastrophic potential – Greater number of casualties per singular event
Children – Greatest multiplier in increasing perception of risk
Magnification by media – Increases focus, escalates anxiety

A noise, a soft thud, came from the apartment's only bedroom. Marus shot up from his low crouch. He hadn't seen the SUV parked outside, but wondered now if he'd overlooked it. The door was ajar, but only slightly, and Marus couldn't see into the dark room. He turned quietly to make an exit, but it was too late. The door swung open, and a man stepped from the shadows.

"Marus?"

His face was familiar. Marus had seen that bald head. The almost comic mustache. It was Rand Harford, the man from the café's customer log.

"You scared the hell out of me," Harford said inching closer. "Did anyone follow you here?"

"Are you one of them?"

"One of who?" Harford crept to the window, pushing the blinds apart for a better look.

"The patriots."

"We don't have a lot of time," he said. He let go of the blind, and it snapped back into place. "Yeah, I'm one of them. Rand Harford's the name." He moved toward Marus and stuck out a hand. "Pleasure to meet you, *officially*."

Marus met his handshake. "I saw your picture," he said.

"Excuse me?"

"In the Rose Café's customer tag log. You bought a croissant and a coffee."

"Did I?" Harford laughed. "How French of me."

"It was an iD swap, wasn't it?" Marus moved closer. "How does it work?"

"That's really why you're here, isn't it?" Harford sized him up. "I hear you're very *attached* to the work. Always working, even now."

Marus ignored the comment. "You aren't overwriting anything. There are too many inputs; it'd be impossible to manufacture that much data."

The system was incapable of iD swap. The data was fixed to the hardware, and the hardware to the person. All fields

were fed by external sources. A person's occupation was updated by the employer, bank account information by the financial institution, marital status by the district courthouse, the
birth of a child by the hospital, recent purchases by the store,
travels by the modes of transportation taken. The only field
that could be updated manually in the file itself was the photo.
Any administrative State employee with access to citizen records was authorized to change it.

"It's a physical swap, isn't it?"

If the hardware was extracted and kept intact, it could,
in theory, be re-implanted in another host. Assuming he or
she was similar in body type, age, and health, to the original iD owner, the biometric data wouldn't read markedly
abnormal.

But a physical swap would limit the host to a single iD,
and the data at the Rose suggested The Hat had used multiple
identities.

Harford was holding his wrist, gripping a black band
that looked, at first glance, to be a Lifewatch. He didn't say
anything.

"You're pretending to be him now, aren't you?"

"Who?"

"The man who lives here."

"You mean Chris?" Harford asked. "Axtell?"

CA. The Hat was Christopher Axtell, the journalist. Of
course.

"The one with the hat."

"Yeah, that hat. Nasty, ol' thing if you ask me." Harford
laughed. "No, I'm not carrying his iD. He doesn't even have

one, at least, not anymore." He moved back toward the window and split the blinds again.

"Why has he been in hiding all of these years?"

"He caught wind of the conspiracy as it was unfolding but couldn't get the break he needed to leak the story. The State put him on the WatchList, probably would have had him arrested or killed if he hadn't gone under when he did. All this time, he's been investigating, looking for the right angle, waiting for backing. That State systems administrator who was murdered a couple months ago tipped him off. From what I gather, there was an exchange mere hours before she was murdered. They've been hot on his trail since."

"And Axtell led the State to Shey."

"And Shey led them to you."

"I had no idea. I didn't know about any of it."

"Doesn't really matter, does it? They don't take any chances. Heard they kicked you out of the IA."

"It was voluntary," Marus said, a bit too forcefully.

"Sure it was."

A dog began to bark from the alley below. One of the young men on the stoop shouted until it stopped.

"What are you doing here?" Marus asked.

"Same thing you are. I came for Chris."

"How do I know you didn't do all this? That you're who you say you are?"

"You don't. You'll just have to take me at my word." Harford smiled. "A novel concept, ain't it? Intuition. Trust. Faith. Seems we've all forgotten what those are."

"And you trust that I'm on the patriots' side?" Marus asked.

"Sure. You got that look in your eye. Like you're seeing things for what they are and you're scared. Well, you're smart to be scared, Marus."

"Is Axtell here?" Marus looked toward the dark bedroom.

"If he was, he isn't anymore. Let's just hope he got out before Novak's henchmen came."

"Novak's people did this?"

"Courtesy of the State's rent-a-thug program." He kicked a plate. "Our tax dollars at work."

"I've seen a black SUV follow me a few times."

"That's them, all right. I'm not sure how much Chris told you, but if they're following you, you must know enough."

"I know about Li. I assume that was Novak's men as well?"

"They took their orders from the Administration, but yeah, they're the ones who pulled the trigger. *Or knife*, in Li's case." Harford shuddered. "Novak's off in Tahiti or God knows where, sipping mai tais while his boys take care of the State's dirty work. Doesn't seem fair, does it?"

"And my son? Was that them, too?" Marus thought of the man in the brown windbreaker leading Cade away.

Harford lowered his chin. A nod.

"Why?"

"They got too close to the truth," Harford said. "Novak's guys started following her around. They must've thought they could scare her away. Devlin didn't want a senior employee with your credentials and level of clearance suspecting them of anything."

"Devlin is involved?"

"I thought you knew."

"No."

"If anyone's in the Administration's pocket, it's the commissioner. They brought him on for that reason. When Shey didn't back down, they hit her where it hurt. The media frenzy supports the I3 launch, so it was a win-win for them."

"So Devlin ordered it?"

"From what I understand, he's done this kind of thing before."

"Could Cade still be alive, then?" Marus stepped closer. "Shey said she thought it was possible."

Harford turned away. "I wouldn't know, but someone at the colony might."

"How do I get there?"

"There's a landing strip about a three day's journey from the colony. That's the only way I know of."

"You're a pilot, right?"

"What gave it away?"

"I saw your profile. So, can you take me there?"

"It's not a question of whether I can get you there. It's whether or not they'll let you in. They're *particular* about who they accept. You have to earn their trust."

"If Shey's there, I have to go."

"Tell you what, I'll talk it over with them. I'm sure they'd be willing to work a deal."

"What kind of deal?"

"You have to earn your way there, Marus. That's the way it works. You have to contribute something. My guess is, being from the IA, you have access they want."

"Devlin revoked my access."

"You can still help us."

Marus straightened, looking back at the door, still ajar. "How?"

"Let me worry about that for now." He grabbed a couple of the Moleskines and handed them to Marus before retreating back into the bedroom. Reemerging with a large gas can, he began dousing the papers along the floor. The pungent smell of gasoline filled the small apartment.

"What are you doing?"

"What does it look like? They'll be coming back for all of this stuff."

"What about the surrounding apartments, the drugstore downstairs? You can't just burn this place down." He picked up a few more of the dry journals and backed up toward the door, his gaze never leaving the match Harford now held in his hand.

Harford walked toward him, "Haven't you heard? The Protectors will keep the people safe." He smiled, the vindictiveness twinkling in his blue eyes as he set the match to the ground.

In the hallway, Harford took a leaf from one of the notebooks and wrote down an address. He handed it to Marus.

"Meet me here tomorrow morning. Don't bring anything you can't carry in a pack. No electronics, okay?"

Marus nodded.

"And you know how to avoid the scanners?" Harford asked.

"Of course."

Harford shot him a doubtful look. "All right," he said, relieving him of the remaining notebooks. "Nice meeting you."

He winked and left Marus at the landing while flames licked the inside of Axtell's apartment clean.

As he made his way back to the motorcycle, a scanner he hadn't seen chirped, *tag, you're it.*

■ ■ ■

The outer boroughs vanished beneath the smog as Marus made his way back to the Isle. Crossing the bridge, he noticed the large headlights, the empty eyes of a beast, closing in. Every lane change, every adjustment to the throttle, there it was. Never more than two car lengths behind him. Whether they were Novak's men or not, they seemed to have been tipped off by the scanner at Axtell's apartment. They had access.

Marus slowed as he entered the residential area. The streets were empty. No witnesses. He'd always wondered why those who could afford the luxury of clean, crime-swept streets were the first to retire in the evening. Perhaps it was because, unlike those farther from the center, they had a comfortable place to retire to, or maybe they had simply been raised differently, taught at an early age to be distrusting of the dark. Hadn't Marus tried to teach Cade the same?

The SUV matched his pace, nonchalant in each turn. A cat to his mouse, they were toying with him. Marus wondered what would happen if he stopped. Would Novak's men take him? If so, where? Not knowing was the most terrifying part.

This was why the system made sense. This was why it felt necessary.

With uncertainty came fear, and, like fire, fear consumed everything.

What was safe when the predator giving chase was governed by the only entity that can provide protection? His home, the Protective Services Center, the city: all were false pretenses of security. The State had manufactured the locks and algorithms. He'd never considered the risk. It never crossed his mind that the State would then pick and decrypt, hand out the combinations to whomever it wanted, and alter the data for its own purposes.

If you have nothing to hide, you have nothing to fear.

But if the State has something to hide, it's a different story. If the State has something to hide: run.

He couldn't run forever. Eventually, he needed a place to hide. Even if he were able to lose the SUV, where would he go? Whom could he trust? He couldn't go to Gene. Certainly not Anj. The woman from the seventh floor had wanted to help. *Roz Roth.* But even if he could trust her, he wouldn't know where to find her, not without looking her up and alerting the system. There were old friends he hadn't seen or talked to in years. Promising acquaintances he hadn't bothered to turn into friends. Time was the problem. It always was. There'd never been enough. Now, he was out of it altogether.

Another pair of headlights had joined the small caravan. He wasn't sure how long it had been there, close behind the SUV. It was a car, he could tell, low to the ground. Devlin, maybe. Or Novak himself.

Marus accelerated, and the SUV and car matched his speed. Sirens wailed through the streets, reverberating off of apartment buildings that looked just like his own. It was the car, he realized, flashing its lights, red and blue. Was this how they'd gotten Li? A traffic stop? Despite knowing what he knew, he had to resist the urge to pull over. A subservience to authority, bred into humanity. As innate as a fear of spiders.

Suddenly, the SUV veered left. He couldn't hear the squealing tires over the engine but saw the jolt of the backend as it lost traction. To Marus's surprise, the cop car went after it, leaving him alone only a few turns before his street.

■ ■ ■

Someone had been in the apartment. He knew even before stepping inside. The door looked wrong, or maybe the handle still held the warmth of a hand. He couldn't put a finger on it, but something had been disturbed. There was a strange weight to the air, and the faintest smell still lingered. *Aftershave and cigarettes.*

Marus scanned his wrist and pushed the door open, half expecting, *hoping,* to see Axtell at the kitchen table. But the table wasn't in its proper place. Nothing was.

There were scuffs on the floor several inches from where the table had been shoved. Dips exposed in the carpet where the couch once sat. The drawers had been pulled open, and every cabinet door was flung wide. Scraps of paper, notes he and Shey had saved over the years, littered the floor as the leaves of paper had littered Axtell's apartment. The sparse contents of his fridge spilled out onto the kitchen tile. Marus moved toward the wooden block on the counter and extracted the chef's knife. The reading chair had been upended in the living room. The lamp lay on its face in the corner. Everything was touched, altered. Everything but the screens.

From the hallway, he could see a light had been left on in Cade's bedroom. Toys trickled out of the doorway. The Luca Valdetti bobblehead looked at him from its contorted position on the floor. Marus rushed to the room and forced the door past a heap of Cade's T-shirts and jerseys. His green bed sheets had been torn from the mattress and thrown in a heap at the foot of the bed. Each of the dresser drawers was emptied, the toys pulled from their containers in the closet. It took Marus a moment to realize the soccer ball wasn't on the bed as Shey had left it, nor was it on the floor or in the closet. It wasn't under the bed, behind the door, or concealed beneath the heap of sheets and clothes. He went throughout the entire apartment, looking beneath each overturned piece of furniture and searching every cabinet and closet. But the ball was gone.

18

The fear had always been there. He knew that now.

A fear of fear itself.

There'd be no coming back. He grabbed what he could and threw it into a backpack. The basics: a jacket, socks, a sweater. Whatever he could find in the dark. There was a photo album somewhere. Photographs from their wedding. Cade's baby pictures. If he knew where it was, he would've liked to go through it. If he'd had the time, he'd pluck out his favorites and tuck them away.

He filled the tub with water and brought the devices. One by one, he shattered the screens against the edge of the counter before dropping them into the bath. Shouldering the pack, he moved quickly from window to window.

The streets were still and quiet. No SUV. No sign of Novak's men. Across the way, several lights were on. Most of the shades were tightly drawn, the windows dark. He looked at his watch, the one Shey had given him. The hands glowed green. Ten minutes before curfew. If he wanted to make it back across the bridge, he'd have to hurry.

The sound of the motorcycle's engine cut through the night as he raced toward the edge of the Isle. He avoided lampposts, mailboxes, and benches, anything that might have a scanner affixed to it, by driving squarely down the centerline. Cameras panned after him. A thousand unblinking eyes everywhere. He kept his head down. Throttle, full. The algorithm couldn't process the video stream the way it effortlessly parsed and analyzed iD data, but facial recognition would trigger an alert if a citywide search were issued.

The bridge hadn't yet been lifted. Large lights flashed on either side, signaling it was almost time. Beneath the overhead scanner, the striped gate blocked the route. Marus slowed behind one of the final cars that would make it across in time for curfew. The passenger car came to a standstill under the reader, and the scanner light blinked green. Marus accelerated once the barrier lifted and shot past the car, clearing the arm. The blare of the car's horn was hardly audible above the whine of his engine.

As he navigated Wells, sirens wailed at his back. It was an ear-piercing reverberation against the flaking stucco that advanced closer with every electric scream. A shot of adrenaline, enough to light up his Lifewatch, had he been wearing it, surged through him.

A tag? Facial recognition from video? A citizen call-in?

He turned down a side street, keeping his head down as he looked for a place to hide the bike. *They'd find him.* His work, and the work of everyone he respected, nearly guaranteed it.

The flashing lights of several police cars blinded him as they flew past, the sound of their sirens following closely behind. When he opened his eyes, they were gone. He took a couple of slow breaths to calm his racing heart. He wasn't the target today, at least not yet.

The address Harford had given him, 499 Flint, belonged to a feeble-looking building Marus now recognized as the old Wells Library. He hadn't known it shut down, but it looked as though no one had set foot inside for years. Come to think of it, he couldn't remember the last time he had visited a library but realized it might have been this very one.

Shey was particularly fond of it and would frequent it whenever she came to visit Reagan. It was one of the oldest buildings in the district, *filled with just the right amount of wisdom*, she told him once when he'd teased her about coming here. To many like Marus, libraries were antiquated institutions. He understood the appeal but could not bring himself to venture through the doors, to breathe the stuffy air and abide by its rules. Anything he wanted to read or research could be found online in the comfort of his home. *You're missing the point entirely*, Shey said and laughed.

God, he missed that laugh.

Cade had come here with her a few times. Whenever his schooling required a book or research for a project, Shey always insisted upon it. Marus encouraged both of them to look at the State's digital archives, asserting that it had anything they could ever need or want and more, without the hassle of having to think about what it was they needed or where it could be found. But he suspected Shey simply enjoyed the time in the aisles among shelves of knowledge she'd never be able to acquire in entirety. She'd wave him off with a wink. *Mother-son time*, she'd imply, heading out, Cade following behind, his soccer ball in tow.

There were jagged, gaping holes in several of the second story's windowpanes, the consequence of a couple rocks and a few kids with nothing to do. Cardboard covered the windows of the main floor like soggy Band-Aids. He wondered if Shey knew the library had closed. Avoiding the single lamppost in case a scanner was affixed, Marus drove through the dimly lit, uneven, and weed-rampant parking lot, parking at the rear, behind a dumpster.

He surveyed the building, looking for a way to slip inside unnoticed. A large sign read DEMOLITION SCHEDULED. He shook his head. *Shey would be beside herself,* he thought. The front door was boarded up with a large piece of plywood but, upon Marus's closer inspection, was still operable. The wood was merely a façade. He pushed it open with little effort. Once inside, he put the door back into place, extinguishing the faint light the dusty building borrowed from the parking lot.

"Hello?" Marus whispered blindly. "Harford?"

He blinked to adjust his eyes, but there wasn't much to see. The checkout counter arced in front of him. He moved past it, around a few toppled bookcases, toward the center of the library. Catching the foot of one of the shelves, he fell forward and landed amid dust and broken glass. A bright stabbing pain seared across his palm.

"Shit."

He couldn't see the cut but felt the warm trickle of blood pool with each pulsation. A deep throbbing.

Righting himself, he scanned the darkness. Shelves stood empty. Most of the books had been taken. A few forgotten or unwanted met the toe of Marus's boot and skid across the tattered carpet to meet a final resting place. It smelled like dust and mold. Damp paper. Yellowing pages. Fumes of some kind. Not gasoline. Paint.

"Harford?"

Thin strips of city light slipped through the sides of the cardboard window coverings, forming dusty columns of light that showed Marus the way to the stairwell.

The second floor was bathed in an orange glow that emanated from the crusted windowpanes. The floor had been cleared; empty bookshelves were pushed together toward the back wall, exposing a large area of tattered carpet. A single book lay face down, spread like a dead bird at the center. He picked it up and studied the cover. Three barren tree trunks. A rock covered in snow. Mary Shelley's *Frankenstein*.

He set it, spine out, on a bookshelf near the wall. Among meaningless loops and names tagged on the wall there, a gleaming shape caught Marus's eye. A symbol sprayed from a graffiti stencil. The profile of a surveillance camera, outlined in black. A circle surrounded it.

He came closer to examine it. Even in the dark, it shined. There were drip marks. The smell of aerosol. He pressed his fingertips to the wall and they came back black, tacky.

"Hello?" he called.

There was a narrow gap between the wall and the bookshelf. A passageway to a small space concealed behind the shelves.

"Harford, are you back there?"

Marus squeezed through the opening and turned a corner. There was a cramped, concealed clearing, six by twelve feet at most, tucked against the back edge of the building. From the stairs, it might as well have been invisible. As safe a place as any to bed down for the night.

■ ■ ■

He didn't think he'd slept, but the next thing he knew, Harford was there, resting at the far end against a windowsill, a book in his hands.

The world outside seeped in at the sides of the cardboard blocking the window, framing him in the sleepy gray light of early morning.

"Morning, sunshine," he said. "Glad you were able to find the place."

"They broke into my apartment," Marus said. "Did worse than what they did at Axtell's. I had to leave."

"Looks like your days as a Protector are done. And your days as a citizen, for that matter. You have to go dark, unless you want to end up like Li."

Marus grabbed at his wrist. "They'd have me killed? For what? I haven't done anything."

"They've got your laptop. They know you've been snooping around."

"How do you know that?"

"Look, Marus, it doesn't matter what you've done. Don't you get it? It's what you *might* do. What you could do. It's what you know. You're a much greater threat to them than Li was. But they can't just off you the way they did her. Not now that the whole world knows who you are."

Neither of them said anything for a while.

"I thought Axtell might be hiding here," Harford said finally. "We rotate rendezvous points as a precaution and treat them as safe houses when necessary. Given the condition of Axtell's apartment, I'd say it was pretty fucking necessary."

"Do you think Novak's men got him?"

"I don't know." He became quiet again, as though weighing the probability. "No one's heard from him. Not a note, no sign, nothing. He's well connected though. It's possible he's hiding out somewhere else. There's a number of other places he could be."

Marus examined his hand. The gash in his palm still ached, but the blood had dried. He scraped it off with a finger and stood.

Harford lifted himself from the brick sill and closed the book. "I never was much of a reader. I kept my head in different kinds of clouds."

"Will you take me to the colony?" Marus asked.

"They're going to want to know you're on our side."

"What does that mean?"

"That you'll fight for the things the patriots believe in."

"I'll do anything to be with my wife again."

Harford nodded idly. "That's the thing about loved ones, they can be a great source of strength and, at the same time, our greatest weakness." He bowed his head and stared at a scuff along the floor.

Marus thought of Shey and wondered what she was doing. Was she safe? Had she thought of him? Did she regret leaving?

As if snapping out of a trance, Harford thwacked the book in his right hand against the palm of his left. "Our reality is so much more complicated than anything you'll find in here," Harford said.

"Truth is stranger than fiction," Marus said without looking at him. When Harford didn't respond, Marus added, "Mark Twain."

"Like I said, I never was much of a book lover." He set the book down on a gritty stack of other worn pages in the corner. "Some of them are pretty unimaginative, if you ask me. Especially those dystopian books. People thought that the Mass Surveillance State would be forced on us. They never thought we'd welcome the cameras and microphones with open arms. That we'd bring the, what were they called—telescreens—into our homes. Shit, we carried them around with us, even before iDs were implanted. And everything their eyes and ears see and hear is stored permanently, forever. The data never goes away. We didn't realize that our whole life, every action and questionable conversation, would be stored on a server somewhere. We didn't think about the mistakes our kids would inevitably make growing up, and how, decades from now, every detail will still haunt them. Haunt us. Every moment of juvenile misjudgment keeps them from reaching their true potential. Every piece of information is available to be spun to meet some third-party objective.

"What citizen would willingly give up their rights?" He raised his hand. "We did. We wore GPS trackers wherever we went—*willingly*. We broadcast our whereabouts, for fuck's sake. *Rand checked-in at Dunkin Donuts.* We celebrated the convenience of it all and never gave a second thought to the potential risks. We put it all in place. Brick by freaking brick, we laid the foundation. And then, to seal the deal, we made it the law just because we were scared of what might happen if we didn't. We gave up our freedom, and it wasn't even a difficult decision for us." He rubbed a circle of grime from the window as though trying to look out, but the pane was too filthy. Encrusted. Disgusted, Harford wiped his hand against his thigh. "Emery is the only one who can help us take the country back."

Marus stood and brushed the dirt from the back of his pants. "Who's Emery?"

"He's the mastermind. He's the reason the colony and the resistance exist at all. Think of him as the leader of the patriots, but try and call him that and he'll insist otherwise. 'I was never elected,' he'll say. Democracy prevails after all." Harford smiled. "The reality, though, is that he's in charge. We're a pretty high-tech operation. Well funded, well staffed, because of him. Turns out there are a lot of entrepreneurial types who don't like the government all up in their shit. Especially once we present them with the facts. You'd be surprised how many State employees we've successfully recruited."

"So that's how you were able to engineer the iD swap?" Marus said, moving closer.

"You won't let that go, will you?"

"Tell me how it works."

"Exchanging iDs was easy enough. The cloaking mechanism we used swapped the photo to prevent any discrepancies in iD confirmation while the individual was switched. A code injection masked the switch. The same one the State uses to hide all of their shady shit."

"And you exchange iDs to vary the data, so that certain behavioral patterns aren't associated with one profile."

"Bingo," Harford said. "We have a large enough pool to make particular behaviors seem arbitrary, when in reality, they're part of a very specific routine."

"And the hardware, you—"

"Let's say we *hacked at* it." He removed the black band and showed Marus the thin, purple scar it concealed. "Before the advancements in the Lifewatch program, it was enough to remove the iD. Of course, the first procedures were pretty sloppy. Literally, hack jobs. Imagine using a scalpel on yourself with your inferior hand."

Marus grimaced at the thought.

"Axtell did it on his own after they mandated insertion. He can barely write with his right hand anymore. Once we amassed a greater following and attracted new talent, we acquired the tools to make it happen. Having an actual surgeon on board is helpful. But it hasn't exactly been smooth sailing since. As the Lifewatch program developed, and the margin of error decreased, we found ourselves having to imitate biological responses so that it wouldn't flag the profile. We had to provide some kind of, what do you call it, *somatic* input?"

Marus nodded. "Heart rate, blood pressure, sleep patterns, hydration, chemical reactions that occur within the body, you'd have to simulate all of it."

Harford tossed Marus the black band. "This can read the basic, external stuff and feeds it to the iD. There's a small compartment that enables the transmission. Everything else is fake, a preprogrammed loop of varied metrics and responses."

"Impressive," Marus said, holding the band closer for examination. "How did you get this kind of technology? How haven't we known about it?"

"The colony. Like I said, we've attracted some very talented folks. That's the power of revolution for you." He took the band back and replaced it on his wrist.

"Can you take me there?"

"I thought you'd never ask." Harford grinned. "I can, but they want your help getting the files first."

"Like I said, Devlin revoked my access. I have no way of getting in."

"You need to visit your friend Gene."

"Gene won't help," he said. "He doesn't believe the State is doing anything wrong. Besides, he'd never jeopardize his position."

"We don't need his help. We just need his computer."

19

MARUS RODE IN the back of the same gray Buick LeSabre he'd seen Shey step into the day she'd left. Harford sat silently in the passenger seat beside a similarly bald man with a goatee who hadn't uttered a single word since they'd left the library. He had no idea where they were going.

The man with the goatee turned on the radio. A staticky symphony trilled from the speaker. Marus looked out the rear windshield for the SUV but saw the enormous face of a bus instead.

Forty minutes later, they pulled onto Takara Place, a neighborhood of faded cottages nestled among large elm trees and a procession of unsightly pylons that sprang from the ground. *Ennis Bates's home.* It didn't look much different from what Marus had seen when he searched the address online, though the overpass was much larger in real life. It towered above, casting a colossal shadow over the high-gabled houses it dwarfed. A thick scrim of smog hung above the road. Even in the daylight, it was hard to see through the dirty pixilation.

They parked opposite one of the houses as if waiting for something. A sign of some kind. Marus watched as an elderly man in denim overalls sat hunched over a cracked and rutted walkway, removing loose pieces of stamped concrete. He flung them over a perimeter of small but neatly trimmed hedges and into a wheelbarrow parked at the edge of the lawn. Bits of loose dirt showered his white hair with each toss. A gust of wind whipped through, tilting the tops of trees, almost blowing the man over. Several crumpled aluminum cans dragged along the curb, then stopped. Even on a Saturday morning, and through the car door, Marus could hear the steady sound of traffic whirring above.

Harford glanced at a screen in his palm.

"Wesley said a car was parked out front for an hour. There were two men wearing sunglasses inside. They didn't get out. He says they left about twenty minutes ago."

Marus wondered if that had anything to do with his search. Had he unknowingly led the Protectors right here?

"Who's Wesley?" Marus asked.

Harford glanced at the back seat but didn't say anything.

"Let's be quick," the driver said.

He pulled the LeSabre past the small cottage and man in overalls to a larger bungalow with green siding and white trim. A red brick chimney bisected the front of the house, reaching up into the sooty sky. The number *150* hung from a pillar to the side of its welcoming front porch. They turned down the narrow drive and arrived at a parking area at the back of the house. Behind it, hidden from the street, was a detached garage with an apartment above. The wooden blinds on the single front window were drawn closed.

"Stay here," Harford instructed.

He and the other man got out and walked around to a side door. It opened from the inside and they stepped through the doorway and out of sight.

Though the windows of the detached building were covered, the windows on the other side of the car, those of the main house, were left wide open. Long, white drapes swelled like sails in the irregular breeze blowing in through the well-scrubbed screens. Music, a soft drumming at first, tinkling piano keys, then the sound of clapping, and the full force of a heady vibrato rushed out through the windows. A French sort of birdsong, if there existed such a genre. It sounded familiar, reminding him of something from a dream or his childhood.

Marus reached for the handle. The white gravel below chattered underfoot like loose change as he stepped from the car toward one of the windows. He could see the kitchen, its butcher block counters tidy, the small table, empty, and part of a sitting room. A couch and grouping of chairs were arranged at the perimeter, angled toward a low, glass table at the center of the room. A small, elderly woman pushed herself up out of a chair and stood for a moment, her hand still clutching the flowery upholstered arm for balance. A white feathering of fine hair was flattened against the back of her skull from the chair. Robed in white, she turned and stared back at him through the window. Swaying a little, she set a few fingertips against the sill to steady herself.

Had he seen her before? In the sunlight, the rumpled blue veins of her hands shone through her translucent, papery skin like a new hatchling's. Sight slackened, her murky eyes looked at everything, but saw nothing. She was looking through him, though she seemed to know he was there. Rosy cheeks, flecked brown eyes. She reminded him of his mother, though she hadn't lived long enough to wear so much as a wrinkle.

The piano music played on to the applause of an unseen audience. A recording of some performance of the past. The woman swayed her head and closed her milky eyes. She tapped a crooked finger against the edge of the window frame. The saxophone started up, and then she opened her mouth. Though the instruments and the audience had been taped, the voice was real, raw, alive. It was hers. The breeze carried it through the window, upward.

"Hey! Marus, get over here," Harford shouted from the door of the detached garage.

He smiled at the woman, though he knew she couldn't see it, and started across the small gravel lot. When he glanced back, she was no longer at the window. But he could still hear her singing.

■ ■ ■

In the apartment above the garage, two men sat hunched around a computer at the kitchen counter. Another was seated in a chair near the front window. Only the man in the chair acknowledged Marus's entrance.

He stood to greet him.

"Galen Thomas. Nice to meet you."

He met his handshake. "What do you want me to do?"

"Why don't we sit down?" Galen gestured toward a wood-en-legged leather chair.

Harford rummaged through the fridge and extracted an apple.

"I'm fine where I am, thank you."

The men at the counter were mumbling to themselves, scribbling notes on a pad of paper, and vigorously striking keys. Through the window, Marus could still hear the movement of music wafting out of the main house.

"Whether he knows it yet or not, we believe your friend Gene has access to information we need."

"He won't help. In fact, he threatened to call the cops on me the last time I was there."

Harford bit audibly into the apple and took the seat offered to Marus. "Like I said before, we don't need Gene to get the data," he said, noshing away in between words. "We just need his computer."

"Even if we could get to the computer, you'd need credentials to pull anything off of it," Marus said. "The VPN requires two-factor, maybe even three-factor, authentication. An on-demand SMS, in addition to the iD scan."

One of the programmers, a fair-faced blond kid with a forward-jutting neck and thick glasses, turned around.

"I can remotely hack his phone to intercept the text and send another one in its place," he said.

"What about biometric authenticators?" Marus asked.

"Think of it like an iD swap," Harford said. Frothy apple juice glistened from his mustache.

"Well actually, Rand, it's not really a swap. Not anymore," Galen said. "Our friends here, have engineered a way to copy the digital fingerprint of an iD and mimic the biometric input, without the use of a physical iD." Galen walked over to the counter and picked up a clear, pill-shaped capsule with a microchip inside. "It can be programmed to assume anyone's identity, including Gene's."

"It won't work. You'll be creating a second set of data for the same iD. It will trigger the system," Marus said.

The kid with the glasses spun on the stool to face them again.

"How do you know that? I mean, the program hasn't encountered dual data sets before, has it? Most likely, it will look like a scanner error, as if the timestamp was off. But after ten or fifteen minutes, a security protocol should flag both sets of behavior for further investigation."

Marus considered it. The kid was probably right.

"I've hacked the building's security system, so I can control their cameras. They'll be looking away as you go through the lobby. The elevator cam points down from the back, so you'll have to put a hat on and keep your head down. I assume Gene is a Privacy Privilege subscriber?" the blond kid said.

Marus nodded.

"Good. So you won't have to worry about anything once you're in the apartment."

"And by the time the system flags the dual datasets, and someone actually investigates the error, you'll be out of there, files in tow," Harford said cheerfully.

The blond kid nodded in agreement.

"The problem, as you know, is that your own iD will give you away as an imitator," Galen said.

Marus clutched his wrist involuntarily. "Neither of you have an iD imbedded anymore, right? So why can't one of you do it?"

Galen moved closer, his head tilted forward in consolation. "We aren't familiar with the system, Marus. But you are. We wouldn't have the first clue where to look for this kind of sensitive information. But you do."

"No, I don't. This is above my clearance. I didn't even know the files existed." Marus looked to Harford for corroboration.

"It has to be you. I'm sorry," he said. "If you want to get to the colony, you have to play the game."

"There's nothing to worry about, Marus. It's an incredibly straightforward surgery," Galen said.

"The iD won't be enough to get me in. There could be iris authentication or a fingerprint scan, maybe both."

The blond kid turned again. "We can exploit those by accessing the database and pulling the target's biometric features. Once we have the iris code, we can use a genetic algorithm to alter the synthetic code over several iterations until a nearly identical template is produced. It's actually pretty basic stuff. We'll literally print out the fingerprint and iris code."

Marus studied the kid. "And as for hacking your way in and obtaining the biometric features? Is that pretty basic, as well?"

Behind him, a throaty voice responded.

"It's stored right alongside the other biometrical data." He hadn't seen the door adjacent to the kitchen open or heard her enter, but there she was. Roz Roth met his eyes and smiled shyly.

"Roz has been instrumental to this operation," Galen said.

"Since when?" Marus asked.

"Since the beginning," she said. "I told you I could help." She winked at him.

"Like I said, you'd be surprised how many State employees we've recruited. We snatched Wesley here before the State could," Harford said, patting the blond kid on the shoulder. "Isn't that right, Wes?"

"Yup," Wesley said, still hunched over the black screen.

"Kid's fucking brilliant. He's already hacked the city cameras and is working on overwriting its broadcast system. Once we have the files, we'll blast them across every network. Every man, woman, and child in the country will know the truth in a matter of seconds. And the rest of the world will be close behind."

"And then what?" Marus asked.

"Revolution." Harford smiled the smile he had when he'd set the match to the ground in Axtell's apartment. The kind of smile that sent a shiver down Marus's spine.

"Even if we do get access to Gene's computer, it doesn't mean we'll be able to obtain the files."

"Wes, show him your necklace," Harford said.

Wesley held up a riveted wafer-like rectangle on a chain. "It's a microcontroller," Wesley said. "All we need is Gene's computer and sixty seconds to establish a backdoor. I can run a script to pull back the files afterward. He won't even know we were there. It cleans up after itself."

Harford stood and grabbed Marus's shoulder. He gave it a firm squeeze. "Don't underestimate us, Marus."

"Are you ready?" Roz asked.

Marus nodded. "Let's get this over with."

Galen moved toward the door. "If you'll follow me downstairs, we can get started."

■ ■ ■

On its first floor, the detached garage was part lab, part operating room. The equipment was sparse, but, as far as Marus could tell, cutting edge. A row of computers rested atop a long, low counter on the far wall. Several machines had been wheeled into a neat line at the back. A spotless porcelain washbasin had been positioned under a faucet in the corner. At the center, an overhead light illuminated a small bed, the operating table, which sat squarely next to a chair and mobile counter with drawers.

Dr. Galen Thomas talked him through the surgery. He would administer a brachial plexus nerve block in the upper arm, which would numb his entire right arm and hand. Rather than be sedated, Marus chose to remain awake. The incision would be one inch long. Permanent weakness in the hand was a risk but only if the ulnar nerve was damaged.

"It's highly unlikely," Galen said. "I've performed many of these surgeries." He offered a reassuring smile, but Marus couldn't shake the image of Axtell's twitching, claw-like hand.

"Have you ever met a one-handed pilot?" Harford said. "I heard of one. A guy who flew out of Helmand Province and was awarded a medal. And he had use of his right hand. I wouldn't trust my livelihood to just anyone. The doc is good."

Marus skirted around the operating table, his eyes fixed on the scalpel shining on Galen's tray. Those who removed their iDs could never legally rejoin society. Without a way to transact, they were forced to live off of handouts. Illegals. They were the ostracized. The homeless. The hungry.

"There's no going back from here," Harford said, reading the hesitation on Marus's face.

Marus removed his shirt and laid back on the operating table.

"There's nothing to go back to," he said.

Galen strapped his arm down and wheeled the portable ultrasound scanning device to his side. "I have to localize the nerves of the brachial plexus before I administer the block. Once I do, you'll feel a sharp prick in your arm, and then you may experience a sudden tingling sensation, like your arm is going to sleep. It shouldn't take long for the entire area to go numb."

"How long does it last?" Marus asked.

"It varies patient to patient. Some people recover full feeling in as little as forty-five minutes; for others it can be several hours, as long as twelve in some cases."

"We'll take care of you," Harford said, patting his arm. "But you'll have to wipe your ass with your left," he grinned.

Galen squeezed the gel onto the ultrasound wand and began rubbing Marus's right shoulder. The small screen of the portable ultrasound machine revealed the indecipherable sonographic splotches of light and dark that were Marus's nerves and tendons. Having found whatever it was that he was look-ing for, Galen asked if Marus was ready.

"Yes," Marus nodded.

Galen inserted the needle.

Marus's arm tingled as the doctor had said it would. He remembered a morning when Cade had run into the master bedroom exclaiming that his arm was paralyzed. He distinctly recalled his pajama-clad son flapping it around in simultane-ous terror and amusement.

It's good that you play soccer and not baseball then, isn't it? Marus had said.

Shey played along, and even Cade laughed about it once the feeling returned to his fingers.

PART FOUR

Disobedience is the true foundation of
liberty.
The obedient must be slaves.

—Henry David Thoreau

20

From the sidewalk, The Harbinger Building looked like an obsidian blade cutting into the midday sky. Marus tilted his head back to take it all into view. He'd imagined life here with his family many times. It had been within reach, the plausible next step. He never would have guessed how swiftly things could change. But here he was, instead of a resident, an intruder.

"The concierge just left for the bathroom," Wesley's voice came through the closed-circuit radio.

"Okay. I'll take care of the doorman," Roz said.

"How?" Marus asked as they crossed the street.

She shot him a look and smiled. "Don't worry about it."

Harford was in a utility van in the parking lot, putting the city cameras Wesley had hacked to use by spying on Gene, who was next door at a restaurant. Wesley was with him, monitoring the Harbinger security feed. The mute man with the goatee was in the driver's seat, in case they required a quick escape.

"Gene's lady friend is fine," Harford said through radio.

No one acknowledged him.

"All righty," he said. "The hostess just led them to a table. You guys are good to go."

Marus waited around the corner until Roz waved the man over. Then he ran. The scanner at the entry's immense glass doors chirped as it read the falsified iD Marus carried in the band worn around his wrist. Gene's plump face appeared on the floating screen at the doorman's post. *Mr. Gene Randall. Tenant. Access Granted.* He stepped inside just as Roz pulled away from kissing the doorman. The man returned to his post, suppressing a grin.

"I'm inside," Marus said. A large, suspended steel loop met the floor to the left, serving as the front desk. The concierge still hadn't returned.

"Use the private elevator. It's at the southwest end of the building, behind that water feature thing. Hurry," Harford's voice crackled.

"The fingerprint and iris scan will get you on," Wesley said.

Marus crossed the lobby floor, a sea of polished black granite that gave the impression that he was gliding atop a sweeping reflection pool. He made his way toward a wall of water, frozen in place. The *water feature thing* Harford described was actually a sculptural glass installation. Behind it, a vast expanse of perforated steel panels towered up from the floor, surpassing the mezzanine to meet an enormous vaulted ceiling several stories high. A colorful undulation of light shone through the small, circular holes, reminding him of Gene's floating fireplace. He would have missed the private elevator doors had it not been for the slender trunks of two trees that appeared to grow from the reflective floor on either side.

He stood between them searching for a button or pad to scan his finger, but there was nothing. The floor beneath him glimmered like an emerald, and two perforated panels opened, creating a large square doorway. He stepped inside, and the doors closed behind him, enveloping him in a crystal chamber. But the elevator car remained still. Through the back and side walls was a lush garden, and looking back through the elevator doors was the lobby floor from which he'd just stepped.

"Are you on?" Harford asked.

"Yes, but I can't find the iris—"

"Voice verification failed. Please state your name," the automatic elevator attendant said.

"You hear that?" Marus said.

"Voice verification failed. Security staff override will be required."

Marus slid his hands up and down the walls in search of an emergency exit button, but there was nothing. He saw a woman emerge from behind the glass sculpture and start toward the private elevator doors.

The woman was on the other side of the glass, her thumb against the pad.

"Security staff override required."

At her feet, the black granite was transformed, glowing green. If the doors opened, he'd push past her and run. There was a side door, an emergency escape that would sound an alarm before delivering him to the parking lot behind the gardens. Harford, Wesley, and the driver were waiting there with the van.

"Marus, take the ear bud out for a moment. It's about to get loud," Wesley instructed. He did as instructed. Pinching it with his thumb and forefinger, he removed it from his right ear.

"Gene Randall." Gene's voice came through the radio. Nothing happened. "Gene Randall," the voice said again.

"Good evening, Mr. Randall." The elevator sailed upward. Marus took a breath and watched as the tops of trees fell away below him. Along the horizon, he could see the distant mountains. The glass tower reflected a fierce sun in front of the eastern range.

"Welcome home." The doors opened to a small marbled entry.

Marus put the bud back into his ear and stepped out. "Thanks."

"No problem," Wesley said.

Harford laughed. "Fucking wonder boy over here."

At the doorknob, a sensor read the replicated iD and blinked green. A small light at the peephole flickered. It was the iris scanner. He blinked to ensure the lens was in place before stepping up to its infrared light. After a second, it, too, turned green. With a mechanical whirring sound, the lock unlatched, and the door popped open to a long hallway.

"I'm inside."

Soft lights pulsed on and then off as Marus walked down the hallway in search of Gene's office. It was the last door on the right. Marus put a hand on the knob. The sensor verified

Gene's iD and unlocked the door. The office faced a different direction than the living room, but the view was just as stunning. Miles and miles of glistening water. An imposing desk was centered in the room, its enormous wooden face angled toward the floor-to-ceiling windows. A storied desk, no doubt. Solid wood. Mahogany, if Marus was to guess. And now it was where Gene conducted his highly classified, morally questionable work for the tenth floor. Marus ran a hand along its smooth surface, noticing a Montblanc ballpoint pen in a silver stand. Etched across the base was Gene's name, and beneath that, the words: *History is written by the victors.*

The laptop wasn't there. It wasn't in the desk drawer, or at the table beside the reading chair, or on the bookshelf. It wasn't in his briefcase, propped up against the left side of the desk. The laptop wasn't anywhere. And yet, it had to be in the apartment because it wasn't with Gene at the restaurant, and Gene knew better than to leave it anywhere else.

Marus left the office and closed the door before continuing toward the living room. The coffee table was freshly dusted. He could smell the lemon oil. The kitchen counters gleamed as if they'd just been polished, and fresh vacuum lines zigzagged their way neatly across the carpets. He wondered if he'd stumble into a maid. At the high counter he saw the sleek rectangle of what was presumably Gene's phone.

"He left his phone here," Marus said. "I can't find his computer."

"What? Did you look in the office?" Harford said through the radio.

"Yes. It isn't there."

"Well he doesn't have it with him, so it must be."

Just then, Marus heard a door shut down the hall.

"I think there's a maid here," he said.

"Maybe the laptop is in the bedroom. Did you check?" Harford said.

"No, I think that's where the maid is."

"Shit."

"What should we do?" Wesley asked.

"We're not going to get another shot at this," said Roz.

Marus surveyed the apartment. He walked toward the couch where he'd sat several nights before to show Gene Shey's letter. He remembered seeing the laptop on the coffee table, the way Gene had glanced at it before closing the lid. He knew that look. It was the same one he'd give Shey when she'd come into the study while he was in the middle of something. The work wasn't going anywhere, but he'd glance at it every so often, as though it might get away from him.

Gene didn't work in the lavish office with the wooden desk, Marus realized. It was for show. He'd probably had the room designed and outfitted because he thought he wanted it. Not having a proper office in his previous apartment, he thought he deserved it. But he was used to a couch and a coffee table and the enormous TV screen for a second monitor.

Marus walked around to the other side to look for a lever or button. The coffee table had an electronic lift-top, which seemed tacky. A lift-top of any sort wasn't suitable for an apartment like this, but noticing it gave Marus a certain amount of pleasure. After all, Gene and tacky went together. Now he realized the table was also a chest, a safe that protected its contents, not with iD verification, or an iris or fingerprint scan, but with a simple three-digit code.

"I think I might've found it," Marus said into the radio. "He's got a lock on his coffee table."

"On his what?"

Marus entered Gene's birthday, 7-2-1, but nothing happened. He entered the last three digits of the year he was born, 0-1-6. Again, nothing. He tried 9-1-1, a tribute to that day, more than a decade before they were born, when everything changed. The reason Gene had cited for wanting to work for the State. And then 7-1-1, a tribute to Gene's love for sugar. Looking up occasionally for the maid, Marus continued to punch in numbers. 1-2-3. 4-5-6. Gene liked those old 0-0-7 movies, didn't he? Apparently, not that much.

And then it dawned on him. *Of course.* With absolute certainty, Marus entered 0-0-1. Bingo.

Gene always wanted to be number one. Now he was.

The lift-top rose and unfolded itself, stretching toward Marus. He lifted the laptop from the compartment beneath and set it on the work surface.

"I got it."

His earpiece rattled with cheering.

"All right. Harford still has him at the restaurant," Wesley said. "Go ahead."

"Okay. Calm and collected," Marus said to himself, taking a breath. He peeled the sticker off its plastic sleeve and pressed it onto his finger. "I'm Gene Randall." He opened the notebook and pressed his new fingerprint to the pad. The screen blinked on.

"You're supposed to say, 'I'm Gene Randall, bitch,'" Harford said through the earpiece.

Roz laughed.

Marus navigated onto the network and inserted the USB microcontroller.

"It's in."

"Okay," Wesley said. "It will behave like a USB keyboard and start typing. It should open system preferences and the terminal."

"It's making an outbound connection from the terminal to the server now," Marus said. "I know it will disable the firewall, but what about network monitoring apps?"

"It will imitate a keyboard to preselect 'any connection' and 'forever' to allow the outbound connection."

"Okay, I see. We're clear. It's tweaking the DNS settings now."

"I don't mean to break up this nerd fest, but you have four minutes before the system registers the dual iD and flags your entry," Harford said. "Just so you know."

"Roger that," Marus said. "It's installing the reverse shell backdoor."

"It will auto-close all of the windows, as well as the *settings* screens to sweep up the footprints, and we'll be good as gold. Nice work, everybody."

Marus turned toward the windows.

"I'd never get tired of this view," he said more to himself than anyone else.

"It's exquisite, even from here," Roz replied.

"Yeah, but I'm sure what you're seeing doesn't do it justice."

"I don't know; that camera you're wearing is pretty good."

"You know, for all of our advancements, there's something about being in an actual place for a period of time that just can't be translated, regardless of medium or technology," Marus said.

He expected a smart comment from Harford, but the only response came from Roz.

"You're right. As far as technology has come, nothing beats being there," she said.

He thought of his dad just then and what he'd said. Photographs were thought to be accurate representations, and yet they failed to capture the smells and sounds, the temperature and feel of a single moment.

"Nothing comes close," he repeated, and it was true. After a moment longer in silence, he looked again at the computer. "All done."

"Uh guys…Gene is gone. I don't know where he went," Harford said.

"He's what?" Roz asked.

"He's gone. I thought he went to the bathroom. But he must've already paid. His lady friend is leaving now."

Marus removed the microcontroller and closed the laptop. He set it inside the compartment and pressed the lock button on the side of the coffee table. The lift-top retracted its arms and closed in on itself.

"Okay, I'm headed for the elevator."

"Gene's in the building," Wesley said. "I repeat, he is in the building, headed for the private elevator."

"Goddamn it," Harford mumbled.

"What about the main elevator?" Roz asked.

Marus shoved the controller into his pocket started for the front door.

"The main elevator is no good. Looks like someone called it in," Wesley said. "Security is there."

"Stairs," Harford said.

"No good, either."

From the back of the apartment, Marus heard light footsteps. Wheels whistling along the marble floor. A door shut. He crept to the edge of the hallway to get a better look. The edge of the maid's cart stuck out from the doorway to the master bedroom, but there was no sign of the maid.

The light at the back door turned green, and the door swung open, revealing Gene's round shape. They locked eyes across the hall. Marus thought about running the other way but dismissed the notion as quickly as he'd thought it. Running from Gene was ridiculous. If anything, he ought to run toward him, punch him in the face, and take the private elevator down.

"Shit," Wesley said, seeing what Marus saw from his lapel cam.

"I knew you'd be by, sooner or later," Gene said. Marus watched as his eyes flashed over to the coffee table and back again. "You never were one to shy away from something you wanted."

"Level the pudgy bastard. You can take him," Harford said.

Marus ignored the chatter. "And what do I want, Gene?"

His conspirators fell silent.

Gene removed a slender, silver rectangle from his jacket pocket. "This," he said.

It was a portable hard drive.

"You were right." Gene took a step toward him. Then another. "All of the files Shey was looking for, the location of Black Mine Bunker, *everything*, it's all on here." Gene crossed the length of the hall and handed him the device.

There was a piece of paper stuck to the side of it.

"No one has to know the information came from me. Okay? I came back for my phone and didn't see anything," he said, sliding past Marus to retrieve his phone from the kitchen counter. "The maid is in the master bathroom. It's her last room. Once she's done, she'll take the private elevator down to the laundry. There's a service entrance at the back."

Marus looked down at the piece of paper affixed to the hard drive. He'd never seen Gene's curly cursive before.

I was wrong.
—Your friend

Gene stuffed his phone into his pocket and made his way back down the hall. "Best of luck to you and Shey," he said, banging his palm against the laundry hamper. He stepped inside the elevator and was swallowed whole.

"What the fuck was all that?" Harford said.

The cart was parked just inside the master bedroom, full of laundry. Marus ran to meet it and began scooping armfuls of the laundry out of the hamper. In the bathroom, a toilet flushed, and the sink came on. He carried the displaced pile into the first bedroom across the hall and closed the door. He ran back to the maid's cart. One leg and then another, he stepped into it. Grabbing the reserved top layer of clothing, he arranged it atop him best he could.

"I'll deactivate the iD so you don't get tagged on the way down," said Wesley.

"They just stopped Gene in the lobby. There are four guys blocking off the private elevator," Roz said.

"That's okay, the elevator should give the maid priority. She'll get to the basement without being intercepted," Wesley said.

Lying in the nest of linens, Marus heard a door open and then close. The light shuffle of feet came closer, accompanied by the tinny, muffled sound of heavy metal being blasted through a set of ear buds. It was perfect. *Too perfect*, really. The maid pressed the door assistance button and wheeled the cart through the open doors and onto the private elevator.

"Good evening, Danica," the elevator greeted the maid, who wasn't listening. "Level one, preselected."

What if they did intercept the elevator? What if when the doors dinged open, the four men waiting searched the maid's cart? They'd be moronic not to. His heart quickened with the thought of it, but he remained still. In that scenario, there were only a few options available to him, all of which ended with him being subdued or shot. The thought of bleeding all over Gene's laundry in a final act of public degradation was, conceivably, the worst death he could imagine.

The doors opened, and the maid pushed the cart out and across the floor. No one stopped her. There were no voices.

There weren't any sounds at all, aside from the repetitive pulsing of the maid's headphones and the whining of wheels against concrete. Then he heard a ringing in her headphones.

"Hullo," the maid answered. There was a pause, followed by the indistinct chatter of someone on the other line. "Yes, Mr. Randall, I'll be right there."

The cart came to a halt, its brakes clicked into place, and Marus listened as the clacking of feet faded toward the elevator. He heard the ding of the doors and their swift closing, followed by silence.

Once he was sure he was alone, Marus writhed up from the clothing like an undead corpse. Reaching upward, he took his fill of air. Oxygen untainted by Gene's sullied trousers. Born again.

"The service exit is back and to your left. We're in position with the van."

"I'll see you all at the exchange," Roz said and signed off.

21

THEY CONTINUED EAST. The four of them, Marus, Harford, Wesley, and the man with the goatee, whose name Marus still did not know, rode silently as the last of daylight bled out of the sky. Their heads jerked and their bodies bounced as the LeSabre made its way along the potholed road. Behind the passenger's seat, Wesley assaulted the keyboard bridged across his lap. His fingers moved forcefully and all at once, crushing the keys beneath in focused fury. The unceasing clicking of his impassioned, whack-a-mole-like effort only amplified the tension that'd been steadily building since they'd swapped the van for the LeSabre.

Roz hadn't been able to contain her smile at the exchange point.

"Nice work," she had said, inching closer. Without warning, she'd wrapped her arms around Marus. He'd felt her breath hot against his neck.

"What did you say to the doorman?" He'd asked, pulling away. "I saw the kiss."

She'd laughed. "I asked him if he'd seen my boyfriend. I said he was cheating on me with a woman who lived in the building. The doorman said any man to walk away from me was a moron, so I kissed him. I would've kissed you, too."

Marus had shifted uncomfortably but couldn't help his smile.

"Good luck finding your wife."

Marus had turned in his seat to see her staring back from the weed-ridden parking lot at the exchange as they drove off. The car swap made everything real. The immediate threat had passed, the adrenaline waned, but the real work still lay ahead.

■ ■ ■

From his cramped and upright position behind the driver's seat, he watched the landscape stream by in a blur of muted color. Brown earth, hard packed and fissured, stretched out for miles on either side of them.

The sky behind them was a violent clash of red and orange at the fringe, a deep blue above. They'd passed the unmistakable faded and peeling pink lettering for Bonshire Fun Park more than twenty minutes ago. The rusted, skeletal remains of steel tracks had stood like fallen heroes, looped and inverted among the dust and tumbleweeds. They were much farther east now, running flat into desert. The abandoned theme park, and a bankrupted development, its first foundations poured and then stranded, crumbled like Roman ruins, were all that stood between them and hundreds of miles of gritty desolation.

Aside from the occasional shack or windblown barn, there was nothing but road and land and sky.

Harford hadn't uttered a word since he'd taken the man with the goatee's spot in the driver seat, but Marus caught several of his sidelong glances in the rearview mirror. His eyes were bloodshot and tired. The creases at their corners were more crinkled than he'd remembered, his brow more deeply furrowed. It might have just been the worry wearing on him, but he looked significantly older and a bit ill.

Marus wondered what Harford's motives were. Was he simply a patriot, as he claimed, or were more sinister pressures at work? Had he joined the patriots willingly, or was he being coerced into cooperation? Marus remembered scrolling through his profile. He had a daughter. Where was she? Harford glanced at him in the mirror again, holding his gaze even when it was met. He looked as if he was anticipating a question or protest, but Marus had neither.

Finally, he broke.

"Jesus, Wesley! What are you doing back there?"

Wesley didn't answer. He only hunched farther over, his lanky figure nearly folding in half as he squinted through black-rimmed glasses at the screen merely inches from his face. Whether he was simply ignoring him or was so entrenched in what he was doing was anyone's guess.

After a long and uncomfortable silence, the man with the goatee turned his handheld screen over and set it on his lap. "Takara's been taken," he said to Harford in a low grumble.

"I thought they were going to pack it up."

"They weren't able to get out in time."

Marus saw Harford wince reflexively in the mirror. "No one?"

"Ennis wasn't there, but Galen and the others were. None of them got out."

"Goddamn it." He hit the steering wheel with the palm of his hand.

Wesley straightened, looking up as though aware for the first time that there were others in the car.

Marus bowed his head, trying not to make eye contact with anyone. He felt responsible, of course. If he hadn't looked up those addresses, the system may not have flagged them at all. Their operation on Takara may never have been discovered. Marus imagined the blind woman singing, un-interrupted, while the entire world came down around her. He'd shown the State where to go. Now, who knew what would happen to Galen, the others, and the woman with white, wispy hair.

"Does Emery know?" Harford asked.

"He's disconnected right now."

"*Can't someone go get him?*" There was no response. "Well, were they able to wipe everything?"

"Yes," he said, picking the screen up from his lap again. "But this is Galen we're talking about. We can't be certain how much he'll divulge."

"You're right."

"I've already warned everyone who's been under his knife. They'll get out of the city and go underground until we see the rest of this through."

"What's our directive?" Harford asked.

"Same as before. Acquire the files and send them over. The analysts are waiting. Once they have what they need from Wesley, we'll schedule the media offensive. Emery wants to coordinate the attack. Is Piper waiting at the hangar?"

"No, she's delayed."

"*What?*" The man said, turning to study Harford.

"Weather's been bad up north."

"I'll call for someone else, then."

"No," Harford said, raising his voice. He took a breath. "She'll get in tomorrow morning. Don't worry, we'll be fine."

"You better hope so," the man said, turning back to the screen in his lap.

Harford looked into the rearview mirror, meeting Marus's eyes for a moment. "What's the status back there, Wes?"

"I'm sending commands to Gene's computer to pull back the files. The connection will automatically upload them to the colony's servers," Wesley said.

"I thought Gene gave Marus all of the files. Haven't you checked the hard drive?" Harford said, turning to look at him.

"I can get them this way. It shouldn't take long."

"Wesley, they're sitting on the goddamned seat beside you. There isn't time to experiment. Stick that thing in your computer and get them over to Emery."

■ ■ ■

Potato Hill had been a fine municipal airport back in the day, according to Harford. Now, like much else they'd passed, it was abandoned and in rough shape.

"It'll serve our purposes, though," he said, pulling into one of the open hangars. The headlights illuminated a make-shift workbench scattered with old, damaged parts and tools. A starter, cracked panels, a muffler, and an assortment of rust-ed screws. In the corner lay a pile of oil-stained cardboard, towels, and rags. "Make yourself comfortable, gents," he said.

There was an unspoken pecking order that entitled the man with the goatee to the backseat of the car, while everyone else was left to lie on the ground. Wesley removed his belong-ings, making a place for himself in the far corner by clearing away the cobwebs with his foot. He pulled his computer from its case and began working.

Marus saw the hard drive, untethered, lying on the cement beside him and relaxed a little. He didn't trust what was on it. He didn't trust Gene.

Harford retrieved a blanket, a flashlight, and a bottle of whiskey from the trunk. "The bare necessities," he remarked, taking a seat in the middle of the hangar. "Would you be a pal and close the doors a bit? Keep the sand out," he said.

Marus obliged, forcing each of the doors with a screech until they were a couple feet from one another.

Harford set the flashlight on its end, creating a column of eerie light. "Let's tell ghost stories," he said, laughing, as Marus took a seat opposite him.

Harford was more relaxed, Marus noticed. Maybe it was that he felt at home here, in the bowels of an airport, and one he had a particular history with. But Marus couldn't let down his guard. He'd fulfilled his promise and was unnecessary now. He couldn't be certain that they would take him to the colony, or that Shey was even there. A glimpse of Harford's gun, spotted when he had leaned over the trunk, confirmed Marus's suspicions. It was best to exercise caution.

Marus looked to the corner of the hangar, where Wesley was. The hard drive still lay untouched beside him.

"It seemed too easy, didn't it?" Marus said.

"What's that?" Harford asked.

"Breaking into Gene's apartment that way and getting away with it. The Harbinger Building is one of the most secure residential buildings in the country, and we just walked in and right back out again."

"Well, technically, you rolled out, and in a rank-smelling hamper, at that. I didn't say anything earlier, but you stink. Your buddy Gene has some nasty BO."

"And there's that, too. The maid being there, Gene coming back at just the right moment. The fact that he gave us the hard drive."

"When you get clear, sunny skies, you don't ask questions; you take advantage of 'em. It's as simple as that."

"I don't know. Thinking back on it, the building's doors should have auto-locked. If I had developed their security program, that would've been one of the first things I'd do."

"Yeah, well, people aren't as smart as you. Lucky us."

"I've worked for the State for more than five years; I've seen its capabilities. Hell, I developed most of them. At the very least, the bridges should have come up. We should have been trapped on the Isle, but we drove through, no problem. It just seems odd."

"Relax, have a drink." Harford handed him the bottle, but he declined.

He looked over to Wesley again, who seemed frustrated. He'd picked up the hard drive.

"I don't think we should use it," Marus said more to Wesley than Harford.

"Why the hell not?" Harford asked.

Wesley walked over.

"Because we don't know what's on it. I've known Gene for almost fifteen years. We worked together at Newbold Corp. before we were recruited by the State. I know him, and he'll do anything to get ahead."

Harford looked up at Wesley, who stood awkwardly over them without saying anything.

"He could have gone to Devlin or someone else. Or someone could have come to him," Marus said. "Otherwise, how would he have known I'd be there? The hard drive was in his pocket, so he must have taken it with him to lunch. Why would he do that?" He repositioned himself on the ground. "The whole thing was orchestrated. They let us walk out of there."

Wesley nodded. "It could be a worm or a Trojan."

"A *what*?" Harford asked.

"It's possible," Marus said. "Or, it could be a tracking device."

"Let me see it," Harford said, looking back at Wesley.

He retrieved it from the corner and handed it to Harford, who was still sitting cross-legged on the concrete floor.

"Newbold Corp.," he read, laughing.

"What's funny about that?" Marus asked, but neither man answered.

"It doesn't look like a tracking device." Harford raised it to the column of light in front of him, turning it as if there'd be a telltale sign that it was or wasn't. He removed the piece of paper taped to its side, Gene's note, and threw it at Marus. "Not a very good friend if you ask me."

"I can run it on an isolated machine and see what it is," Wesley said.

"Have you made any headway with the backdoor you established?"

Wesley pushed his glasses back and nodded. "I'm querying their databases now. It's just taking a little longer than I expected. From what I can tell, though, they have no idea we're in."

"How long until we have something?"

"It's pulling back files as we speak. There's a lot there, but I've asked the colony for help. With their capabilities and more people on it, we should have everything we need by tomorrow, maybe a little later, but definitely by the time we reach the colony."

"Don't worry about checking the hard drive then. Smash it. Burn it, whatever. Let me know once you have something worth looking at."

"Yes, okay," he said. Looking newly energized, Wesley walked back over to his corner.

Harford turned to Marus. "Thanks for your help," he said. "You were in a tough position, having to go against what you believe in without even knowing you could trust us."

"My family is all I believe in anymore."

"I can appreciate that," Harford said taking a swig from the whiskey bottle. "I'm a family man myself. My daughter is twenty-three. You'll meet her tomorrow when she comes with the plane."

"She's a pilot, too?"

Harford nodded. "My pride and joy."

"Twenty-three is a good age. It was a long time ago, but I remember it being very transformative."

Harford took another sip. "How old was your boy?"

"Seven" Marus said, "going on twenty. He is...*was* a serious boy."

"I'm sorry." Harford handed him the bottle.

Marus took a long pull.

"We weren't trying when Shey got pregnant. In fact, we didn't even know if we wanted kids. We didn't think we were ready."

"No one's ever ready."

"He almost didn't make it. Through the birth, I mean." Marus brought the whiskey back to his lips and swallowed hard. "I'd spent so much time thinking about what he was going to be like, you know, building him up in my mind, that it was like I already knew him. The thought of losing him—and now—" Marus swirled the amber-colored liquid inside the bottle and passed the whiskey back.

"If I was you," Harford said, taking it from him, "when all this is over, I'd find Devlin and kill the bastard."

"You really think he's behind it?"

Devlin was cold, calculated. A politician. But a murderer?

"I know he's fucking behind it," Harford said, taking another drink.

"How?"

"Just do." He set the bottle down. "He's a creep. I wouldn't be surprised if he's in a bunch of bad shit."

"My dad almost died. Maybe he was behind that, too."

"What makes you say that?"

"He had a heart attack. He's perfectly healthy, no history of heart problems. The doctor said she didn't know what caused it. But he told me he fell and that a nurse took him home and hooked him up to an IV because he was dehydrated. He woke up in intensive care."

"Potassium chloride," Harford said. "Nasty stuff, hard to detect. I'm surprised he survived."

"They resuscitated him."

"If they were trying to kill him, why would they do that?"

"I don't know. Maybe it was a warning, or punishment. Could be both, I guess."

Harford studied the bottle. "It's a fucked up world we live in."

■ ■ ■

Forty minutes later, Wesley walked over with the laptop. His glasses were crooked on his nose and his hair, nearly vertical.

"Hey, *guys?*"

"There he is. Taking a little break?" Harford gestured toward the bottle between them. "Here, have some before it's gone."

"I, uh, found something," he said. He took a seat between Marus and Harford and turned his computer toward them. "I'm still scraping their servers, but I was able to pull back a few encrypted files. There's a folder called *Collateral*, and there's some interesting stuff in there."

"Like what?"

"There's some information about political hostages."

Marus shot him a look.

"Let me see," Harford said, taking the computer from him. He scrolled through, squinting at the screen. "Wow. Nice work, Wes."

"There's, uh," Wesley cleared his throat. "There's a folder in there titled, *CVW.* You might want to look at that," he said, meeting Marus's eyes.

Marus went rigid. He felt his chest expand. A fleeting rush of air he couldn't hold. He extended his arm, reaching for the laptop, and Harford set it in his hand.

In the folder *CVW* were documents and pictures. The documents were surveillance notes, where Cade went at which times in the days leading up to his abduction. The pictures were similar, snapshots of him, in the school parking lot, at soccer practice, and on the way home. Some included Shey. There was a video. He clicked on it and forced himself to breathe.

Cade was sitting on a white chair at the center of a white room. He was wearing white shorts and a white T-shirt.

What is your name? a voice said.

Cade. Cadien.

What is your full name?

Cadien Vanguard-Winde.

Who are your parents?
Marus Winde and Shey Vanguard.
Would you like to tell them anything, Cadien?

Cade bit his lower lip. It's what he did when he was trying not to cry, when he was trying to be brave.

I—I miss you and I…
Cadien?
I want to go home.

Wind rattled through the hangar. The smell of gas and dust was temporarily cleared by creosote and sagebrush. The ghoulish cackles of coyotes came in gusts. Marus couldn't speak. Wesley had taken the computer from his lap. He pushed his glasses back and looked at each of them in turn.

"So, your son is *alive*?" Wesley asked.

"The video is time stamped. It was filmed yesterday," Marus said.

"He's alive, then," Wesley said. "He must be."

"I'll drink to that," Harford said.

■ ■ ■

The golden glow of morning beamed in where the hangar doors had been pulled apart, illuminating Harford's inert body at the center. Wesley was stirring beside him, pawing desperately at the light with a limp hand. He moaned and turned over, his bare cheek against the oil-stained concrete. The car was empty.

Marus had fallen asleep sitting upright, slumped against one of the ribbed, metal walls of the hangar. His back ached in places where the steel had pressed into him. He felt foggy from lack of sleep and a night of drinking and woke not knowing where he was. The incision on his wrist pulsed with pain. It hadn't been a dream, after all.

He scanned the hangar and found Wesley's computer and the overturned whiskey bottle, empty, beside it. They had celebrated. The video of Cade was not a figment of his imagination. It existed, which meant his son still existed. He was out there, somewhere, waiting for his father to take him home.

Across the taxiway, the man with the goatee was standing in the middle of the uneven runway. His back to the hangars, he looked beyond the desert floor toward the distant hills where the sun was rising. A cigarette dangled in his right hand. He brought it to his lips.

Marus crossed the pavement to join him.

"Good morning," he called as he approached.

The man squared his shoulders but wouldn't face him. "I heard the good news," he said.

"For a second, I thought I'd dreamt it." Marus took a breath and listened. The chirping of crickets and the uncertain song of a lone cactus wren rose from the desert floor. "You know, I don't even know your name."

The man was silent for a long time.

Marus shifted uncomfortably. "When are we leaving?"

"Harford's daughter will be here in a few hours with the plane." He flicked the cigarette to the cracked asphalt and continued to study the horizon.

"I want to help take down the State," Marus said. "There's more I can contribute."

"You've already earned your place at the colony, if that's what you're worried about."

"No," Marus said, shoving his hands into his pockets. "It's not that."

The man squinted into the rising sun. "Vengeance is a powerful motivator, but it clouds your judgment," he said. "We don't need people intent on executing personal vendettas. The cause has to come first." He looked away from the horizon and turned to face Marus.

"I want to make things right, that's all. I feel responsible."

"We're all responsible."

Marus nodded. "Just tell Emery for me, will you?"

"He'll want to meet you once we're at the colony. You can tell him yourself," the man said. "Just don't tell him about your son."

"Why not?"

"There's a reason they kept your boy alive. Whatever it is, you wouldn't want Emery doubting your allegiance."

"Why are you telling me this?"

"Because I know you're not stupid enough to trust the Protectors again. And I believe people can have more than one cause." The man turned and began walking toward the hangar. When he'd crossed the cracked, weed-ridden taxiway, he looked back at Marus. "My name's Mike."

22

MARUS HAD NEVER flown like this. Aboard the AirBuses he'd take cross-country to conferences on the East Coast, he could never get a sense of the gravity he was defying. He couldn't hear the thoughtful purring of the engine or look forward out into the open sky as he moved closer to the sun. He'd watched the ground peel away on takeoff, but it had never felt like this. Here, in the Cessna, it was different. He felt as though he could touch the trees and scattered buildings as they glided over the tops of them. Suspended in sky, Marus was utterly untouchable.

"Wave goodbye to your friends," Harford said through the static of the headset.

Wesley clutched his stomach in the back beside Harford's daughter, Piper. She'd had a rough night. The weather had been bad, with no indication of letting up, so she'd flown a lengthy alternate route to reach them. When she landed, Harford ran up to the plane and pulled her from the cockpit like he hadn't seen her in years. Marus watched, imagining his own reunions.

What would he say to Shey as he pulled her close? Would he ever be able to let Cade go?

Mike sat across from Wes and Piper. His elbow was propped up against the armrest, and his chin, in the crook of his thumb, as he gazed out the window.

Marus couldn't see the Isle, but imagined it there in the distance. The glass tower, a second sun ablaze in fiery reflection, refracting light into the atmosphere, radiating certitude as it engulfed the city in its light. Gene would be there, on the tenth floor of the IA, going about his Monday morning without consequence. He'd played his role expertly. How he'd been able to even look Marus in the face, Marus couldn't understand, though Gene's conscience seemed clear enough.

■ ■ ■

An hour and a half into the flight, the distant mountains had transformed into sleeping giants that loomed straight in front of them. The sheer stature of them left Marus uneasy. It was an odd thing, he realized, to be in an aircraft, the rest of the world shrunk beneath him, looking *up* at a mountain. They would hit it head on if they continued flying straight. Still, he didn't say anything. *Harford knows what he's doing*, Marus thought, trying to halt the images of the plane smashing into its side, disintegrating on impact, that flashed repeatedly in his mind.

In just a few seconds, they had moved much closer. The mountain dominated the entire view from the windshield, but the Cessna kept on. Marus watched the control wheel in front of him mimic the slight movements of the one in Harford's hand on the left. It barely moved at all.

They'd be dead on impact, strewn across the mountainside like garbage. A convenient meal for the wildlife. An article he'd read not too long ago stated that the gray wolf was flourishing now.

Marus couldn't shake the image. Harford lying limp with the others among the wreckage, a quick death. His own legs and arms broken, awaiting the sound: a lone howl, followed by many. The wolves chewing greedily, their teeth abnormally white, as they worked the grisly pieces of flesh in their mouths. He'd never be found. The truth, never told. Shey wouldn't even know he'd come for her. Cade would never come home.

Without thinking, he took the control wheel firmly in his hand and pulled back. The plane lurched up fitfully, pinning its passengers to their seats, revealing a bit of blue sky at the mountain's peak. Piper and Wesley screamed. Mike choked on his own saliva. A fearful cough.

Harford reacted swiftly.

"Jesus fucking Christ!" he shouted, striking Marus square in the chest with his right hand, forcing his control down with his left. Marus released the wheel and the plane pitched forward. The craggy shelf of mountain below rushed toward the windshield, like a scene from a video game. Would he feel any pain, or would he just be, and then a moment later, not be?

Harford banked hard to the right, slipping into a canyon Marus hadn't seen. Having made the narrow opening at just the right angle, he leveled the wings.

"What the hell were you thinking?" The wiry blond hairs of his mustache fluttered up with his pointed exhale.

"I didn't see the canyon," Marus said.

"So, *what*, you were going to try to fly over the mountain? Are you fucking nuts? That mountain is fifteen *thousand* feet tall. Even if our service ceiling wasn't about that, the rate of climb wouldn't get us there in time. Not to mention that we'd stall before we even got close. Jesus." Mountains rose up on either side of them. A line of trees snaked its way through the canyon below, growing thick and close together. "*Jesus*," he said again, fixed on the sliver of open sky ahead. "I'm the pilot. You're the passenger. Do not touch the controls again. Understand?"

"I'm sorry," Marus said, feeling the weight of the collective gaze emanating from the back of the plane.

■ ■ ■

Water spouted from a crevice high up the mountain wall. White foam trickled down the rocky face and disappeared into a grove of trees, ablaze. Reds and oranges. Neon yellow. Soon, the leaves would drop, and the chute would freeze. Falling snow would replenish its stores before spring's thaw unleashed the full fury of the falls.

Harford seemed at ease in his seat. His mustache had settled, and his lips were pressed into a thin, contented line that stretched straight across his face. Though Marus couldn't see his eyes behind the sunglasses, a slight tilt of head suggested that he, too, was transfixed on the waterfall to the right.

Marus wondered how many times he'd seen in it, and in how many seasons.

Here, among the gray, knobby escarpments and groves of flame-colored trees, the world was vast, timeless. And he, merely a blip.

The canyon widened, offering them up to the open air and revealing an expansive valley below. Farm country. Acres and acres of it. Well-plotted fields butted up to the same, large river that ran through the canyon where it was fed by the falls. Brown and black spotted cows grazed sleepily beside immense, golden oaks dotting the fields.

Only Marus and Harford were wearing the headsets. Piper and Wesley were asleep in the back, Mike was still looking at the window, but none of them would be able to hear Marus anyway for the loud thwacking of the prop.

"Yesterday in the car, Mike said Takara was taken."

Harford's voice sounded hollow through the headset.

"That's right."

"How do you think the Protectors knew about it?"

"What're you asking me for? You're one of them, aren't you?"

Was. He didn't say it aloud. He didn't need to.

"It can't be helped. It had to be somebody. They knew the risk. We all do," Harford said.

"You think they're dead?"

"I don't know why Devlin would keep 'em alive. He doesn't do that unless he's got a reason to."

"And the old woman?"

"You mean Emery's grandmother, Clare. I don't know what they'd do with her. Send her to a bedchamber. It's a shame. She's a sweet lady," Harford said.

"How old is Emery, then?"

"A hell of a lot younger than me. Younger than you, too. Thirty-something, I think." Harford banked to the right. "See those mountains off in the distance? That's where we're headed. We'll be on the ground in about an hour. Then the real fun begins. You might want to do like the children and get some shut-eye." He motioned over his shoulder and smiled.

"I'll be okay."

"Suit yourself. Supposed to be one hell of a climb, though."

"You've never done it?"

"I've never been to the colony."

"Why's that?"

"Haven't proved myself yet, I guess. They won't even tell me where it is."

Marus expected a laugh, but Harford didn't make another sound.

The farmland ceded to rolling hills and steeper terrain with more vegetation. Marus watched from the window as birds flocked beneath them.

"What about Axtell? Do you think he's at the colony?"

Harford nudged the plane right. "Couldn't tell you."

"In the car earlier, Mike said something about a coordinated attack. I thought the plan was to distribute the information."

"That's part of the plan. But the government's stored a lot of data on folks, and Emery wants to make sure they don't plan to use it to dissuade the public from revolting. A clean slate, that's the goal."

"Will you wipe their servers, or physically destroy them?"

"I won't do anything. It's not up to me," Harford said, agitated.

"Do they know where Black Mine Bunker is?" Marus asked, trying to sound indifferent.

"I don't know."

"Mike didn't say anything about it?"

"Jesus, Marus! I don't know. Would you mind keeping quiet for a while? I'm trying to concentrate."

Marus watched as Harford guided the plane, his limp left hand the only point of contact with the control wheel. He didn't appear to be concentrating. He looked as if he was about to fall asleep.

■ ■ ■

The airstrip Harford and Mike had referred to was an uneven field with a dark line down the middle where the grass struggled to grow. It looked too short. At one end, the front, Marus could make out the low profile of what looked to be a stone foundation. The roof and walls were gone, pilfered for firewood, or else worn to splinters by weather and time. At the other, the far end, was an enormous stretch of pine trees that grew tall and close together. A Christmas tree farm never cut, Marus guessed.

"It'll look like we're going to land on our nose. I have to come down like that. Whatever you do, don't touch the controls. If you do, we'll all be dead. Got it?"

Marus nodded and clasped his hands in his lap.

Harford pulled a lever back and then took some of the throttle out before lowering the flaps ten degrees. He eased the throttle back again and lowered the flaps another ten degrees.

"We've got a little bit of a crosswind," he said. He used the ailerons to keep a steady line, but the nose kicked over, and it looked like they were going to come in sideways. They were pitched pretty far forward as they descended, and it seemed that they might run the prop into the ground. Harford eased the thrust and pulled back on the yoke as he stepped on the rudder to straighten the nose. The stall horn went off just as they touched down. Marus exhaled an audible sigh of relief.

"Cake," Harford said. He pulled a knob and the engine sputtered. The plane coasted to a halt. "Kids, we're here!"

Marus helped unload the cargo, four packs they needed to take to the colony.

"Not this one," Harford said, putting it back in the plane.

"You're not coming to the colony?"

Mike looked up from what he was doing. "That wasn't the plan, Rand."

"The plan's changed. I got a call on the radio while you guys were snoozing. Emery wants me to make another stop. Whoever I'm picking up knows the way and will get us there in a day or two."

Mike didn't say anything. Marus didn't remember any call.

"Well, we better head out, Piper. Looks like a storm is coming, and we need to make a pit stop for gas." He put an arm around her and kissed the side of her head.

Piper nodded and returned to the plane, assuming Harford's seat on the left.

Harford shook Mike's hand.

He patted Wesley on the back. "See ya, Wes." He waved a hand in the air. "Adios!" he said to no one in particular.

Once inside the plane, Piper and Harford pulled the headsets over their ears. A moment later, Piper yelled, "clear" and the prop started spinning. Marus watched as the Cessna made a sloppy turn and took off in the same direction from which it'd come.

■ ■ ■

The edge of the pinewood stood at the end of the field like an impenetrable wall. Across the ridge, the spire-like tops of trees trended, black against the sky, in upward and downward spikes, concealing whatever waited beyond.

"Why couldn't the helicopter take us?" Wesley asked.

"It's tied up elsewhere," Mike responded.

"So, it'll take, what, three days?"

"Three days, as long as we keep a good pace," Mike said.

Clouds tumbled and rolled behind them. Heavy. The wind howled in Marus's ear, carrying the low groan of the retreating Cessna, almost out of sight, in a wash of gray sky overhead.

"Is Harford allowed at the colony?" Marus asked.

Mike plowed through the dried shoots of grass, his focus fixed ahead. "How do you mean?"

"I just wondered since he hasn't been there before."

"Everyone's allowed once they've proved themselves."

"Three days, huh?" Wesley said behind them. "What are we going to eat? Where will we sleep?"

Mike patted the pack he'd hoisted onto his shoulders. "We'll be fine. Just keep moving and stay close."

They walked through the last of the waist-high grass without a word. The pine trees stood tall and close together, in equal distances on all sides. A dozen dark doorways to the world beyond. Mike motioned toward one of the black portals before them, but Marus and Wesley waited for him to go first. The dead grass plunged in violent gusts across the field behind them. The sky was marble.

Mike disappeared between the trunks.

He called a moment later from the darkness. "Come on, let's go."

Marus allowed Wesley to go before stepping through to the other side.

■ ■ ■

The pinewood harbored a silent and colorless void between its towering trunks. A dense ceiling of branches blotted out the sky, transforming the alleys into a network of tunnels cloaked in perpetual dusk. Marus took a deep breath and felt as though he might choke. The air was thick, damp. Decades of fallen pine needles carpeted the forest floor, contributing their stale perfume.

Mike started down one of the narrow alleys. He walked fast, with purpose. Marus and Wesley followed, blinking into the dimness.

Had the public known about the colony, had curiosity carried them this far, Marus now understood why they wouldn't continue. It wasn't difficult to imagine the inclement weather and unchecked predators, the basic dangers that awaited those who dared to venture beyond the safety of the cities. He'd played out numerous possibilities in his mind, electrical storms and ferocious winds, conjuring encounters with bears and wolves. Even the gypsies who were known to reside in these parts. But this, the pinewood, a barrier between the known and unknown, was something else entirely.

The deepest of breaths wasn't enough for his lungs, and for a moment, he thought he might suffocate. Resting a hand against the trunk beside him, he stopped to draw in a long breath. When he closed his eyes he could see their faces, his wife and child standing there beside him.

The shifting of rotting pine needles beneath careful footsteps wafted out of the piney corridor to his left. He heard a murmured padding sound. When he squinted through the grainy dark, he could see that Mike was already well ahead.

"What was that?" Wesley said.

Marus didn't respond. He put a finger to his lips and listened instead, ears upturned, rigid in his stance. Everything was gray and quiet around them. He motioned Wesley on.

They heard it again.

"Should we yell to Mike?" Wesley whispered.

Nothing lived in the wood. Harford told them that, despite never having made the trek himself. It was a three-day journey through the mountains, and not without its dangers, but the eeriest part, Harford said, the pinewood, was uninhabitable. *Nothing lives in there, except maybe the Devil. If you believe in that sort of thing.*

Marus peered into the shadows and saw a row of black figures standing uniformly ten feet from one another in all directions, except for one. The harder he looked, the more unsure he was that it was standing there, staring back, and then it was gone.

"What was that?" Wesley said. "Did you see it? What the *hell* was that?"

"Shh—" Marus turned a circle, but there was nothing to see. Nothing concrete, at least.

Trunks seemed to split and become whole again as shadows darted across corridors, disappearing before either of them could get a better look. Mike was barely visible. Marus could see his stocky silhouette moving at a rapid clip toward a pinprick of light in the distance. They were almost through. Marus grabbed the arm of Wesley's shirt. They started walking once more, but the footsteps followed. They stopped and started and stopped again, and the faint padding of feet did the same.

Marus spun around to try to catch the predator. But the wood was silent and empty except for the trunks, dark and crusted and infinite in their succession. Wesley was shaking. He turned to face the speck of light ahead. It wasn't any closer, and Mike was out of sight. Marus scoured the alleys, and they both quickened their pace. But after a moment, they could hear the quick clip of footfall right behind them. Getting lost was just one of the dangers here, and the only gun was holstered to Mike's waist.

"This way?" Wesley said.

A bead of light blinked at the end of another corridor. It was possible Mike had turned to meet a trail there. Marus could feel the trickle of sweat percolating from the rimmed creases of his brow, the fear edging, electric, up his spine. They started down the right corridor, passing the fissured trunks of several trees before Marus changed his mind.

"This way," he said.

Straight had been the only direction they'd gone, the only way they would go. He looked to the left and headed for the first small circle of light in the distance. Wesley followed.

"Ya lookin' lost." The voice was raspy. Harsh as gravel.

The black trunk beside him erupted in laughter. It was one of them.

He looked exactly as Marus had always envisioned a gypsy might. Cast away from society, starving, sick, and surely insane. His teeth were rot, his hair, grease, and his skin dusted with days of dirt. Maybe weeks. His head bobbed unsteadily as he laughed. A series of small, jerky movements. He was twitching with delight.

"So fancy."

He spat, kicking Marus's boots with his own as he reached for the arm of Marus's coat.

Marus pulled away. Wesley was frozen three feet from him. Laughter reverberated from trunk to trunk. *Where the fuck was Mike?*

"We're headed for the colony. Which way is it?" Marus said, taking another step back.

"You haven't felt it in a while, have you?" The rancid warmth of his breath clung to Marus's cheek as he moved closer.

Wesley made a muffled, high-pitched sound. Like a cat being slaughtered. He was trying to say something, Marus realized, but couldn't.

"That frost in ya blood, a quicken'n in ya chest like ya heart might burst out'n do the runnin' for you. There's nuthin' ta keep you safe out here, you know? Fear's gonna eat y'all alive."

"Can you tell us where the colony is?" Marus asked again. Keep steady, he thought. *Breathe*. The air was too dense. Too putrid.

He needed to assert himself, to look the gypsy in his eyes and show him he wasn't afraid. But there was something wrong with them, something *in* them. Gray eyes flecked with oily smudges, hungry like an animal's. Wesley was frozen, shrunken against a large trunk, watching as the man stroked a nest of hairs at his chin.

The gypsy swayed, looking to Wesley, who looked quickly away, before stepping to the side and leaning his lips forward as if to whisper. They almost grazed Marus's ear before he jabbed his index finger into Marus's temple.

"It's in there, brotha!" He moved away smiling, repeatedly prodding at his own skull, as he encircled Marus in the pacing of slow and unsettling steps. "Any place you wanna be's right here!" He shouted it over and over again.

He pulled a pistol from his waistband and pointed it at Marus. Wesley cried out. He dropped his pack and started to run. Marus wondered if the gypsy would shoot him. Unstable men, it seemed, rarely had an unsteady hand. They knew how they'd kill you long before they knew why.

He didn't seem to care about Wesley. The animal-eyed man was at his side, the mouth of the gun caressed Marus's temple.

"You feel it now? Ya feet stuck in tha dirt, but ya heart's tryin' ta get free."

The pistol's cool snout dug at the soft flesh above his cheek as the gypsy brought his own to Marus's chest. His heart was pounding.

"I hear it. 'Run coward! Run!'" He shrieked with laughter.

Marus felt the pressure at his temple, the breath on his neck.

"What do you want? What can I give you? My watch?" Marus tried to keep his voice steady. He pried at the buckle at his wrist, the watch Shey had given him.

The gypsy flashed a smile. Some teeth were yellow, some black, some gone.

"I don't want nothin', 'cept you." He pressed upon the pistol at Marus's temple. It did not waver.

The man wiggled the muzzle, screwing it further into Marus's flesh, and he wondered if anyone had ever died this way. Not by being shot, but *stabbed* with a gun.

Pine needles murmured underfoot in the darkness. A figure emerged from the perfumed dusk. He saw its bald head. The goatee. It was Mike. Out of the corner of his eye, Marus watched as Mike inched closer until a twitch in the gypsy's right hand took precedence, and he lost sight of Mike. Maybe it was too late.

Then, an ear-piercing explosion. The gypsy was limp on the forest floor, his eyes wide, and his mouth, agape. Blood pooled on the ground beneath his matted hair. Marus felt the damp warmth of the gypsy's life flecked across his own face. He touched his cheek and pulled back to examine the blood thickening on his fingertips.

Wesley emerged from the trees, mumbling to himself.

"Oh God, oh God. What the fuck? Oh God." He bent over, throwing up.

"Pick up the gun," Mike said. "And keep up."

■ ■ ■

The true forest met them at the edge of the pines. Out from under the dense roof, the pine-made twilight surrendered to the muted light of late afternoon, hazy and refracted, through slender, bone-colored trunks. A seamless, gilded canopy of quaking aspen and narrowleaf cottonwood danced above in the wind. They weren't like the trees in the city, confined to boxes or breaks in the concrete. They sprang wherever they pleased, growing tall, in tandem, or sloping sharply toward their roots, unrestrained and undecided, as though their course might alter tomorrow. Marus wondered if they were different kinds of aspen and cottonwood, or if it was the environment that changed them.

Mike led with quick, calculated steps. Wesley, still sick, but too terrified not to keep up, remained a few paces behind. Marus made up the rear, the gun under his belt hard at his hip. There wasn't a path or indication that people had walked the

c

route before. The dirt wasn't packed or smooth, and the yellowing grass was undisturbed. Knotty roots broke the surface of scattered leaves to grab at their ankles.

Mike walked on, his squat legs powering up each incline, navigating effortlessly through the undergrowth between stones and fallen branches, never looking down.

There weren't any birds, as Marus thought there might be. It was quiet and colder than he'd expected, and though he couldn't see anything but the blur of trees and Mike's stout figure moving fast ahead of him, he felt eyes all around. The terrain was unforgiving and unfamiliar, but it was what it might conceal that preoccupied him. In every space, each pocket of sun or shadow within the leafy tapestry, he saw the gypsy's undying eyes.

There was unequivocal truth in the gypsy's words that he couldn't quite shake. They were far from the influence or guarantees of the civilized world. He could feel his own vulnerability crawl across his skin. Poisonous spiders, malarial mosquitoes, ticks ridden with Lyme disease. He knew they were out there; he'd read the articles, watched documentaries. And so he swatted in futility at the arm of his jacket and the leg of his pants.

The brush thickened and the sky darkened as the three men continued: the guide and the guided. Marus didn't know how long they'd been walking or how much further they had to go. It was best not to think about it. Head down, one foot in front of the other. That was the task at hand. Whatever came next was anyone's guess. Another gypsy? A storm? Wildlife?

He chose to think of Cade, instead. His grin. The way he watched the world around him. A studious curiosity, like a light beaming from his wide eyes. He was alive. He would grow up and go on to do things, important things, Marus was sure. His own flesh and blood. His legacy.

He thought of Shey. Her eyes, her hair. Her lips against his. Her thighs around him. He loved her. *God, he loved her.* But love wasn't all that kept him going. There was a need deep within him, in the pit of his stomach, a beast kept in the well of his mind, tugging at the rope.

Redemption wasn't just guilt's saving grace; it was everlasting life in the eye of the redeemer. It was forgiveness and immortality, all at once.

23

THEY SPENT TWO nights in the trees.

Huddled close to a low fire, they listened to the distant cry of wolves and the *hoo hoo hoo* of a watchful owl. The slightest ruffle of leaves, a snapping of sticks, was enough to set Wesley on edge. Tormented by every sound, he sat rigid, his body as close to the fire as he could stand, while his head swiveled in search of the source.

With his boots off and his socked feet turned to the flames, it was obvious Mike was at ease in the woods. He led each day's hike and built every fire. At the end of the evening, he'd set his pack behind him, wedge the pistol underneath, and recline. He clasped his hands across his stomach and closed his eyes. A moment later, he was asleep.

"Have you been to the colony before?" Marus asked Wesley on their last night.

"No." He threw a stick into the fire. "Supposedly, it's pretty cool. They've got a full lab. A cooling system, and everything."

"They plan on putting you to work when we get there, I bet."

"Of course," Wesley said. "But I don't mind. I know everyone has to pull their weight. It's a privilege just to be able to go."

"How did you get involved with the patriots?"

"They recruited me."

"From where?"

"A darknet." Wesley broke a twig in two and tossed it into the flames. "A couple of us were building a video feed. It was stupid. Kid stuff. We'd hack cameras all over the city—security cameras, web cams, phones—and piece the footage together for fun. Eventually, we started selling subscriptions to friends of friends. I don't know how, but other people heard about it. Sales were through the roof. One day, we hacked some random guy's phone. At least, that's what we'd thought. By this point, we'd automated a lot of it, so we didn't always know who we were hacking. Anyway, he turned out to be one of Novak's men. Not a gangster, either. Someone higher up. He was meeting with a couple State officials, talking about a job. It sounded shady, but we didn't really know who these guys were or what they were talking about. Apparently, though, one of our viewers did. A patriot. I got a message the next day. It was Emery himself. I quit the feed and joined the cause."

"Do you trust him?"

"Emery? Sure. He's brilliant. I mean, he'd have to be to do what he's doing, but it's more than that. You know, when I was with the feed, I never thought about the consequences. I didn't think about how what I was doing could affect people. I separated it from real life. But to Emery, everything's connected. He acts like he's—*responsible*. Like everything that's happened is his fault, and he won't stop until he makes it right. He says people like us—engineers, scientists, technologists—have to make things right. That we're the only ones who can. We have to take responsibility for our work. *Forward* isn't the right direction if we're headed the wrong way."

The fire hissed and cracked. Somewhere in the distance a coyote called out.

"We better get some sleep," Marus said.

Wesley nodded and lay down. "Good night." He zipped his sleeping bag up to his neck and drew his knees in close.

On his back, Marus could see a hexagon of sky where the trees gave way. Stars among stars. Varying brilliance and size. More than he'd ever seen. More than he'd known existed. They'd been there all along and would be there long after he'd gone. And yet, not even they were everlasting.

■ ■ ■

On the third day, after following a creek bed most of the afternoon, Mike stopped just before a shadowy grouping of trees.

"It's through there," he said.

Marus couldn't see anything at first, but as they moved closer, he saw a trampled path and a humble hunting cabin or ranger's quarters positioned among firs and aspens.

"That?"

Mike didn't respond. He kept on. Marus and Wesley followed. A chipmunk skittered through fallen leaves to the right, and a bird launched from a nearby branch at the left as they moved closer. Through the dim windows of the cabin, Marus could see that it was poorly stocked. Along the far wall there was a bench-like bed topped with a thin, tattered sleeping pad and a moth-eaten blanket. The shelves were bare aside from a coffee can, a can of beans, and a tin of SPAM.

"I don't understand."

Mike forced the door open.

"Set the packs down," he said and took a seat on the bed.

"What are we waiting for?" Marus asked, but Mike didn't respond.

A helicopter flew by somewhere in the distance. Marus set the pack inside the cabin and went out to see.

Some time later, he heard footsteps. A twig cracked underfoot as someone approached. Marus pulled the gypsy's gun from his waistband and walked around the cabin's perimeter. Knocking on the window, he spoke through the filthy glass.

"Someone's here."

Mike didn't move, and Wesley, though visibly concerned, remained at his side.

A man and a woman emerged from the trees behind the cabin. The man registered Marus's gun and moved his hand to his waist, on the butt of his own pistol.

"Easy, Jonas," the woman said.

The man dropped his hand but kept his eyes trained on the gun in Marus's grip.

The woman called out, "You're Marus, aren't you?"

"Yes," he said, eyeing the man, Jonas. "I'm here with Mike."

"I'm Leah," the woman said. "Emery's just landed. He's waiting for you."

Marus hesitated.

"I'll take you."

Marus glanced back through the window. "Let me grab my pack."

"Leave it," Leah said. "Jonas will take it for you."

Leah led Marus through the trees to a large clearing and a much larger cabin. It was lighter in color than the first, clean and modern, with enormous glass windows that consumed the front face. Beyond it, Marus saw another cabin, and another. Modular, some were as tall as three stories high with angled roofs that overhung large patios and balconies. The grounds around them were clean, hard packed, and clear of undergrowth. As the woman brought Marus closer, he could see that the cabins were built in a wide arc. They curved around what looked to be a large, communal fire pit encircled by wooden benches and flanked by a massive outdoor oven. People were cooking at the oven, while others watched from the balconies above. On the far side, two men were chopping wood. A woman passed the split pieces to hands that received them from the inside of a square shed.

Marus's guide led him through the heart of the colony and continued on. They passed what looked to be a large common house, a greenhouse, and a grouping of smaller cabins before they were back in the trees. A narrow, well-groomed trail wound them through the woods and over a considerable creek to a large boulder flecked with orange and black lichen. Through the trees he could see a clearing and a helicopter.

"The stairs are just there," Leah said. She turned and left him standing beside the rock.

Looking up, Marus didn't see it at first. It took him a moment to locate its edges and corners. The structure was long, but narrow, and outfitted with strategically placed mirrors that made it look more like an apparition floating among the trees than a building.

Marus climbed the winding wooden staircase to the treehouse. In the canopy, among the branches and birds, he came to a large mirrored panel with a circular knob at its center. He twisted the knob and pushed the door open.

"Hello?" he said, stepping inside.

A large trunk came through the floor on his left and exited through the ceiling. The branches inside had been cleaned of their twigs and tapered, sculpture-like. Dark wooden floors met the seams of horizontally placed, stone-colored planks that ran from the walls to the ceiling. Enormous windows, squares and rectangles of glass, let in gold and green light that danced with the leaves.

"Hello?" Marus called again.

He walked through the foyer into a large living room. The back of the treehouse was mostly glass. He could see a wooden deck stretch out into the trees. Large wooden recliners were positioned at its end in the sun. A tablet gleamed on a pedestal table beside one of the chairs, but there was no one there.

Marus heard the muted sound of music around a wall to the left. As he rounded the corner, he saw a man sitting, eyes closed, in a white reading chair beside another living tree trunk and a bookcase. Large headphones were cupped over his ears.

He looked familiar, though Marus couldn't place him. His dark hair was pulled back into a bun and a thick, reddish beard concealed the lower portion of his face. He was bare-foot, wearing jeans and a T-shirt. When he opened his eyes, Marus saw the blue in them and was sure they'd met before. Emery removed the headphones and set them on the arm of the chair.

"Marus," he said warmly, rising to his feet. "I didn't hear you come in. Welcome." He walked across the hand-stripped hardwood floors and extended his hand. "It's been a long time." His handshake was firm, trusting.

He smiled, as though waiting for Marus to make the connection.

"Emerson Keller? Founder of Newbold Corp?" He remembered meeting a clean-shaven, shorthaired Emerson six years prior, for a split second, at a developer's conference a few months before he was recruited by the State.

"I prefer Emery."

"You're behind all of this? You're their *leader?*"

"Think of me more as an advisor, a resource."

"But the technology, the infrastructure, it all came from you. Newbold Corp is the reason the Protector Program exists at all."

"It is."

"I don't understand. Why undo it? Why self-sabotage?"

"Would you care for something to eat or drink?" Emery started toward the kitchen.

"I'm fine." Marus stood, trying to make sense of it. Was it a test? A misunderstanding? Recruitment? The cascading sound of music was still coming from the headphones clamped over the armrest.

"You didn't run into any trouble on the way, I hope." Emery pulled the handle of a wooden panel and retrieved a glass.

Somewhere in the forest, the gypsy's undying, animal eyes still stared into the stillness. At the bottom of the pack he'd carried to the hunting cabin, his shirt was still splattered with the man's blood.

"No."

"Good," Emery said, taking a pitcher from the fridge and filling the glass. He set it on the white counter in front of Marus, who took a drink though he hadn't wanted one.

"How do you define patriotism?" Emery asked.

Marus set the glass back on the counter. "Loyalty," he said. "Defending one's country against its enemies."

"For some of the people here, what we're doing, what we're about to do, is first and foremost, an act of patriotism. They are defending principles this country was founded upon. They fight for the nation that once was, and that should be."

Emery took a seat on one of two facing white couches beside a slab of stone that flickered with fire. "Please, join me." He gestured to the empty couch.

Marus did as instructed.

"There's value in making mistakes," Emery said. "At Newbold, we champion that kind of thinking. It's a simple equation: the more you make, the closer you come to success. In fact, I think that's painted on a wall somewhere. Anyway, that *MO* continues to serve us well, so long as three rules are followed. The first: be accountable for your mistakes. The second: make amends for your mistakes. And the third: never make the same mistake twice. I'm the first person to admit I'm wrong. When the State contracted Newbold, I saw it as an opportunity to strengthen the nation. The possibilities seemed endless. We could systematically decrease crime, improve the nation's health, and curb poverty. In the absence of fear, with the aid of machine learning and algorithmic absolutism, we could progress much faster than what was previously possible. Technology would pave the way to Utopia. That's what I thought. But I was wrong."

"The program isn't perfect, but it's progress," Marus said. "The economy is in recovery; people aren't afraid to leave their homes anymore. That's something. The nation's still healing. We have to give it time."

Emery shook his head. "The Protector Program was designed to make the country safer and less prejudiced, enabling society to become proactive, rather than reactive. But it failed. The system didn't eradicate fear; it only altered its form. It's a mistake we have to atone for, Marus, while there's still time."

"What if we start over? If we expose President Sacha and Commissioner Devlin and anyone else involved, we can take the administration down. We can increase transparency and salvage the program."

"Do you know what they do on the tenth floor?" Emery asked.

"I assumed something to do with international affairs."

Emery leaned forward, his elbows coming to rest against the worn denim at his knees. "The tenth floor isn't just a level of the IA, it's an international cyber warfare program. The algos they're developing will enable the State to control the economies of the first and second world. It will give them the ability to override foreign financial markets. Power grids, water supply, public transportation, even healthcare systems could be programmed against the countries that own and rely on them."

"Why?"

"Because the State can. Because they have the technology. It's a form of insurance, a step forward."

Marus remembered the pen on Gene's desk. *History is written by the victors.*

"There is no transparency, Marus. It can't exist. Surveillance doesn't go both ways. There are those who watch, and those who are watched; the powerful, and the powerless. The government wants us to believe that privacy is dangerous and frivolous. Antiquated even. But it's necessary. If we give up our privacy, we risk our individualism, too, and with it, innovation and progress itself.

"Think about the process of innovation. Many times, you have to step outside of what's considered normal or acceptable. You have to take risks and make mistakes. But under surveillance, we learn to censor, to conform. Our values and morals become fixed as a society. Over time, we atrophy. We become more easily controlled. A mass surveillance state can't remain a democratic one, Marus."

Marus leaned forward. "When the public learns the truth, people will lash out. They'll do terrible things, and without some kind of system in place, there will be no way to prevent or stop it. It will be chaos."

"There are good people out there, Marus. Trustworthy politicians, dedicated cops. They still exist. When the State falls, they will rise and put the nation back together."

The floorboards creaked from the loft above. Marus stole a glance, but there was nothing to see but the trees on the other side of the window billowing in the wind. "I was told my wife was here," he said.

"Not anymore."

"Where is she?"

"Up north, on a recruiting mission. She's been a powerful asset to us."

"When will she be back?"

"I'll send my pilot after her. It shouldn't be more than a couple days."

"Harford?"

"The helicopter. It'll be faster," Emery said. "Mike told me you thought you could help us."

Marus nodded, surprised. "I know the State's systems better than anyone. With access to your lab, I can help you bypass security and get the information you need."

"We'd be grateful for your help. The team is in the process of mapping the State's networks and pulling back the rest of the documents. If all goes as planned, the first wave of stories will break tomorrow evening. Once we have what we need, you'll have to dismantle the program and execute a system-wide wipe. Every last bit of code has to be destroyed. Are you willing to do that?"

Marus hesitated.

"Yes," he said, finally.

"Good." Emery stood, indicating that it was time for Marus to leave. "Leah will take you to Shey's cabin. You'll be comfortable there."

"Thank you." Marus extended his hand.

"I'm glad you are with us," Emery said, meeting Marus's handshake with both hands. "I hope you like it here." He returned to his reading chair on the other side of the fireplace and Marus showed himself out.

When he glanced back, he saw that Emery had already replaced the headphones over his ears and closed his eyes.

24

THE QUARTER CABINS, as Leah called them, were four-hundred-square-foot wedges, stacked and scattered around the fire pit. Each had its own bedroom and bathroom, a small living area equipped with a wood-burning stove, a kitchenette, and an outdoor landing. Some appeared larger, nicer, with better accommodations. Marus wondered who resided in them and why.

Leah led Marus around the colony, appearing to take pleasure in the tour. "People think the colony will be like one of those crazy camps, all tarps and cardboard, but really it's nicer than any resort I've ever been to."

"How did he keep it secret?"

"It wasn't so much a secret as it was an early investment. Before the New Era, when the tiny house movement went bust and the largest modular, mobile cabin manufacturer went bankrupt, Emery scooped its units. He donated dozens but saved quite a number for himself."

She led him past several of the quarter cabins and over the creek.

"Water is clean and plentiful," she said. "It's captured from the creek and collected when it rains. We run it through an advanced filtration system Newbold developed."

"What about power?"

"A combination of solar energy, hydropower, and generators provide electricity and radiant heating."

Marus remembered Newbold's early efforts in solar. Hadn't they taken to building their own generators, too?

"Does Emery pay for it all?" he asked.

"He set us up to begin with," Leah said, "but every resident has to pay for extraction and their place at the colony. It's not cheap, either. It's several thousand dollars just to remove the iD and get here. Not to mention the cost of the cabins, supplies, food. There aren't any freebies—you have to earn your keep. Emery wanted to make sure that people were committed, both to the colony and to the cause."

Suddenly, the weekly transfers Ballo had found from Shey's bank account made sense. She'd been buying her way in, maybe buying Marus's way in, too.

"Most supplies are airlifted in via drone," Leah said. She glanced down at his shoes. "We can get you some more clothes, if you like."

They continued down a path, and Leah pointed out the lab. Even through the trees, Marus could see that it was massive.

"I still don't understand how the State doesn't know about any of this."

"Emery purchased his privacy, just like the rest of the higher ups," Leah said. "Besides, Newbold is their greatest asset.

Why should the government be concerned about him, when he's profited from the Protector Program more than anyone?"

They wound down another path, and Marus saw what looked like a deer trail snaking its way through the trees toward another large structure with a wide rolling door. An army cargo truck was parked beside it.

"There's a road?"

"You could call it that," Leah said. "It's an old forest service road. It hasn't seen much use in recent years."

"And what's that building?"

"That's just storage," she said and turned the other way.

Through the trees, Marus could see several men lifting crates out of the warehouse and loading them onto the truck. They nodded at him and continued with their work.

Leah led Marus back toward the fire pit without another word.

"This one is Shey's," she said, stopping in front of one of the cabins. "Dinner is at seven around the fire pit. You should come and meet everyone."

Shey's cabin looked no different than the rest. Several steps led to a small patio at the foot of the front door. He had to step around a woven chair to knock. Several seconds passed. Someone laughed from a nearby patio. Marus looked back at the fire pit. Two people assembled a large teepee of wood at the center of the pit. Marus opened the door.

There was a small sitting area and wood-burning stove flanked by a short stack of wood. Books were piled atop a tiny table that separated two chairs in front of the stove. Marus picked up the top book and leafed through. It was the same collection of essays and poems he'd seen Shey pack the day she'd left. The same faded, yellow note bookmarked Ralph Waldo Emerson's essay, "Self Reliance."

Emerson. Emery.

He wondered how long they'd known each other and if Emery could be trusted. Marus set the book down and continued toward the kitchenette. There was a short counter, a sink, two electric burners, pantry space, and a mini fridge.

A narrow hallway led to two sliding doors. To the left, behind the kitchenette, there was a small bathroom, outfitted with a toilet, sink, and shower stall. He picked up the toothbrush on the counter and examined it. Wouldn't she have taken it with her to go up north?

At the end of the hallway was the bedroom. A bed and closet took up most of the space. He slid the closet door open. There were her things. The sweaters he'd seen her pack, the duffel bag she'd thrown over her shoulder before leaving. Opposite the closet, centered on the back wall, a small window provided a view of the forest floor and another modular quarter cabin, stacked three high. In the corner of the room, a foot from the window, Marus saw a small wooden shelf. A triangle that served as a nightstand. Atop it, propped up against the wall, was a photograph of the three of them: Marus, Shey, and Cade.

■ ■ ■

He woke from a dream to the sound of laughter and shouting, the quiet thrum of a lonely guitar. It was getting dark out, and for a moment, he'd didn't know where he was. The picture of his family rested beside the pillow. He'd fallen asleep clutching it and had creased one of the corners.

It had been taken on their wedding day at the gardens. Shey was wearing a simple, white dress, and he, a white button-down shirt and khaki slacks. He was looking at her, and she was looking at Cade, who was only one year old at the time. He sat between them, smiling as big as he could, looking at someone next to the photographer. It was Vic, Marus remembered. In that first year of Cade's life, only Marus's dad could make Cade smile that way.

Cade had been Vic's second chance. A shot at redemption. As a grandfather, he was more attentive, more caring, more patient. Somehow, in becoming a grandfather, he'd become a better father, too. He'd made amends, or at least tried to. Marus had forgiven him. The past was in the past. He'd told him that, hadn't he?

He wondered if he'd get the chance to tell his dad that his grandson was alive. Maybe that would be a reason for him to continue living. Maybe one day, when everything had blown over, they'd take Cade to a fútbol game, after all.

Marus smoothed the corner out as best he could and replaced the photo on the shelf.

■ ■ ■

Outside of Shey's cabin, the colony had come to life. There was a sweet, smoky scent in the air. An enormous fire danced in the circular pit as people ate around it. Someone was passing out plates of food. Many were sitting and talking. A young woman stared blankly at the flames as children laughed and ran between the trees beside her.

Marus watched them play, astonished that children lived here at all. What a strange and magical upbringing a child would have in the forest. The possibility hadn't occurred to him before. But now, seeing the tiny silhouettes in front of the fire, as they wove in and out of the trees, brought the possibility the weeks and months and years ahead of him held back into view. His family would be reunited, and they could live here in the cover of trees, far from the chaos, confusion, and uncertainty that awaited the city.

On the far side of the fire pit, Marus saw Mike sitting beside the same man who'd come for them at the hunting cabin. The two talked seriously, quietly, to one another. On the other side, Wesley was eating by himself. His lanky figure hunched over the food reminded Marus of The Hat.

Marus continued down an aisle toward the fire pit, aware of the eyes all around him. A woman approached with a plate of food.

"Baked beans, carrots, and pork," she said, handing it to him.

"Thank you," he said.

"Thanks for being with us." She smiled and returned to the counter near the outdoor oven.

Eager to sit beside a familiar face, Wesley called him over.

"This is nuts, right?" he said, pushing his glasses back.

"It's something," Marus said, taking a forkful of baked beans. A boy and a girl, about Cade's age, were throwing rocks at a bullseye carved into a nearby tree trunk.

"Have you seen the lab?"

Marus shook his head. "Not yet, tomorrow."

"I thought what we had on Takara was cool. This one, it's serious stuff. Everything is state of the art from Newbold." Wesley shoveled the rest of the pork on his plate into his mouth. "I just found out who Emery really is. That guy, Jonas, told me. I didn't believe him at first. But then I saw the cabins, the server room, all *this*, and realized he's the only person—maybe on the planet—who could make something like this happen. Have you met him yet?" he said, his mouth full and his words barely decipherable.

"Yeah, we spoke earlier."

"In his treehouse?"

Marus nodded.

The lenses of his glasses reflected firelight, but Marus could still see his wide, curious eyes.

"*Well*, what was it like?"

"It's nice," he said, turning toward the flames. The woman across the pit was still staring, transfixed.

"I bet it was more than nice," Wesley said. "You know why he built it, right?"

"Because he could."

"He came up with all of his early ideas in his treehouse as a kid. Said it had something to do with being elevated, away from everything else, and close to nature. Sound like any place you know?"

"Sounds like this."

"I would have thought, at best, it'd be all dorms and common showers and stuff. But he's not lying when he says privacy is important." Wesley wiped the rest of his plate clean and set it on the bench beside him.

"Have you gone through any more of the files?" Marus asked.

Wesley nodded. "Some stuff. It's all pretty fucked up. Remember that school shooting back east? Well, I found the State's file on the guy who did it. He was in trouble for tax fraud. Owed a ton of money to the government and had racked up crazy debt in hospital bills because he's got a daughter with special needs. Well, lo and behold, his debt is expunged, and his family is gifted a million dollars just three weeks after the cops laid him down in the school parking lot."

"And it ties back to the Administration?"

"Even the president is a puppet. It's someone else, manipulating him. Or at least, that's what it looks like. The way the data was organized and encrypted, I don't know if anyone knows the whole truth."

"What about my son? Were you able to find out where they're keeping him?"

Wesley shook his head. "Not yet."

"And the data repositories? Have you guys been able to locate them?"

"Yeah, we can get all of them remotely, except for one. It's completely offline."

"Black Mine Bunker," Marus said.

"Yeah. I didn't think it actually existed, but they found it."

"Where?"

"Apparently, just a couple hundred miles from here."

A woman gathered up most of the young children and led them back to the row of quarter cabins. Without their play, the circle grew quiet. Voices hushed as eyes fell to the fire, which cracked and hissed. Slowly, those sitting around the fire dispersed. Marus watched as they peeled away in small groups and pairs, and walked toward the cabins.

"Well, I'm going to call it." Wesley stood and tossed his napkin into the pit. "I'll see you tomorrow," he said, and started off toward a far cabin.

Marus watched the napkin ignite. Soon, it was nothing more than a flame itself.

On the other side of the pit, Mike hardly moved. He stared straight into the fire, as though he were looking through it. A woman Marus hadn't seen yet sat a few feet from him. Her dark eyes moved with each undulation as though she were watching a performance.

What was it that was so mesmerizing about fire? Its ability to give life? To take it away?

Marus remembered how Cade was drawn to it as a baby. Most babies were, it seemed. Their heads bobbed as they sought sources of light. A fixture on the ceiling, lights above the mirror, the flames lapping at the glass in the fireplace. Their young, round eyes gaped, captivated. Just like the woman's now.

But when he looked closer, Marus realized it wasn't the fire she watched with such interest. The black discs of her eyes moved not with the tongues of flame, but with what they consumed. Moths. Dozens of them dove headlong into the inferno. Spinning and twisting, they crumpled like paper before falling between charred logs and out of sight. The woman looked pleased, as though she were happy to watch them burn.

When Mike stood to leave, Marus rose and followed. He didn't move in the direction of the cabins, but away, toward the woods.

A few minutes passed before Mike acknowledged him.

"I thought you'd be in bed by now. Early morning for you, you know," he said, continuing through the trees.

"I don't need much sleep." Marus followed Mike's familiar silhouette as he had during their journey to the colony. It was much easier now that his pace was leisurely. His route, less direct. "Where are you headed?" Marus asked.

"Nowhere in particular," he said without looking back. He tipped his head up at the dark figure of a tree. "People get so used to walking with a destination in mind. Out here, it's easier to wander. To lose yourself."

"And that's when you find yourself," Marus said, more to himself than Mike.

Mike's shadowed shape turned toward him. "Yeah, something like that."

Somewhere above them, the hasty purr of a helicopter grew louder.

"What happened on Takara?" Marus asked.

"Novak's men got to it. That's all we know, but I'm not holding my breath for any miracles. They're as good as dead if they aren't already. I just hope it was swift."

Mike continued on, and Marus matched his pace.

"There were going to be casualties," Mike said. "That's just how it goes. The only thing we can do is press on and make sure it wasn't for nothing."

"And you think Axtell could be one of those casualties?" Marus asked.

"What do you think?"

If you go looking for the truth and you find it, it becomes part of you. And from then on, you'll live either trying to change it or learning to accept it. Axtell hadn't said anything about dying for it, but Marus suspected the journalist would have done anything to expose the truth.

"I think if he was, it'd be how he'd want to go."

Mike's silhouette turned toward Marus, but he said nothing.

"For the truth, I mean," Marus said.

"We all die sooner or later. Might as well be for something."

"What's your something?"

"My cause?"

"Yeah. Why are you here?"

Mike thought about it for a while. "To matter," he said finally. "I guess that's all it comes down to. Not very profound." He laughed.

"I understand what you mean, though. That's why I went to work for the State. I thought I could make a difference."

"I'm sure you did."

"Not the difference I wanted to make," Marus said.

Mike stopped and faced him. "None of us makes the difference we want to," he said.

The helicopter was almost directly over them. It threw wind through the trees, rippling the collar of Marus's jacket as it passed. A moment later, it came down. Marus heard the whine of its blades as they slowed to a stop.

"Do you need help finding your way back?" Mike asked.

"I'll manage."

"I'll see you tomorrow." Mike disappeared down a trail to the right.

It was the deer path, Marus realized.

25

MARUS PUSHED BACK several branches for a better look. From his low crouch, he could barely make out the building's edges against the blackness of the surrounding forest. The rolling door had been lowered, but not closed. A bar of light near the bottom revealed two pairs of legs inside the warehouse. Mike and someone else.

Ten minutes passed. It started to rain. The drizzle was slow and soft, but cold as it clung in fat droplets to his hair, trickling down his forehead and the back of his neck.

The large door was rolled back, revealing the silhouettes of those inside. The crates were gone, and a third person had emerged. One of the men was shorter and thinner than the other two. Marus was almost certain it was Emery. He could hear them talking but couldn't make out their voices or any of the words. His legs burned from his squat among the weeds. If he moved now, he'd risk his position. Slowly, he lowered a knee to the ground and leaned forward.

An owl sounded from the canopy above before taking flight. One of the men walked from the light of the warehouse around the front of the truck and climbed inside its cab. The truck roared to life, and the headlights shot beams directly at Marus. He pitched forward into the undergrowth to dodge the light. The sharp end of a twig grazed his left cheek as he met the ground.

The truck pulled forward. Turning a tight circle, it disappeared through the trees at the back of the building. The sound of its engine grew faint until it was barely audible above the din of rain.

Leaves rustled, and a stick cracked under the weight of footsteps to Marus's right. The taller, rounder of the two remaining silhouettes switched on a flashlight and threw its beam into the trees.

The warehouse went black except for the small thread of light in Mike's hands. Marus could hear the crash of the rolling door as it was pulled shut. Another light switched on in the hands of the other man, and they went their separate ways. One beam, deeper into the trees, and another, across the path and out of sight.

■ ■ ■

By the time Marus returned to the row of quarter cabins, the rain had picked up. A column of steam rose where the massive fire had roared. The air smelled of smoke and earth. Somewhere among black branches, an owl called into the night.

He climbed the steps to Shey's cabin and twisted the knob, looking over his shoulder for Mike or any passersby, but he was alone. No one watched out here. No one but the owl who kept the forest's secrets. Marus shook off the rain and stepped inside.

The cabin glowed from the warmth pulsing in the stove. Someone had stoked it, he realized, though much of the wood had burned down. He kept on his coat and crept further into the room. The books on the table had been straightened. He looked toward the end of the hallway but couldn't tell in the darkness if the door was open or closed.

"Shey? Is that you?"

The bedroom door slid open, and the light flipped on and there was his wife staring back at him.

She ran toward him. Rain flung from his jacket as she collapsed into his arms.

He held her as if his grasp could bind them forever. She cried into his chest and tried to speak, but the words were indiscernible. He straightened his arms to look at her. Fat tears streaked her cheeks and rolled off her chin. The front of her T-shirt was wet with tears and the rain he'd brought inside.

"Sorry," he said, peeling off his jacket and flinging it to the floor.

She closed her eyes and opened them again, as though she thought it might be a dream, and he pulled her into his chest again and breathed in the smell of her hair, so different than he remembered.

"I didn't know if I'd ever see you again," he whispered, crying.

"I didn't know you were coming," she said, the tears glistening in her eyes. "I wouldn't have gone if I'd known."

"It's okay."

"I'm so sorry, Marus. I—I—"

"Shh. We're together now."

There was so much to tell her. An entire lifetime had passed in the weeks she'd been gone. An eternity between them. He wondered if she knew about Reagan. So much had happened. He'd been drugged and dragged from their home. There'd been the promotion. The falling out with Gene. Then there was Anj. Had Shey known about Devlin? Did she know what the tenth floor really was? He would have to tell her about his father. About Axtell. But, more important than any of that, he needed to tell her that their son might still be alive.

"There's a video of Cade. It was filmed just a few days ago."

Now it was she who straightened her arms to look at him, a question forming in her glossy eyes.

"He's still alive."

She inhaled hard, choking for air. Her lips quivered, and her eyes flickered, and she fell into him. Grabbing the fabric at his chest, she let out a single sob.

"You were right," Marus said. "He's alive."

He's alive. Our son is alive. As though understanding the news for the first time himself, he wanted to say it again and again.

Shey shivered under his arms, too stunned to speak. Marus led her to the fire and set a fresh log atop the embers in the stove. It erupted in flame. Wrapping her in a blanket, he sat down beside her. Her face glowed orange in the firelight. To him, she'd never looked more beautiful.

"Where is he?" she said, finally.

"I don't know yet," he said.

She turned from the fire to meet his eyes. The fear he'd seen that morning on the soccer field was gone. Something else had taken its place.

"What happened?" His flesh burned as she traced her finger across the fresh cut along his cheek.

"Nothing." He took her hand and noticed the thin, red incision along her wrist that matched his own. Gently, he kissed it. "I'll find him, Shey. I will. I promise."

"And then?"

"Then I'll never let either of you go." He brushed the hair from her face and brought her lips to his. The kiss was long and slow and sweet.

The rain fell hard outside, and the fire pulsed in front of them as they opened their bodies to one another.

26

IT WAS STILL dark when Marus heard the first knock.

Shey's body, warm at his side, had barely stirred all night. Her breath was deep, but easy. Though he could see only the dark outline of her head against the pillow, he thought she looked peaceful, happy. Perhaps she'd dreamt of Cade. Of the reunion that awaited them. He didn't allow himself to think in ifs.

He hadn't expected much sleep, himself, but it washed over him, tossing him wholly into its depths the moment he closed his eyes. The knock came again, louder this time. He slid out of bed and met the cold floor with bare feet. The stove at the entry had been reduced to a pile of smoldering embers. The blanket and his jacket were still strewn across the floor.

Marus cracked the door. The familiar shape of Mike's round, bald head waited in the faint light of the patio. A red glow burned between his lips.

Mike took the cigarette from his mouth. "Time to work," was all he said.

"I'll be out in a minute," Marus replied with eyes half open.

He fumbled in the dark for his jeans and shirt, remembering the way they'd come off only hours before. Shey stirred but didn't wake. He wished she would if only to reassure him that she'd still be there when he returned. He kissed her forehead, his lips barely grazing her skin, and lingered a moment to see if she'd open her eyes, but she was somewhere far off, dreaming.

Mike exhaled a cloud of smoke as Marus descended the steps to join him. The rain had stopped but the air, cool and clean, carried its weight.

"What happened to your face?"

"I tripped last night on my way back. What time is it?"

"Four thirty."

Mike crouched and pushed the cigarette into the wet earth. He stood and slid the butt into his pocket. "I told you it was going to be an early morning," he said, switching on the yellow flashlight in his left hand.

A column of light illuminated their way past other cabins and into the woods. The trail wasn't as established as those that connected the quarter cabins to the common house, greenhouse, and fire pit, but it was decipherable, three feet of semi-packed ground that wended through the trees.

"I didn't realize it was going to be *this* early," Marus said, struggling to match Mike's pace.

"There's a lot to do yet."

Marus could hear the water gushing just beyond the trail to their right. On the other side of the creek, somewhere among the trees, Emery's treehouse hovered. The flashlight came to a break in the trees atop a small incline. As they emerged, Marus saw it. Several small external lights cast a dim orange ring around the building. Long and narrow, it was much larger than he expected, constructed from reclaimed wood and concrete at the water's edge. The creek likely fed a cold-water cooling system that prevented the server room from getting too hot. He'd come to expect nothing less from Emery.

Mike pried open the heavy wooden door and turned on the lights.

"No security?" Marus asked, stepping inside.

"It isn't necessary."

The building's ceilings were vaulted, with large, trapezoidal panels of glass off of the rafters. Wide, weathered boards coated in polyurethane extended lengthwise from the door. Rows of desks and computers lined the perimeter of the room. At the center, several round tables provided areas for collaboration. As with the IA, there was even a ping pong table at the back.

"It's impressive."

"Emery wanted you to get a jump on accessing the rest of the State's networks. The first stories break today. He wants to wipe everything before then. The security patch needs to go live as soon as possible."

Marus nodded.

"Wesley and the others will be here around seven. Enjoy the quiet while you can."

"Will you turn off the lights?" Marus asked, taking a seat at the computer.

Mike shook his head and sighed but flipped the switch on his way out.

The code was a tunnel. A string he wove, then tugged. But he had to be careful, methodical. If he wasn't, he'd leave a trail, his very own set of digital footprints.

In the dark, with the screen in front of him, he felt most alive. Every sense was turned and tuned to the lines in front of him. There was a slow separation of self, a oneness with the code. It was automatic, fluid. Effortless.

Sometimes, he'd catch himself humming along with the machines and wonder how long he'd been doing it. The sound was nearly indistinguishable from his own breath, the rush of blood through his veins. Time surrendered, and there was nothing but the thread spun from his fingertips. The moment of creation, of triumph. A point of no return.

Afterward, he'd try to follow the logic, the mental process, but could never keep up. It was best just to let go, to succumb to *flow*. How many hours had he spent in dark rooms like this? That was a stereotype he found to be true. Programmers didn't always work in basements, but they did enjoy working in the dark. The rest of the world faded to black. *The only way out is through*. Robert Frost said that. Coding was writing, after all.

Marus opened Nmap. Wesley and the team had used the tool to take inventory, mapping the State's networks and auditing security while they were pulling back files. He was supposed to add to it, to make the map larger, deeper, more complex. Hacking was a form of guerrilla warfare. The lines were the trenches.

The backdoor they'd established on Gene's machine had given them access through the VPN. But there were other networks they needed to infiltrate to manipulate State security.

Once he was in, Marus and the others could override protocol in the same way Wesley had infiltrated street cameras and accessed major publishing platforms and media outlets. The patriots would use the infrastructure the IA had built with the help of Newbold Corp. technology and turn it against the State. All of the data would be destroyed. The networks, the program, everything. But it would all be pointless if the patriots didn't destroy the final repository. The State's backup, Black Mine Bunker.

Marus thought suddenly of the crates from the warehouse. The truck, riding low with their weight. *Were they weapons? Explosives?* Were the patriots planning to blow the facility up, and with it, everything and everyone inside? *Jesus.* There would be hundreds of people at that facility. State employees just like him, and maybe, his son among them. What had Axtell said? *If the State was keeping hostages, it might keep them there.*

Marus left Nmap open and moved to another machine. His fingers glided swiftly over the keyboard as he typed. It was a simple piece of code. Simple questions that required simple answers. *Where is my son? Where is Black Mine Bunker?* He pressed *enter*, and the thread went out. A string of characters—parameters and queries—probing for clues. For vulnerabilities. That's what hacking boiled down to: exploiting weaknesses. Flaws tucked deep inside a system. Quiet, but telling.

He found Cade's file, the one Wesley had retrieved from one of the State's servers, and pored over the details. He watched the video to see if it provided any hints, but white walls were white walls, regardless of where they were located. Marus read and reread descriptions and notes, observations

Cade's abductors made about him. *Luca Valdetti is the key*, one wrote.

Of course.

Marus imagined the man in the brown windbreaker and baseball cap. It didn't matter how much time passed, he would never be able to shake the image of his son being led away. Now, at least, he knew why Cade hadn't put up a fight.

He went through every single document cached in Cade's folder, but there was nothing to confirm or disprove whether or not Cade was being held at Black Mine Bunker. Even if there were, Marus would have to find where the repository was hidden. Wesley and the others had scraped and decrypted hundreds of thousands of State documents. Over the years, the State had commissioned hundreds of kidnappings, most before the New Era began. Documents showed ransoms requested and paid. Checks cut to criminals. Balances pocketed by the State. Marus's query went through each of these, too, searching dates and times, visual cues and geotag data, but he couldn't find anything on the repository.

The sound of laughing children came from just beyond the wall of the lab. Marus straightened, straining his ears over the thrum of machines. Not children, he realized, coyotes. Their ghoulish cries could carry for miles, but the volume told him they were right outside. He crept toward the back windows and peered into the darkness in the direction of the creek. The orange rim of light around the building illuminated their backs as they drank. He'd thought coyotes were solitary beings, that they hunted and lived alone. Yet, here were three, taking turns lapping up the water and watching the night. Together, they increased their odds of survival. Or so it seemed. In another instant they were gone, skittering off into the trees.

The sun rose behind the mountain, washing the lab with gray light. It was 6:14 a.m., and Wesley and the others were due in less than an hour. He hadn't run a single script to map any of the State's redundant networks, but the script he'd written had gone through thousands of video logs, photographs, and assessments for many of the State's hostages and still hadn't found where they were kept. Black Mine Bunker seemed the only viable option, and yet, he had no way of proving its existence, let alone the possibility that Cade was there. Marus had been able to infiltrate some of the most secure networks in the world, but he hadn't been able to find his son.

■ ■ ■

By the time Wesley and the others arrived, Marus had moved back to the first computer and written, run, and rewritten several programs, but he'd only infiltrated and mapped two redundant networks out of dozens. Maybe hundreds.

"Huh," Wesley said, a thermos of coffee in one hand and a plate of bacon in the other. Hunched over, he scooted closer to the machine, examining Marus's work. "Well, looks like we've got some work to do." He extended the plate of bacon. "Here, have some brain food."

Marus took a strip, greasy and translucent at the middle.

A dozen people shuffled in and took their seats at empty machines. A thin woman with short, spiky hair moved to sit beside Marus, at the computer that was still querying databases for anything pertaining to Black Mine Bunker. He reached for the chair to stop her.

"Do you mind? I was using this one, too."

"Double fisting," Wesley said.

When the woman had moved on to another workstation, Marus whispered. "I think they're going to blow up Black Mine Bunker."

Wesley dangled a piece of bacon and dropped it into his mouth. "I guess they'd have to, huh? There's no way to access it remotely, and hacking in once they're there would take too long." He looked at his watch. "We're pushing it as it is. Emery wants everything wiped by three o'clock. I kind of thought you'd have a couple dozen networks mapped by now."

"There have to be hundreds of people who work there."

"I'm sure they'll get everyone out in time."

"How?"

"They're going to use a security override to replace the existing protocol so they can get to the server rooms."

"I think Cade's at Black Mine Bunker," Marus said. "Axtell mentioned he thought the State kept hostages there."

Marus wondered how far the cargo truck had gone by now. Even if the patriots infiltrated the facility's security and led the hostages out before sending it up in flames, there would be casualties.

That's just how it goes, Mike had said.

"If the facility is offline, how did they get the protocol?" Marus asked.

"I based it off of what we've seen at the PSC. I'm sure it's relatively the same. Security protocols usually are. Lock doors.

Seal exits. I reversed the facility's lockdown procedures so that it will automatically unlock and open every door." Wesley's lips shined with bacon grease. "If we found out where Cade was in the facility and knew where State personnel was stationed in relation to him, we could use the building's systems to separate them and get Cade out."

"How are we going to find out where Cade is in the building if I can't even locate the building?"

"I don't know, but if we don't map the rest of the networks and wipe the data in time, we're going to have bigger problems."

"I have to find my son."

Wesley pushed his glasses back and surveyed the room. "Yeah, yeah. Of course," he said, nodding. "Don't worry, we got this. If you can't get to Emery, try talking to Mike. I think he's the one coordinating the ground strike. He could tell them to keep an eye out for your son, or else, buy you a little time."

"Thanks."

"Good luck, Marus."

"You too."

■ ■ ■

Around the pit, the colony was awake and active. The fire was already crackling, and a man stooped over it to ladle black liquid from a pot into several coffee mugs. On the other side of the oven, a woman passed out pancakes. The smell of bacon hung in the air. There was no sign of Emery or Mike.

Shey sat in the first row of benches around the fire. Her slender frame folded forward as she picked something from the ground and tossed it into the pit. A man in a red Baja jacket approached and whispered something into her ear. He nodded seriously at Shey's response and left as though taking an order. She was the axis of this place, Marus realized. As if in orbit, everyone moved around her, aware of her presence. Groups of two and three watched her as they ate; others smiled and nodded while passing by. She directed people here and there. Even the children seemed quieter around her. He wondered how much she really knew.

She turned and spotted Marus by the trees. A shy smile spread slowly across her face. It was the same look she used to give when she caught him watching her with Cade, or in the kitchen, or across a crowded room. The same smile she'd worn at the end of their first date. An invitation to know and be known.

"I need to talk to you," he said, taking a seat beside her.

"Good morning to you, too." She brought her mug to her lips and looked out at the others gathering nearby.

There was an energy about the colony. A quiet excitement building.

"We've waited for this day for a while," she said.

Things were different now, he could tell. They were different. There was a delicate reality that hung in the air between them. They danced around it, unsure how to move forward, not knowing if it should be discussed or left alone.

"I really need to speak with you. Can we go someplace quiet?"

"What is it? Is it Cade?"

Marus walked back into the trees, and Shey followed. At the bridge, he stopped and faced her. The creek gurgled below. Somewhere ahead and above, Emery's treehouse loomed in the canopy, invisible.

"Have you heard about Black Mine Bunker?"

"I knew they were looking for it."

"Did you know they were planning to blow it up?"

"I heard that Emery might send a team on the ground, if they weren't able to access the servers remotely."

"Well, he has. They loaded a truck up with a bunch of crates late last night. I think they were explosives."

"They have to destroy the servers. The plan won't work if the data isn't destroyed."

"Whose plan?"

"What do you mean, *whose plan*? The patriot plan," Shey said. "Our plan."

"If the repository is what people say it is, there will be hundreds of State employees at that facility."

"Don't pity the State, Marus. You've seen what they've done."

"I'm not talking about the State. I'm talking about people. Hundreds of them, Shey. People no different than me."

"They are different. They're the upper echelon. They know what they're a part of, you didn't. They are the State."

"So, you just blow them up? Jesus, Shey. You're starting to sound like a fearist."

"Don't you dare," she said, taking a step away from him. "You have no idea what I've lost."

"*Really?* Because I've lost those things, too, Shey." He stepped toward her. "We don't have much time. Who knows how close that truck is now. We need to go to Emery."

"He won't—"

"Listen to me, Shey! We can't let them blow up that facility." He reached out a hand. "I don't know for sure, yet, but I think Cade might be there."

Her eyes went wide and she lurched forward, as if to strike him. "Why didn't you say that to begin with?"

"Because…it can't be about that. Emery won't listen if that's our only argument. It's not just about our son anymore, Shey. It's about doing the right thing. Period."

27

SHEY KNOCKED FIRST. The front door was cracked open, but no one answered.

"Before you say anything, let me try talking to him," she said.

"What will you say?"

"I'll think of something." She pushed the door open and stepped inside. "Emery?"

The foyer was clear, as was the great room. Marus looked to the corner by the bookcase, half expecting to find Emery the way he had the day before, but the chair was empty. The headphones, gone.

The wind had picked up. Tree branches clawed at the glass on all sides. The entire structure seemed to creak as though it were a swaying ship. Through the skylights, the clouds were slate and darkening.

From the bedroom above, they heard voices.

"Emery?" Shey called again.

Emery appeared, barefoot and shirtless, at the top of the stairs. His long hair was wet and down around his ears. There was something about his demeanor that reminded Marus of the gypsy and sent a shiver down his spine.

"Oh," Shey said, startled by his appearance. "Sorry."

"What can I do for you?" Emery patted at his chin with the small towel he was holding. He'd shaved his beard and was starting to look more like Emerson than Emery.

"We were hoping to speak with you."

"Speak away," Emery said, descending from the loft to meet them in the kitchen. His eyes were bloodshot. His skin, pale and gleaming. From water or sweat, Marus couldn't tell. He leaned back against the counter, flashing a fresh, red pinprick in the crease of his arm. Upstairs, the floorboards creaked as someone moved about in the bedroom.

"We wanted to talk about Black Mine Bunker," Shey said, "and what your plan is."

"My plan," Emery said. It wasn't a question, but he didn't say anything else.

"I saw the crates and the truck," Marus said. "You're going to blow it up, aren't you?"

Emery didn't speak. Instead, his eyes fluttered backward, and he fell sideways to the floor.

"We need help," Marus called to whoever was upstairs.

Shey rushed to Emery's side and turned him over. There was the sound of a door shutting and then another one opening, and Mike was at the landing.

Mike and Marus carried Emery upstairs.

"He's a junkie?" Marus said.

Mike heaved Emery onto the bed. "No," he said. "He's sick."

■ ■ ■

Emery's room was outfitted with several machines. Clear plastic bags hung from a metal arm above his bed.

"It's sickle cell," Mike said. "His body can't fight off infection like yours or mine can. He should've gone to a doctor days ago." Mike moved closer to insert an IV, but Emery waved him off.

"Leave it alone, Mike. I'm fine."

Mike disappeared through a large sliding door at the back of the room and rolled it closed behind him.

"You were saying something about Black Mine Bunker."

Shey glanced at Marus as if to tell him to keep quiet.

"Yes," she said. "We're concerned about the people there. We understand the need to destroy the facility, but we were wondering if there wasn't some other way."

"You think your son is there." He rolled his head to the side to cough.

"There are hundreds of people there," Marus said. "We have no idea how much they know. It's likely most of them weren't involved at all."

"He isn't there," Emery said.

"What?" Shey asked.

"Cade isn't at Black Mine Bunker."

Marus moved to the edge of the bed. "How do you know?"

Through the door came the sound of Cade's voice. "I just want to go home."

"Baby?" Shey pushed past Marus and pulled the door open.

Mike was sitting on a chair looking at the far wall and a large screen that hung there. On the screen, Cade spoke quietly into a camera. The Protective Services Center loomed behind him. A hand streaked with short, black hairs gripped his shoulder. "I miss my mom and dad," Cade said. Below him, the news ticker scrolled. PROTECTOR'S SON PLEAS FOR PARENTS' RETURN. The camera panned out. The hand belonged to Commissioner Devlin, who waved the reporters away.

A woman at a news desk leaned into the camera. "Earlier this week, authorities learned that formerly accused Anthony Jennings did not act alone in the abduction of Cadien Vanguard-Winde. Police apprehended this man, a known fearist leader, who, despite an early altercation, proved cooperative, leading investigators to the home where Vanguard-Winde was being held."

A large photograph filled the screen momentarily. It was The Hat. Christopher Axtell's right eye was rimmed in black and blue. His lip was cut open.

"The fearist leader was found dead in his cell this morning after an apparent suicide. In related news, investigators say the knife found at the home on Takara Way, where Vanguard-Winde was being held, is the same knife that was used in Reagan Meyers's execution-style killing earlier this month. Police arrested five people found at the home, though it is still unclear what their involvement is."

Again, Commissioner Devlin appeared on screen. "It's been an eventful couple of weeks, and we're grateful for the program as well as the law enforcement who have helped bring closure to these cases. As a city, we continue to mourn the loss of Reagan Meyers and Li Syun. Mindful of their deaths, we've made system-wide improvements to ensure our community never goes through this kind of loss again. However, we're glad to have found Cade alive and are looking forward to reuniting him with his parents."

"A happy ending," the woman at the news desk said.

"That's right." Devlin smiled.

Propped up in bed, Emery pointed his remote. The TV went quiet, though the anchorwoman continued talking.

"You knew, didn't you?" Marus said, turning to face him.

"You were already on your way, and Harford had taken off. Even if we did send the helicopter for you, it wouldn't have been in your best interest to go back."

"My best interest? That's my son; he's my only interest."

"It's a trap," Emery said. "Devlin wants to lure you back so you can help him stop the movement. Then he'll kill you and your son. Nothing good will come of it, trust me."

"Call your helicopter pilot. We're going," Marus said.

"I won't let you jeopardize the movement."

"Fuck your movement!" Marus rushed him, and Mike intercepted. Locking his thick arms around Marus's chest, he brought him to the ground.

"Stop!" Shey yelled. "Let him go."

Mike listened, and Marus stood up.

"That's my son!" Marus pointed toward the screen. "I have to go."

Emery let out a single cough. Lying there on the bed, he looked small and weak, and Marus despised him.

Shey went to his side. "Emery, please. We have to try. It won't change anything. You can still go through with the plan, and Marus and I can go back to the Isle for Cade."

"You won't make it out alive."

"It's a risk," she said. "But it's the only choice we're willing to make. With or without your help."

■ ■ ■

Shey scanned the walls of the cabin, looking for anything to pack. There was nothing except for the books, a few items of clothing, and the photograph. Marus took it from the shelf.

"Emery's right," Shey said, moving toward him. "Devlin wants you to come back so he can coerce you into helping him fend off the patriot attack. If you don't, he'll kill Cade. Kill all of us."

"I know."

"What do you think the likelihood is of getting Cade out?"

"It doesn't matter. There could be a ninety-nine-point-nine percent probability of failure, and it wouldn't change my mind."

"What about a hundred?"

He put a hand at her waist and met her green eyes. "Not even a hundred percent could keep me from my son or from trying to make our family whole again."

"But what do you think your algorithms would predict?"

Marus studied the photograph. In it, his head was tilted toward Shey, Shey's turned down at Cade, and Cade's lifted up toward his grandfather. All three of them smiling, looking at a loved one.

"If I've learned anything, it's that it's impossible to quantify love," he said. "No system can predict what the heart is capable of. We have to follow it blindly or not at all."

Overhead, they heard the sound of the helicopter's propeller slashing at the air.

A slight knock came at the door. Wesley stood as though he wasn't sure what to say. "I wanted to come by to wish you luck," he said, pushing up his glasses.

"Thanks."

Wesley extended a small, black device. "If you keep this on you, I'll know where you guys are."

"We're on our own on this one, Wes. Emery doesn't want it to affect the mission."

Wesley looked around to see if anyone was watching. "It's still a free country, right?" he said, making air quotes. "Don't worry, Emery won't even know." He set the device in Marus's hand. "I'm sorry we didn't get to work together more."

"Did you get the rest of the networks mapped?"

"We're close."

"What about Black Mine Bunker? Were you able to find it?"

Wesley smiled. "I guess Emery was the only one who knew where Black Mine Bunker was because he built it. It's a Newbold facility. The ground team is going there to secure it.

They'll wipe the servers, but they won't be blowing anything up."

"Oh," Marus said. "Well…Good, then."

Wesley descended the steps. "Once these stories break, though, a whole bunch of people are going to want to blow up the PSC. You're flying straight into the hornet's nest."

28

From their vantage point in the helicopter, it was a Friday like any other on the Isle. The lunch rush was in full swing as people stepped from the street to the sidewalk. Cars inched forward, dropping passengers at the curbs of cafés and restaurants.

Marus could see their building, the reflective panes of glass that obscured the view into their apartment. What had become of it since he'd left? Had it been pillaged by the neighbors? Raided by the police? What had Ballo made of it all? Now that Marus thought about it, he wasn't sure he'd even closed the door.

A few blocks over, The Harbinger Building rose, dwarfing everything around it. Everything, but the PSC straight ahead of them. The monolith. And somewhere inside it, their son.

"The Protectors know we're coming," the pilot said. "I've been granted permission to land on the pad."

The pilot navigated to a small concrete circle perched atop the parasitic Intelligence Annex. Devlin's very own helicopter

pad. It was a speck among steel and glass and seemed peril-
ously inadequate for Emery's high-powered helicopter, yet the
pilot kept it coming down.

Marus could see the men waiting by the door. Two suits,
impossibly large. Were they State employees, or did they answer to Novak? Was there even a difference?

The pilot set the bird down and mumbled something un-
intelligible. Marus and Shey stepped out. A moment later, the
helicopter's skids left the ground. They were on their own.

The men didn't move. They waited for Marus to come to
them.

When Marus and Shey had reached them, one turned to
open the door. The other ushered them into a long, harshly
lit hallway. Neither of them said anything. Marus and Shey
walked side by side toward the elevator at the end. The red eyes
of cameras blinked all around them.

Are you watching, Wesley? Can you see us?

There weren't any buttons in the elevator. Just a small,
sleek square: a scanner and a speaker.

One of the men waved a wrist over the scanner.

The other said, "The tenth floor."

A tiny light by the speaker turned green.

The elevator lurched and fell. Marus counted, *one floor, two,
three, four.* They passed the tenth floor, the ninth, and eighth,
and continued down, down, down. Until, at last, the elevator
stopped and the doors opened. The men remained still, their
faces revealed nothing.

Shey was the first to move. She looked at Marus and then
through the doors into the blackness that awaited them. And

then she walked into it. She was almost wholly consumed when Marus pitched forward to follow. He didn't look back but heard the doors close once he'd cleared them.

The whirring of cables announced the elevator's departure, and with it, the suits.

"I can't see anything. Can you?" Marus asked, his hand at her side.

"No."

They slid along the wall, feeling for a door, a hallway, anything. But the way was straight and narrow as far as they could tell.

They'd been down there moving along the walls for forty minutes, or maybe it had only been five, when the first sound came. It was hollow. Familiar. Rubber and air and cotton meeting cement. Shey stiffened under his grip. Together, they froze, turning their ears for the slightest clue. *Was there any other direction but forward?* Marus wasn't sure if it was Shey's heart he heard, or his own.

Then it came again. And again. The bouncing of a ball. But not any ball. Shey hadn't been there the night someone broke into their apartment and took their son's most prized possession, but the significance of the sound was not lost on her. She sprang into a run, slipping his grip and moving fast along the wall. Her footsteps clapped down the hall.

"Wait! Shey!" Marus called, stumbling after her.

The sound of dribbling reverberated down the corridor, echoing alongside the striking of soles until Marus was no longer sure whether he was running toward the sounds or from them. His hand met a corner where the wall fell away and opened to another hallway. He called ahead to Shey to see if she'd turned as well, but he couldn't source the sound of her voice. It was above and below, in front and behind him, all at the same time.

Beyond another corner, a feathering of light emerged. He ran toward it, reeling through the labyrinth until he saw them at the end of a long stretch of hallway. His wife and child, embracing at last.

He called out, sprinting toward them, only slowing when his mind caught up with his heart and he realized that Shey and Cade were on the other side of a two-way, floor-length mirror. And he had run straight into a trap.

The doors rushed from the walls, closing with a definitive thud behind him a second before he could spin on his heels. The light from the other side of the mirror flickered as Shey clutched Cade, holding him as Marus had held Shey the night before, a prayer and a promise that they'd never be lost again. He leaned hard against the glass as he watched, the fear and the joy streaming hot down his face.

"Touching," said a voice.

It was Devlin's.

Marus turned toward the source, seeing the commissioner's outline in the low light. He sat with crossed legs in a chair angled at the far corner of the room. The soccer ball rotated slowly in his hands.

"The love between a mother and child," he said. "I can't think of anything more beautiful. Can you?"

Marus had envisioned this moment. Facing his son's abductor, he'd thought about what he'd say and do. He wasn't a violent man, but he'd pictured his fist making contact. The vibration of force beneath his fingertips upon impact. A rearranging of Devlin's face. Skin and teeth and blood. A reckoning.

But now that he was here, all he wanted was to be on the other side of the glass with his son and wife.

"Your own mother was gunned down in a shooting at a shopping mall, isn't that right? Isn't that why you were interested in predictive policing in the first place? You thought you could make a difference. You did, Marus. You made a tremendous difference."

"Take me to them," Marus said, turning back toward the glass. He watched as Shey, one arm still firmly around Cade, pressed her other hand to the wall, looking for a trigger, a switch, a way out. She was calling his name.

"Let's talk first," Devlin said. "Why don't you take a seat?" He gestured toward a chair in the opposite corner, but Marus didn't move.

On the other side of the glass, Shey had begun banging on the walls.

"Come on, take a load off," Devlin said. "That three-day trip must have been exhausting."

Surprised, Marus turned toward him.

The commissioner smiled.

"Harford was helpful, but you've been our greatest asset, Marus. Thanks to you, we finally know where the enemy is." He rested his hands on top of the soccer ball. "And *who* it is. Newbold," he said, shaking his head. "Emerson Keller, himself. That was a surprise to some people, but I'll admit I wasn't shocked. Those entrepreneur types are all the same. They're happy to disrupt. Develop now, deal with the repercussions later. It's when they lose control that they actually start thinking about the consequences of their innovation. Not you, though. No, you're better than that. You know going into it what's at stake. It's a calculation for you. Isn't it? A matter of probability. Risk versus reward."

He threw the soccer ball at the wall, hitting the two-way mirror. Shey turned toward the sound, pressing her face to the glass, trying to see the unseeable. Cade watched wide eyed as she pounded her fists against the glass.

"Marus? Is that you? Marus, can you hear me?"

The ball rolled toward Marus. He resisted the urge to pick it up.

"So tell me," Devlin said, "in joining the fearists, did you think the reward would really outweigh the risk?"

"I just want my family."

"You took an oath to protect your country at all costs. The people still need you."

"The truth will protect them."

Devlin shook his head. "Don't be naïve, Marus. You, of all people, know that good must be sacrificed to achieve greatness."

"You call the senseless murder of thousands of citizens a *sacrifice*?"

"How many lives have been saved because of the Protector Program? How many *will be* saved? Nothing has changed, Marus. Our goal is still the same."

"The truth changes everything."

"We have the ability to *prevent* war. Not just here, but across the globe. Think about that for a moment. Think of all of the progress we will make."

"You kidnapped my son."

"We did what was necessary to ensure the future of the State."

"What about Reagan? And Li? And Axtell?"

"At some point, we have to decide what kind of legacy we want to leave. We have to choose a fight and, in that fight, a side. Ms. Syun made the wrong choice. As did Ms. Meyers and Mr. Axtell."

Marus turned back toward the glass. Shey bent onto one knee and put her hands on Cade's shoulders. Her lips were pursed. The point of her chin tipped forward. He'd seen that expression before. She was telling their son something important. Something very serious. That, no matter what, she wouldn't leave him. That she loved him. That he shouldn't be afraid. That they would all be okay.

Cade nodded, and Shey hugged him.

"There's still a way out of this, Marus. It's not too late for you, or your family. Whatever you did, you can undo it. Help us defeat the fearists. Give the public another headline. Show the people what it means to be a hero. A true patriot."

What did Devlin know about patriotism? What did Emery know?

The commissioner stood and came forward.

"You could be the new face of the program," he said. "We can win, Marus. Together, we can write history."

He thought of Gene's Montblanc pen. His office. The view of the water and the Watchtower. Even now, he could picture Gene waddling down the plush hallways of his luxe apartment at the Harbinger. It was what Marus wanted. What he deserved.

A future for his family. Their safety, their freedom. Happiness.

He'd thought he was entitled to these things. He'd put in the time. Made sacrifices. And yet, here he was. Here they were, on the other side of the glass.

Nothing was certain. Nothing guaranteed. Through all of this, he'd learned that much. Whatever dangers awaited them were far less threatening than the pretense of safety Devlin offered.

"No," Marus said. "I won't do it."

"Don't be foolish, Marus. There's a reason we've got a room with a view."

"If you even touch them—"

"Oh, it won't be me," he said. "It'll be one of Novak's men. A real nasty fella. He'll take his turn with each of them. Your father was lucky he got to go the way he did."

"My father—"

"Oh, right. You hadn't heard. My condolences." Devlin moved forward. "The way I see it, Marus, you have two choices. You can help us and in doing so help your family. Or you can do nothing, in which case, *I'll* have two choices. Will it be your wife first, or your son?"

Marus lunged at Devlin with his right hand. The commissioner's nose cracked against his hand. A terrific crunch.

His knuckles met his brow, the flesh surrounding his left eye. Devlin staggered backward, and Marus matched his step, throwing his fist again. This time the hit was low. A collision of hand, lips, and teeth that drew blood. Then another. Devlin wheeled back, tripping and falling to the ground. In an instant, Marus was on top of him, striking again. Harder.

Blood sprayed from Devlin's face. A spattering of dark droplets across the concrete floor. He'd heard of men being beaten to death. He'd seen the movies and always wondered how a man could go on hitting. How he wouldn't tire of it as the focus of his force was pulverized. Marus's hand was numb, and Devlin was unconscious, but he kept hitting. He would have continued that way, would've beaten him dead, if it hadn't been for Shey's shouting and Cade's crying.

Marus went to the glass.

"I'm right here! Cade, it's Dad. Can you hear me?"

"What's happening? Are you okay?" He could see her mouth move, but her voice was very far away.

"I'm fine. We're going to be fine."

Cade was clutching Shey's hand. He put his free palm against the glass. "Dad?"

"I'm here, buddy."

Devlin lay motionless next to the soccer ball. Blood dripped from the corners of his mouth. His nose. A cut above his left eye. Marus's own hand was cut and bloody. He pressed it into the end of his shirt and watched the red come through.

"*Dad?*" Cade said again.

"Yeah?"

"Can you take me home?"

Marus looked around the room. Cement floors. Cement walls. The two-way mirror. A steel door. Two chairs. A camera in the left-hand corner. No way out, and Novak's men would be there any minute.

He slid to the ground in front of the glass. Cade was inches from him. He could see the concern lining the corners of his small mouth.

The tracking device Wesley had given him was still in his pocket. He took it out and set it on the ground.

If what Devlin had said was true, the colony was doomed, if it hadn't already been destroyed. And without the colony, they would die down there, whether Novak's men came or not. Regardless of what happened to the world above.

Shey and Cade on one side. Marus on the other.

Marus got up and walked over to Devlin.

"We're going to go home," he yelled back through the glass.

He felt the commissioner's pockets and retrieved the small screen. Lifting Devlin's limp hand, he forced thumbprint authentication and unlocked the device.

He hadn't pressed a single button on the screen when he heard the whirring of locks. A gap at the middle of the wall widened as the steel doors came apart, revealing the long, dark corridor from which he'd come.

He squinted into the darkness trying to make out an approaching figure, the outline of Novak's men, but there was nothing.

Returning to the glass, Marus came so close that his lips were nearly pressed against it. He knocked as discreetly as he could.

"Shey? Can you hear me?"

She walked closer. "I hear you," she said.

"The door just opened. I'll be right there. If anybody comes for you, scream."

He started into the darkness, a hand along the wall. Then, thinking better of it, he turned and ran back toward the room and Devlin's unconscious body. He grabbed the soccer ball and tucked it under his arm, looking once more at his wife and son through the glass.

In the corridor, the ball in one hand, the cement wall cold against the other, he hurried but didn't run. He didn't want to miss a turn. His fingers sought the sharp edge of a corner and found it, a right turn. Crossing the opening, he felt ahead to see if the hall continued straight. He tried to remember the turns he'd taken to finally end on the wrong side of the glass. Maybe it was here that he'd turned where Shey continued straight.

He took a left and began to run, wondering how he'd get the door open.

Up ahead, beyond another turn, Marus could see the bouncing glow of a flashlight moving quickly toward him. When he stopped to listen, he heard the tread of advancing feet.

He should have brought the chair, something to defend himself with, he thought. Turning, he ran back toward the split in the hall and took the right. He set the soccer ball down. A moment later, he saw the light beam bounce against the opposite wall and threw himself at the source.

The flashlight flew from the hand that had been holding it and crashed to the floor a few feet ahead. Marus pinned the person to the ground and wrapped his hands around their neck. It wasn't one of Novak's men, he realized. It was a woman.

She gasped as he pressed his fingers into the soft flesh beneath her jaw. The smell of peppermint wafted up with the sound of her labored breath.

"Mar—Marus—It's me. It's Roz."

In a moment, he was off of her. He pulled her up from the ground and retrieved the flashlight, throwing its light at her, just to be sure.

"Where's Devlin?" she asked.

"I knocked him out. My family's in a holding room on the other side. We have to hurry."

"I have the building's schematics. Let me pull it up." She retrieved a small screen from her pocket. "It's this way."

Marus followed. "How'd you get down here?"

"Biometric duplication," she said. "I replicated the commissioner's iD." She turned a sharp corner. "Wesley called me. He was tracking you, said you might need help. I think something happened at the colony. I heard gunshots through the radio, and then I lost him. Everyone's offline."

"That's my fault."

"What do you mean?"

"Devlin said I led them to the colony. Harford was involved somehow. He said I showed them the way."

Roz stopped and turned toward him. "Of course. *That's it.*"

"What?"

"The night you were drugged. It was the same night your sister-in-law was murdered. I thought at first they might've done that to frame you. You know, to turn the public against you. But that wasn't it," Roz said.

He could see the sheen in her eyes against the dark as she looked him up and down. Something of terror and awe made its way across her face. She continued down the hall.

"You think they *bugged* me?" He hadn't considered it before. He hadn't given much thought to the night he awoke in the park. Knowledge of Reagan's death and Devlin's request that Marus leave the PSC had commanded his attention the following day and thereafter.

"It makes sense," Roz said. "Right from the start they were using the system against you. Your son's abduction wasn't an act of retribution against Shey—it was the trigger. It was a part of their strategy. Your wife leaving, the response from the media, Gene's promotion, the Protectors predicted your response to it all."

"The Internal Indicator Initiative," Marus said. "They must've added me to beta months ago. It might've been why they gave me control of the project in the first place. Once they were able to amass an adequate data sampling and model different scenarios, they set their plan in motion."

"The active tracking device is still inside you. They probably inserted it somewhere where you wouldn't be able to see the point of entry. Then they roughed you up that night in the park so the pain wouldn't be localized," she said. "They turned you into a rat and let you lead them right back to the nest."

Roz pressed a button on the illuminated screen in her hand and the wall split, revealing another hallway.

And just like a rat in a maze, Devlin had corralled him here, Marus thought. Leading Marus down one hall and Shey down another.

"It's hell up there, Marus. The whole building is being evacuated. People are storming the mall and ransacking apartments. The safest building in the world is now the most dangerous, because of us."

He couldn't tell if she was proud or horrified.

"Wesley must have reversed the security override to unlock all of the doors so Devlin and the other officials wouldn't be able to hide from the public. I didn't even think about people looting."

"Yeah, well, the stories broke an hour ago, and it's already the third world up there. There are fires in the street."

"The security override should have affected the entire system. So why didn't the locks on this floor disengage?"

Roz lifted the device as if to show him.

"It's controlled through another system. Wesley was able to get me access. Everything is manual," Roz said.

"The tenth floor is a bunker."

In the dim light of the screen, Roz nodded. "Looks like it."

"So, if it's chaos up there, where is everybody?"

Roz shined her flashlight on two steel plates ahead of them. "I don't want to find out." She pressed a button and the steel doors came apart.

The room was dark. Someone had turned off the overhead lights. Roz angled the flashlight's beam inside, illuminating Cade who was sitting at the center of the room.

"Shey?" Marus called.

Shey was in the corner, as if to jump whoever came for them. She ran for Marus, almost knocking him over.

"Oh thank God!"

"Dad!" Cade said, running toward him.

Marus dropped the ball and lifted Cade to his chest. He closed his eyes, casting aside the small eternity that had separated them.

With his son in one arm and Shey in the other, Marus dropped to his knees. The fear and uncertainty that had lodged deep within his chest loosened and tears of gratitude fell freely to the floor.

"Are you okay?" Marus ran his hand through Cade's hair, tipping his son's head back to examine him. "Are you hurt?"

Cade's face was red and wet, but he looked fine. He looked as perfect as the day he was born.

"I'm so sorry." Marus pulled him close. "I promise, I'll never let anything happen to you again. Either of you." He buried his face between them; his wife and child. He could have stayed that way forever, but Roz was pulling on his jacket, saying something incomprehensible as she tried to usher them out.

"He's gone!" she was yelling. "We have to go."

Now that both rooms were dark, the two-way mirror had become a window. And through it, Marus saw Devlin's blood on the floor. But Devlin was no longer lying in it.

■ ■ ■

He ran faster than he thought possible. With Cade in his arms, clutching at his shoulders, he flew through the hallway. Shey was two steps ahead with the flashlight. Roz, two steps behind with the ball. All together, they were a flash of color against the sheen of concrete. There one moment, gone the next.

Cade's breath was warm at his ear. He wanted to stop, to kiss the boy and tell him how much he loved him. *I'll never let any harm come to you again. I promise.*

But he had to keep running.

Beyond the walls, the world was turning inside out. Even here, underground, shielded by steel and concrete, Marus could feel the thrum. A new world order. Would he like what it had to offer?

It was too late now.

Turn the corner. Don't look back. Keep running.

Somewhere up ahead, they heard the elevator doors open. A rush of voices. The *clack clack clack* of black dress shoes slapping against the floors.

Shey jerked to a halt, throwing the beam of light in the direction from which they'd just come.

"There's another way," Roz said. "We can take a different hallway and circle back once they've cleared that area."

Walls split and became whole again as they moved through the corridor. Marus held onto Cade a little tighter. He kept an eye on the silhouette of Shey's body moving fast in front of him. As long as he didn't let go, didn't look away, he wouldn't lose them.

Someone was behind them. Or maybe ahead. The shuffling of shoes echoed all around, so that it was hard to tell.

"Just up here," Roz said. "Turn left."

The wall split and opened as they approached, revealing another dark expanse.

"Elevator's at the end of the hall."

The pounding of feet was closing in behind them. Marus didn't dare turn to look. He ran faster.

"Run, Shey."

A shaft of light leapt up behind them, throwing their shadows in front.

"They're coming, Dad!" Cade cried. "Go faster!"

A moment later, they were puffing and wheezing at the elevator bay.

"It's almost here," Roz said, eyeing the screen.

They could hear the cables, the descent of the car.

But Novak's men were coming faster. And right behind them, Devlin. Marus could see the commissioner's bloodied face spread into a triumphant smile. There was nowhere for them to go.

By the time they selected the floor and the doors began to close, Devlin and his guns would be right on top of them. Marus knew it as well as he knew anything.

This was it. The end. They'd made it this far, and now...

The elevator doors parted and five people in SWAT gear, guns raised, met their gaze.

No one moved.

One of the men in the middle glanced at Cade, then Shey, and back to Marus. He motioned to his associates, who cleared a space in the middle of the elevator car. Marus, Cade, Shey, and Roz stepped inside as the others moved out.

Just before the doors closed, before the sound of gunfire carried the elevator along its cables to deliver them from that dark hell, Marus met the man's eyes.

Underneath the goggles and the helmet, in the boots and bulletproof vest, was Ballo.

PART FIVE

I learned that courage was not the
absence of fear,
but the triumph over it.
The brave man is not he who does not
feel afraid,
but he who conquers that fear.

—Nelson Mandela

29

THE STREET WAS aglitter. Broken glass flickered atop the asphalt like flame in the midday sun. Small fires cleaned out the insides of garbage cans beneath traffic lights. People ran in every direction, not knowing where they were going. Others yelled from the roofs of cars. Cheered from curbs. Several men threw bricks at the glass front of the IA. The windows spider-webbed up and outward.

High above, the screens showed images of faces. Names and headlines raced across the bottom. Atrocities spelled out. A collection of neat, little sound bites. Carefully crafted and packaged, the truth circulated.

People pointed, the rage building behind their eyes as they stared at the billboards or read from the screens in their hands.

A child wailed from her clutch around her father's waist. He patted her hair and looked around, frantic. Marus watched the smoke rise above the buildings overhead and held Cade tighter. Birds flocked from their perches to find a safer place.

The end of the world. This is what it had looked like in all of their minds. It's what they'd seen on-screen, after all.

He scanned the streets, looking for danger, but it was all around. Sirens wailed. Tires screeched. A helicopter buzzed overhead. *Emery*, Marus thought. But the bird belonged to a news station. He glanced up at it. The black camera more powerful than a gun. Three reporters safe above the chaos. Since when did journalists have enviable jobs?

The screens shuddered and went black. People in the streets stopped their fighting, yelling, looting, and crying, and turned to watch. When the picture was finally restored, it was Emery looking back at them.

His enormous blue eyes peered from the sides of buildings. The backs of benches. Up from the palms of hands.

They were eyes that saw everything. Consumed everyone. Every single man, woman, and child watching. All of the city. The entire country, rapt. Every ear, waiting.

And then Emery spoke.

"Today we are liberated. Today, we return to the principles our nation was founded upon. Today, we decide who we are and what we stand for. Fear can no longer rule us. Convenience shall no longer command us. We are a nation of thinkers, of doers. And today, we must stand united in the understanding that our destiny is not to be handed to us, but to be created. Crafted. Earned. Together, we must rise. We must unshackle ourselves. Not from fear, but from our fear of fear itself."

■ ■ ■

A crowd of people moved through the street. Some joined hands in their march. People cheered. Others went back to their shouting, their crying, their looting.

A community in transition.

Transition had been Emery's word for it. And with it, *transformation.*

There were those who became common criminals simply because the opportunity presented itself. They pumped their fists in the air, shattered storefront windows, took what wasn't theirs. Because they could. Because it was there to be taken.

But there were others. Quiet heroes. Men like Ballo, who took it upon themselves to right wrongs. To do the difficult thing.

Roz handed the soccer ball to Marus.

"Thank you," Marus said.

"I suppose I'll be seeing you," Roz said. "Maybe back at the colony." She nodded in Shey's direction before moving into the street. In an instant, she was gone. One of many who moved as one.

Marus and Shey looked on as the throng grew longer, wider. Strangers strode side by side in the march toward a new beginning. They, *the people*, would decide what it meant. Not just here on the Isle, but in cities across the State. Everywhere there was a screen, there was Emery. His call rang through every speaker; his petition met every ear.

"Can we go home?" Cade said, turning his head toward Shey and then back to Marus.

In his son's eyes, Marus saw the reflection of the smoke drifting behind them. He saw flames. The glitter of glass. He saw Shey and saw himself. The past and the future. The entire world.

The people would rise up to lead, to care, to fill in the gaps. To take the country forward. Emery had been sure of it. And now Marus saw it, too.

Cade took the soccer ball from his dad. "I really want a sandwich."

Shey smiled. "All right," she said. "Let's go home."

In the absence of fear was love. The love for a country. For a people. An idea. The love of a family. It was Marus's greatest strength and weakness. It was his cause.

He kissed his son's head. Taking Shey's hand, they moved into the street.

"Home."

ACKNOWLEDGMENTS

I ONCE READ an article against acknowledgments in *The New Yorker* by Sam Sacks (here's to you, Sam!) and found some truth in what was written. Acknowledgments *can* be gratuitous, even braggadocious, and often serve as the literary equivalent of the pop-up ad. But, having few professional shout-outs to deploy, no MFA program to thank, and zero fellowships or grants to recognize, I'm hopeful my acknowledgments will be interpreted as they are meant: sincere and boundless in gratitude. In short, there are no ulterior motives here.

For however solitary the act of writing may be, a book is a labor of love sustained by many. Even those who were not directly involved in the novel itself had to endure seemingly inexplicable swings in my demeanor, frequent absences or, conversely, appearances, and, at times, my excessive whining and/or consumption of wine. To all of you: Aubrey and Ilya Oyzerskiy, Lindsay Wolf, Loryn Wilson, Trent Ashton, Nathan Marsala, Aaron Munro, Allie and Derikk Henderson, Meredith Pike-Meher and Jordan Meher, among others, I am thankful for your tolerance and unwavering friendship.

For their support and involvement in the book, I am also grateful and indebted to:

My editor, Alan Rinzler, for his guidance, patience, advocacy and zero-tolerance for bullshit. Also, the croissants.

Karen Concannon for her close eye, sharp wit, and ample polish.

My wonderful writing group for their kind words and willingness to read more.

Early readers and critics: Ginamarie Marsala, Stephanie Carter, Ben Henderson, Sam Funk, Tim Ash, Deborah Moore and my mother-in-law, Jane Roxbury. Your feedback was crucial and greatly appreciated.

The *LAOF* marketing dream team: Ted, Gina, Steph, Mauri, Wil, Tim, DJ and Marty.

LAOF supporters: Those who backed the Thunderclap campaign and others who shared the book with their own readership, family, and friends. #thankyou

Phil and Mauri Hansen for offering their home as the venue for the *LAOF* book launch.

My dog, Po, for keeping my feet warm and my mind sane during all those days of writing.

There are no words to adequately express the love and appreciation I have for my family, including all of those I cannot mention by name because our family is just too big, though I'll try. I am profoundly grateful to my parents, Bill and Vicki, for their tireless encouragement, and to my sisters, Chelsea and Cailey, for standing by my side. I don't know what I'd do or who I'd be without you.

To all of these people, I am beholden. The book would be very different without you (as would I). But there's one person, without whom the book simply could not exist (and I would not want to), and that's my best friend, chief supporter, and husband, Ted Roxbury. Thanks for believing in me when I struggled to believe in myself and holding my hand as I leapt.

Made in the USA
San Bernardino, CA
22 November 2015